HIGHWAY
ZERO

HIGHWAY ZERO

A Novel

BILLY LAWRENCE

Broken Tribe Press

New York

FOR ELEANORE

The car hugs the icy road as the snow pelts the windshield. Specks of snow splatter my vision of the road ahead through the break in the fog of the windshield. I lean forward to focus on the road. My eyes are strained. My back is stiff. My hands grip the steering wheel. The heat pumps in through the vents, but I shudder at the possibility that a breakdown could strand me in the cold. I must keep pushing. This will be a long journey with time to reflect, just enough time to rewind back to the beginning of where it all started.

Ronkonkoma, New York, Fall, 1995

Hell was on the highway. The wildfire out east raged all summer, or at least it seemed to. The fires hadn't started until August, but everything before it was a blur. The heavy smoke drifted in the sky along with the smell of burning wood. The reddish glow lit the night sky from miles away.

There used to be increasing solace as you moved east through Long Island away from the city. The further you got, the more peace you found, but the fire had caught up with us. It had followed. The wind was its helper, blowing something bad east toward the beginning of land. The Hamptons were cut off from the rest of the island with fire on both sides of the highway. Nowhere left to go. I imagined it burning out of control until evacuation boats arrived. The wealthy were swooped off to safety on their private jets. The rest of us huddled on ferries heading to the mainland of Connecticut for refuge, never to return.

The fire stopped in September, and we were spared for now. When it was over, 7,000 acres of forest had burned to a crisp. With such destruction, it was time for the land to start anew. But starting over is always a long process.

☆

In October, I took a drive out east on the Long Island Expressway. I was restless. I drove to the end in Calverton and wound around Flanders Road until I came to Sunrise Highway. I passed the wasteland of burned forest and drove out into the fog of the Hamptons. I kept going farther east. At once in the air, I could smell and taste both the fire and the wealth.

I drove through Water Mill, Bridgehampton, and then East Hampton, almost to the end of the island, where the Atlantic Ocean begins its stretch back to Africa and Europe. I stopped eighteen miles short of the lighthouse at the end and found myself wandering around Amagansett, a small, wealthy, south shore village. I drove down a long road with big properties, homes set back from the road, fenced in by walls and shrubs. I wondered which one Billy Joel lived in and pictured him playing the piano in the window of a big home behind a big white gate.

Big Shot.

Big Man on Mulberry Street.

No Man's Land.

I drove around in circles for a while, lost, unsure what I was doing out there. The fog was overwhelming. I had to pull over. Never had I found myself so confused in my direction. My headlights were ineffective, and so I turned them off and sat. I slid my seat back and watched the fog cover my car until I was gone.

Don't Tell Me (What Love Can Do)

I was still working at Jerry's Healthy Alternative after graduation, but the drive west to Bay Shore was getting to me. I didn't know if I wanted to leave because Jerry treated me good, but it wasn't feeling like I fit in anymore anyway. I didn't know how to tell him.

Instead of yelling my name like he usually did, Uncle Al showed up at my cracked door and gave a knock.

"Jack, you have a call."

He looked serious but didn't say what it was. I went out to the kitchen and picked up the receiver.

"Hello…Oh…Oh…All right, thanks."

What else was there to say? Jerry was dead. There would be no notice. The store would be closed immediately, and the man would be cremated on Sunday.

I called a coworker, and he said Jerry had suffered heart failure at a New York City club. A concoction of drugs had been in his system. I called someone else and asked her.

"Is it really true about Jerry and drugs?"

"I'm afraid so, Jack."

The idea that Jerry was a sham angered me. I wondered how a health food store owner could fall into such late-night city life. He had had his own adversity tale of beating a rare disease with herbs, vitamins, juicing, and diet, yet he dabbled in street drugs? It didn't make any sense to me.

It soon occurred to me that Jerry had had a decently successful business, but that was it. Everything else in his life was empty. He lived in a sterile townhouse. No family. No love.

He had invited me out to the city clubs, but I knew it wasn't my scene, especially when he told me they'd be out until four or five. Jerry pushed though.

"Come on, Jack. It's fun. Dance music. Girls. Guys. Ecstasy. Whatever you're into."

"No thanks, Jerry. I think I'll stay in."

I hadn't touched much more than a cigarette and coffee the entire year. After what I had been through the previous winter—homeless and burnt out, some dance club was the last place I wanted to be. And look where it got him.

☆

At Sunday breakfast, which Al and I always tried to keep, he asked what I was going to do next. I told him I didn't know, and that I'd be looking for jobs closer to home.

"You could always try being a porter," said Al.

"A porter? What's that?"

"You don't know what a porter is?"

"No idea."

"Someone who cleans up."

"Like a janitor?" I asked.

"Yes, same thing."

"A custodian."

"Yes, same thing," he said again.

Hadn't I been a porter already? That was the point of going back to school, so I wouldn't have to clean up after others anymore. I moved in with him, went back to school day and night for six months, all to end up a porter? It just didn't feel right. I didn't even know why he was asking when he knew I had done that kind of work before.

"I guess I can look around."

"I thought because of your experience, that kind of job could be something to help put you through college."

"Yes, I have to get down there to get signed up."

College was an idea Al and I discussed a bit. He threw it out to me even before I had finished high school, but I wasn't ready yet. I was starting to think about it more as the summer went on. My only option was the local community college. But fall was approaching, and I hadn't enrolled. It was looking like I would be taking a year off from school.

☆

I took a job at a local HESS station. Since the company offered tuition benefits, I knew the job might be nice to have when I enrolled in college. All I would have to do is sit in a booth behind thick, bullet-proof glass and take money through a slot.

The station manager was a thin man in his fifties named Cliff. His face was clean-shaven, and his hair was slicked-back, long ago overtaken by gray. He wore the white uniform with worn white sneakers. His face had a distinct look like he could've been a Hollywood star from the '50s. He tilted his head down when he spoke, and the words came out in a deep grumbly sound.

"Hey Jack, just be sure your drawer is good at the end of the shift. Do your measurements outside at the beginning and end of the shift, and you should be fine. Smoke all you want," he told me with a cigarette burning in his yellowed fingers.

"Sounds like a plan," I said.

"There's coffee in the back. You want some?"

I nodded. "Yeah, thanks."

"Let me go make a pot. Try out your first customers on your own. I'll be back here."

I rang through a few customers.

"Ten on one," said the first man.

"Great, thank you. Have a good day."

I quickly realized that that was even too much for someone with a foot already pointed back at their car.

"Fifteen bucks on pump four," said another guy.

"Thank you," I replied through the microphone.

That worked, but soon enough I learned it would be a good idea to repeat the amount back as confirmation.

"Twenty dollars, please. Pump eight," a woman said.

"Twenty dollars on eight. Thank you," I replied.

For that customer who lingered for a moment, I snuck it in— "Have a great day."

"Hey, Jack, coffee's up. Might put some hair on your chest."

"Thanks, Cliff."

"Hey, you sounded good. You got it down. Good idea to repeat what they give you. I've had some shysters try to pull a fast one on me. They come back up after pumping their gas looking for change and tell you they gave you a bigger bill. I once had a guy who was convinced he had given me a fifty. I had to break it to him that I didn't even have a fifty-dollar bill in the drawer! Cover yourself."

"Will do, Cliff."

He returned to the back room to check supplies and left me alone a while. The Van Halen song "Don't Tell Me (What Love Can Do)" started up on the radio station. I lit a cigarette and got to work.

Counting Blue Cars

For the next five months, I was a gas station attendant. It wasn't so bad. Time on my shifts flew when it was busy. I read a bit during downtime. I had more cigarettes than I knew what to do with. I had a radio to listen to. Great songs played over and over.

An incredible song called "Counting Blue Cars" by Dishwalla played every few hours. The song chorus didn't mention blue cars, but I caught the title one night and couldn't forget it. Every time it came on, I'd look over to my blue Camaro and wonder where it would take me next.

"All I Really Want" by Alanis Morissette usually followed on the radio. This was the age of alternative rock artists— Gin Blossoms, Lisa Loeb, Soundgarden, Pearl Jam. The music of the mid '90s was surreal to me. It seemed like the whole world had transformed. At home, I'd pop in a CD or cassette and listen to music every waking moment. I was overwhelmed with euphoria.

Music was my savior because without the job at Jerry's Healthy Alternative, I wasn't feeling as healthy. Just being around the herbs, fresh food, and fitness-centered people made me feel better. During my five months at the station, I smoked cigarettes and consumed chaotic amounts of caffeine, but I stayed clear of the rough stuff. This was easy because I didn't go back to that old town anymore. I knew to stay away.

I felt like I was finding myself. Doing some real soul work. In between customers at the station, there would be slow periods where I'd sit and smoke, pondering my existence. On my days off, I would sit at the lake in my car and stare out at the water while zoning out to music, just the way I had when I was stoned out a year before, wondering where I'd sleep that night, what I'd eat, how I'd survive. I was a scared teenager with nowhere to run.

But those days were at the mercy of the ocean.

This was a lake. I was used to the waves, so there was a stillness here I could not understand. I spent hours gazing out at this lake as if it were a great sea I dreamt of sailing. Now that high school was conquered, I thought I was slowly finding myself, but of course, this was only the beginning of adulthood. The more I found, the more I wondered and questioned. My life had been in such a haze for so long, and I had finally stepped out of the bubble, but the adjustment was challenging and lonely. I found myself at that lake. I lost myself at the lake. One closed window in my mind opened another.

One day, I spotted my old health teacher Mr. Cavanaugh from across the store in the 7-Eleven by the lake. I wasn't sure if he saw me, and I didn't approach him. I had no confidence, nothing to tell him. It was a reminder of what I needed to do. I'd never forget his act of kindness as he took me out of school suspension one day to teach me how to change a flat tire on an older teacher's car. He did what he could for a troubled kid. It's the little things that add up.

No one is going to swoop down and save your life in one instance. If they do, there might be reason to be suspicious. It's all about planting the little seeds in the heart, so you can do the changing yourself.

☆

On the way home from my shift one night in December, I stopped at the grocery store—the same chain I had briefly worked at in high school. I'd never forget the miserable managers and how they mistreated their workers. An odd feeling of nostalgia was there as I walked in the front doors under the big red sign out front, but this was a different location, a different world. The villains who had made me feel bad were all gone.

I went in and roamed around picking up a few odd things like Raisin Bran and Yoo-Hoo. This was my life, and I was so damn bored. But I really should have embraced it—

Quit smoking—

Take up yoga—

Eat more vegetables—

Meet some new people—

Go to college—

That's what I should've been doing. I wish I had. But first I had to learn a little more about life, even if it meant taking a big step back into the darkness of the cave.

Shuffle It All

Living in Al's house was surreal to me. The house was just okay, but there was a feeling of safety I had never known. For a while, I felt so alive through the quiet nights as he worked night shifts. But I felt like a stranger in this town. I didn't know anyone and wasn't doing much. I was waiting for something and didn't know what that something was. A great loneliness crept in from somewhere cold.

Perhaps I had too much time to think, but I had a feeling I still wasn't far enough away from the old town.

In January, my aunt Annie and uncle Russell from my mother's side tracked me down. They had finally heard what had happened to me the previous winter.

"What a year! What's going on now?" asked Annie.

"Ah, it's okay. Just trying to figure out what to do next."

"Why don't you come down and work for our new frozen drink company? We have a job for you."

"Key West? Oh, I don't know. I was down there on vacation with Mom and JP when I was a kid. It seems far."

"It's so nice here. The Keys are beautiful. Everything is so easy going. It's not like New York, Jack. I'd never go back."

"Oh, you're a poet," I said, and she laughed.

"No, really, there's a college here too. You could do it all."

"All right, let me think about it."

☆

I decided to go to Florida, but I wasn't sure I would take the job. First, I needed to see an old friend. He had since moved to Lake Worth in the Palm Beach area. Maybe I could live near him and start college there.

I got into my car on January third and set off on my journey, just as a huge snowstorm started to bombard the northeast. I hit the road at ten o'clock. The traffic wasn't too heavy on the Long Island Expressway, but there were plenty of intimidating big rigs. I wasn't used to this. It seemed they all came out at night. In comparison to those big trucks, I was so low to the ground in my blue Camaro. I lit cigarette after cigarette, and looked side to side, back and forward. At one point, I turned the tape deck off to concentrate on driving. The snow was coming down hard. I needed to get out of the city.

I crossed the bridge out of New York for the first time on my maiden road trip and entered New Jersey as the snowstorm ripped past me. The snow finally dissipated by the time I got to southern New Jersey. The sky cleared. Stars twinkled. My southern route was a road right out of trouble.

Alone on the interstate late at night, I gripped the steering wheel tight. The trucks were out and aggressive. They shook my car and startled me with their massive size and speed. One sinister Mac truck pulled right up behind me. It didn't have normal headlights. Instead, a giant smiley face with teeth lit the front grill. It was demonic looking. I pulled over into the right lane. A series of big rigs blew right past. I was both anxious and impressed.

I continued down the rest of the east coast on I-95 out of Jersey through Delaware, and then onto Maryland and DC, arriving in Virginia. The drive was exhausting, and I couldn't get much farther south on my first try. I saw a sign for a Red Roof Inn just before Richmond, and I pulled off the exit past some fine-smelling pine trees. It was almost four in the morning, and I collapsed into the motel bed for the rest of the morning. I needed to rest before the sun came up.

After about five hours of sleep, I got back out on the road to head to Palm Beach. It was a long way down, but the road was great. I burned through a box of cassette tapes, singing along, smoking cigarettes, and drinking Yoo-Hoo. I popped on a song called "Shuffle It All" by a guy named Izzy Stradlin. He sang all about packing up your life. I sang along loud.

The temperature warmed as I approached the south. I passed some odd South of the Border scene. All along I-95 in South Carolina, billboards featuring half naked women from strip clubs were followed by ads with Biblical verses instructing me to save myself with Jesus. A giant peach sign popped up in Georgia, and then the welcoming natural flags of palm trees started to line the interstate highway. The climate had changed in a matter of hours. I was in Florida, and I could smell it.

Lake Worth, Florida, Winter, 1996

I headed to Lake Worth in the Palm Beach area. My once again estranged father lived directly across on the opposite west coast of Florida. We were just terrible at returning calls. I thought about visiting him, but I needed to be out on my own with my old friend.

I pulled up to his condo and put the car in park. Out stepped the old friend who had taken me in when I was kicked out of my house only seventeen months earlier. He walked out to meet me and embraced me with a hug.

"How you doing, buddy?"

"Great to see you, Paul."

"Come on in. Let me help you with those bags."

Only a month after high school, while I was starting my gas station job, Paul Roma got smart and packed it all up. He led the way and was the first to go. His mother had a three-bedroom condo in Lake Worth. She had the master bedroom but was staying up north with her boyfriend for a while. Paul had his own room. Then there was a third furnished bedroom, which a friend of his mother's had just moved out of.

"I've got an extra room. My mom says you can stay as long as you want and take over the small rent if you want."

"I'm going to consider it. Thanks."

"I know you have family there, but it'd be great to have you."

"Thanks, Paul. I appreciate the options."

"It'll be like the old days."

"Yes, except I sleep on beds these days."

"Ha, I know, buddy. I know," said Paul.

☆

We had a good time for several weeks. Paul's place was only a quick ride down to the beach. On his day off, we went and spent a few hours at the ocean. On the days he worked, I stayed around the house and listened to his CD collection, which consisted of a mellow band I hadn't heard of. A world of a difference from the Led Zeppelin, Guns N Roses, and all the other stuff we listened to in school. This was a fresh start.

"All Right" by Toad the Wet Sprocket came on, and I was entranced. Are you kidding me? I asked out loud. The songs took me away to another place. I listened through several other albums by the band. Where had these guys been my whole life?

Some days, I drove around the city, sometimes just up and down on a road called Military Trail. It gave me a feel for the area. I found a great spot for breakfast where I'd sit by myself reading the job ads and thinking about whether I should stay. It felt like a place I could live and enjoy. Sometimes out on the roads, I'd see a young guy cruising in his freshly waxed car with his hand high on the steering wheel, blasting his bass-filled, disco-like freestyle music, and I was reminded of my old town. I was trying to get away from that place, and sometimes it felt like it was following me.

One night, Paul and I went out to a nightclub with one of his new friends. I never liked clubs. The music was always too loud to talk. Dancing seemed like a bunch of strange movements. As usual, I stood on the side observing the spectacle. There were mostly guys in this club. It wasn't my scene. Paul disappeared for a while. His friend Tom and I just stood there bored.

When Paul came back, we all took off for the night. A night on the town always had some kind of disappointment for me. At eight o'clock everything was ahead of you and by twelve that was it, nothing new, nothing had changed, at least from my experience. I had high expectations, I guess.

If I was going to stay for good, I would have to figure out a game plan to keep me productive. I looked into Palm Beach Community College and got excited about the prospect. I could stay in Lake Worth with my friend and start college, or I could have the safety of having a room and job waiting for me in Key West.

I decided to make up my mind on the trip back up to New York to get the rest of my things. I would be moving to Florida either way, so I parked my car and jumped on the Amtrak. It would take twenty-four hours to get up there. I gave myself just forty-eight hours to pack and say my goodbyes.

Back in New York, I went over to my mother's house, my old house, in the old town. I went in to say goodbye. She was home alone. It was strange to be back in the house. It felt like it had been so long since I'd been there, almost like I never even lived there. Everything was smaller than I remembered it. I didn't stay long.

I went and had a meal with Uncle Al. He understood my need to try out Florida, but he seemed sad, like he was losing me, like it was the end of something. I told him I'd be back to visit. He wished me luck and reassured me I could always return home.

☆

With a suitcase and a black garbage bag full of stuff, I rode back to Florida on the train. I sat up most of the night, smoking in the lounge car, thinking about my next step. Would I stay with Paul in Lake Worth, or would I go farther down to Key West?

I stepped off the train in the morning and got in my car, which had been parked in the lot. I went to Paul's place to talk.

"Jack, I want you to stay, but if you want to go and check it out down there for a while, we'll keep the room open for you. It's no rush," Paul said.

"You know, maybe that's just what I'll do. I have no idea what the place even looks like."

"Yeah, what if the place or the job isn't a good fit?"

"Thanks, Paul. I can always count on you for good old logic."

☆

I headed farther south in my Camaro with a few new mixed tapes made from Paul's CD collection. Just before getting to Miami, I popped in Phil Collins so I could feel "In the Air Tonight" playing as I surfed the road like Sonny Crockett. I rewound the song three times to get those drums going in my head as the green and yellow traffic lights above flew past me. Then I started up a new heavy metal tape by Iron Maiden. The song "Lord of the Flies" blasted as I crossed through the south end of Miami. Within an hour, I arrived in Key Largo to begin my descent to the edge of the world.

Key West, Florida, Spring, 1996

The island was only a mile by a mile. The feel of the place was different from the mainland. It was more tropical. It was wilder. But it was fresher and cleaner. I needed this.

Annie met me in the lot and gave me a big hug. It was good to see her. I had fond childhood memories of her before she moved away. She was always full of laughter and excitement.

"Annie! So good to see you."

"Yes, Jack, Yes! I'm so happy to see you. You're going to love this place. I'm telling you. We love it. The work is going really great too. We hope you'll be a part of it," Annie said.

"Sure thing. I'll check it out."

"Let's get your bags up and then I'll take you downtown."

She took me up to the second-floor apartment and I dropped my bags on the bed of the guest room where I'd be staying. The apartment was fairly new, something you don't really see much in New York where most homes and apartments are older. Most Long Island apartments are in people's homes in the attics or basements. A new apartment complex with a pool and a gym for a fair price was an impossible find in the north.

Annie brought me downtown to the cart where they sold tropical smoothies. Russell was busy at work and seemed happy. It looked like a nice place to work. Shops lined the property of a courtyard with a placed called The Garden Café over in the corner. She showed me around and introduced me to some of the locals. The café owner Carla was also from New York, so I felt at home. Carla made me a chicken sandwich on the house as a welcome gift.

The next day I took a drive back downtown to explore on my own. I parked the car on a side street and walked a few blocks in to get to Duval Street. It was warm for early February. Palm trees lined the street. I walked the brick sidewalk under giant signs and colorful awnings from the gift shops, bars, and restaurants. Capt. Tony's Saloon, the original Sloppy Joes where Ernest Hemingway downed drinks, had a giant fish over the sign just about sticking out into the road.

I dropped by the cart to see Russell. It was quiet so he introduced me to some of the other vendors I hadn't met the day before with Annie. Everyone seemed nice. Suddenly a wave of business started up.

"It happens like this. Up and down. All day! Go explore the city. We'll have time to train you tomorrow," he said.

I got out of his way and went to have another addictive chicken sandwich at the Garden Café.

Then I took a walk down to Hemingway's old home. The green painted balcony from the second floor overlooked the property. Inside there was a weird old bed where he supposedly slept. Descendants of his cats lay around the house, some on the bed. His office where he wrote was the highlight. There was a deer's head on the wall just over a case of books. Red tiles lined the room around a bland carpet in the middle. A reclining chair was set right next to a small round table with a typewriter on it. More stuffed animal heads and fish lined the walls over more bookcases. Right on the wall where you are allowed to peek into the room via a gate, is a painting of Hemingway wearing a sport coat and red pants standing outside the front of his house. An orange tabby cat sits near his feet. I walked back downstairs and then out past the pool, which was preserved just the way Hemingway had left it, a world of its own hidden away behind tall shrubs.

The ride back to the apartment wrapped around the south part of the island. You could pull over and see the ocean from your car. I got out and walked over to the edge of the walkway that dropped out onto a short beach. The clear shallow water stretched out for what appeared to be miles. Puffy white groups of clouds gathered low in the distance. I blew the smoke out from my cigarette and tried to mimic the clouds.

Some of the way home was just like the trip down from Key Largo. The high water seemed to crowd the land and the road seemed to snake around with the changes in the landscape as dominated by the waterline. It seemed like you could reach out your car window and skim the surface with your hand. The roads here were clean, unlike the New York roads, which were battered with litter and cigarette butts. The tropical feel of the islands was a world away from my old town.

And so I decided to stay.

Into Another

The courtyard was an exciting place to work. Tourists from all over the world stopped in. Pretty girls on vacation paraded around in bathing suits. The Hard Rock Café was right across the street. All kinds of folks sold their art from booths in the courtyard.

For a couple of hours at sunset, some would close up shop and head to Mallory Square to sell their work at the sunset celebration. It was an art haven. Bill the sunset photographer would do this a few times a week, and then he'd stay in the courtyard other nights hoping to remind people of the sunset they saw the night before. "Take the sun home with you" was Bill's slogan.

One man would ride his bike back and forth past my cart. He had no shirt on like a kid out playing in the summer. He would stop and stare, perhaps waiting for acknowledgement. I usually greeted customers, but I could tell by his circling that he was a vulture looking for meat. After a few times, a blond girl stepped in and put her arm around me pretending to be my girlfriend. He winced in surprise and then shook his head.

"Thanks for the save," I said and smiled.

"Anytime. I'm Ashley. You new around here?"

"I'm Jack. Nice to meet you. I just moved down from New York to help some family out."

"New York, wow. What's it like?"

"Fast, busy, crowded…"

"I dream about getting out of here. Maybe I'll go somewhere like New York," she said.

"Really? It seems like paradise here," I said.

"How much sun can you get?"

"Are you from here?"

"Yes, born here. Still in high school in twelfth grade."

"Wow, young."

"How old are you?" she asked.

"Nineteen."

"So, you're only about a year older."

"Well, so you're looking to get out of here after school?"

"Yes, maybe Orlando. California. Vegas. Who knows!"

"Who's going to save me when you're gone?"

"I can get you started, but you'll be on your own soon."

"What if I convince you to stay?" I asked.

"What if I convince you to leave?" she asked.

I didn't want to get wrapped up in another serious relationship. It was too soon. But this girl was tempting and assertive. She invited me out on my day off. I couldn't say no.

☆

On Sunday, I knocked on Ashley's door. Her mother answered the door with her and asked us a few brief questions about where we were going. I assured her I'd keep her daughter safe. We said goodbye and drove off in my Camaro to head downtown. Deciding to cruise down Duval Street, we found ourselves parked at the beach, which was empty besides the two of us. The windows were rolled down and there was a slight island breeze. It was bizarre for February, at least to me, but to everyone else who lived on the island this climate was the norm.

"What are you going to do if and when you go?" I asked.

"I'd love to do something in entertainment."

"Are you an actress?"

"You could call it that," she said.

"So what happens in the scene we're in?"

Ashley and I leaned into each other for a kiss. I smelled strawberry and it melted me.

She was different than any girl I'd ever known in New York, but maybe the contrast was a good thing to move my mind forward away from the ghosts.

We basked in the winter sun for a while before heading downtown. She said she wasn't feeling hungry for a meal, so we decided to just get something to drink at an outdoor café.

"You want to go to a party Friday night?" she asked.

"Sure, what time? I work the stand until 9."

"I'll pick you up then," she said.

"All right. It's a date."

So Far Away

The shirtless guy got the message and stopped circling around. Replacing him was the Garden Café delivery guy who would eye me every time he drove past on his motorbike with a delivery. He was a tall, built, black man with a shaved shiny head and diamond earrings. One day, he stopped and shut the ignition.

"Hey, handsome."

"Hi there, man. I'm not..."

"Don't worry. I saw you with the girl. I'm not going to bite. I can still look and wish, right? You know how that is?"

"Sure," I said laughing.

"You do know it's very gay here?"

"I see that now. You must have a lot to choose from."

"Oh, but of course the one I want is always straight," he said pointing to me with a smile. "I'm Rodney."

We shook hands.

"Hi Rodney. I'm Jack."

"I won't embarrass you, sweetie, but I'll see you soon."

"All right there, big guy."

This guy was funny.

From there on, Rodney would give a wave or wink every time he'd scoot by. I was glad I got to laugh a bit with him because the other guy on the bike hadn't made me very comfortable.

Another guy came over to say hello one day from the booth across the way. He was a thin metal head with long curly light brown hair. I just knew he was into music.

"Hey, man. I'm Freddie."

"Hey, Freddie. I'm Jack. Good to meet you."

"That's my mom's jewelry booth. I came down from Michigan last year. You must be Annie's nephew."

"Yeah. They recruited me down here from New York."

"How are you liking it so far?" Freddie asked.

"So far so good. How about you? Have you adjusted?"

"Yes, it's a nice break from Michigan winters," he said.

"You into music?" I asked.

That was it. Instant connection. We spent an hour talking about bands before my busy wave picked up again.

Freddie invited me over to his place one night to watch some concert tapes. I went after work. He had his own room out in a shed-like guest house. He closed the door behind us. There on top of a black chest was a huge, packed bong.

"Do you smoke?"

"Sure, but I haven't had any in a while."

I had kept away from this, yet I thought about it. It had been such a long time. Cravings for it were still there, stronger than my desire for any drink. Maybe just a little wouldn't hurt.

Freddie lit the big pipe up and passed it. I took a hit and slowly inhaled. I held it in for a few moments, and then coughed it right back out. I had to take a gulp of water after that first one. I passed the pipe and waited for the effects to hit me. The Alice in Chains concert started up on his TV. The thin singer named Layne Staley came out on the stage shirtless, in ripped blue jeans, and wearing dark sunglasses. He was still in his prime in this video before it became difficult to tour. The music lured me in, but the song was called "We Die Young" and the lyrics were miserable.

"What a show!" I said.

"They're the best. They're doing an MTV show in April."

"Really? I thought he was really messed up now."

"Yeah, we'll see. I hope it's not disappointing," he said.

After a couple of songs, Freddie repacked the bong and handed it to me for a fresh hit. I was back in the saddle.

"Here, check this out too. Let me put this on."

He stopped the VHS tape and flicked on the CD player.

"This is from a new supergroup Layne's been in with the guitarist from Pearl Jam, Mike McCready."

A haunting and heavy song titled "Lifeless Dead" started up. I was frozen. Toward the end, the band got into a hypnotizing groove and the singer just repeated over and over— "lifeless dead" "lifeless dead" "lifeless dead..."

"Jesus, Freddie. That was crazy."

"You said it. I know."

☆

Freddie and I got together two nights later to watch more concert videos and listen to tunes.

"Check this out."

He popped in a CD and hit play.

"Dude, that sounds like GNR," I said after hearing the first twenty seconds of vocals. I was shocked and for a minute I thought this was some kind of lost release.

"It's an early 90s band called Wildside, like the Motley Crue album. They made this in 1992 but it didn't take off."

"Ah man, they missed the '80s boat."

We laughed and listened to the rest of the exciting lost album. A song "So Far Away" captured my feelings of confusion and past rage. I realized I was starting to feel far away from the rest of the world, down there on the island.

I was content for a while just smoking a little pot with him, but then an urge crept in to smoke alone like I had done so often in my car back home.

"Could you get me a small stash to smoke before bed?"

"Yeah, I can. You can have the rest of this bag," he said.

He handed me a bigger bag than I'd ever had.

"Whoa, I don't think I need this much."

"Go ahead, I have a whole new bag," said Freddie.

"How much do I owe you?"

"Don't worry about it this time."

I slapped down a twenty-dollar bill.

"At least let me leave you something," I said as I walked out.

The ride home around the island was always strange. The speed limits were lower, so cars just crept along with the motorbikes in slow motion. I lit a cigarette, rolled down the windows of my Camaro, and blasted music all the way to the other side of the island. Some nights I'd stop at the IHOP and get breakfast at one or two in the morning. I'd sit there all stoned out with dozens of other folks all dazed out on who knows what. None of us talked to each other. This was a place to stop, eat, and zone out in before we'd have to go home to our regular everyday lives. Yet our regular everyday lives were a world away from those on the mainland.

Lifeless Dead

Ashley picked me up from work for the party. We walked a few blocks to a large house. Music was playing. Kids were in and out of the house. Some just hung out on the lawn with beers. The ages ranged from about fifteen to early twenties. She introduced me to a few girls. We did rum shots with one group before finding our way to the kitchen for strawberry daiquiris. I was feeling good.

A while later, Ashley led me up to a bedroom on the third floor. It wasn't empty though. We walked in and saw a daughter of one of the other vendors in bed with two older guys. There were other people in the room kissing, smoking, and talking like everything was completely normal. One guy just sat there staring at everyone, occasionally breaking into a smile. Ashley and I ducked out and went to the next room.

In the next room, we were greeted by three dudes and a gal. They told us to come in and lock the door behind us. One guy unzipped a bag with needles in it. I turned to look at Ashley.

"I'm not into this."

"You don't have to try it if you don't want to," she replied.

"You do this? You don't have to…"

"Don't hog it all up this time, Ash," said a man over me.

They were starting to load the needles.

"Did you think this was going to impress me or something?"

"No, I'm just being upfront with you. Right? You didn't want to find out who I am a week later, did you?"

"This is who you are? You define yourself by a drug?"

"I'm just being honest. It's really not a big deal," said Ashley.

"I'm sorry. I'm out of here," I said.

"You're not going anywhere," said one of the guys firmly.

"You're going to sit down and put some of this shit in your veins. We can't trust that you're not going to go out there and call the cops," said the biggest of the three men.

"Listen, I don't want trouble. This just isn't my thing."

"Too late for that. Watch where you walk. You could step on a viper," said the other smaller guy.

There were three of them. Even if they were junkies, they hadn't shot up yet, so there would be a fight. I wasn't sure I could fight off all three of them, but I wasn't going to just sit there. I bolted for the door. Just as the bigger of the three men grabbed my arm, a loud knocking hit the door.

"Hey, Jack, are you in there?"

I had been saved. It was Freddie.

The burly man let go of my arm and looked at his buddy, who just shrugged it off. I unlocked the door, opened it, relieved to see my friend.

"What are you doing? I've been looking for you," he said.

"Perfect timing."

I looked back at Ashley. She callously waved me on. The mean guy next to her put his finger to his mouth.

"See you around, Ashley. Be careful."

She just laughed.

Once out of the house with Freddie, I turned to him.

"What are you doing here? You saved my ass in there."

"The vendor two carts down told me who you were with and where you were heading, and I just knew. I wanted to be sure you knew who you were getting in with."

"They were about to strap me down and shoot me up."

"Ashley got in with some bad people just recently."

"Man, she had me fooled. What a disappointment."

"You can meet someone and have no idea how messed up they are. They'll lead you right into the demon's den."

"Thanks for showing up when you did."

"I'm glad I could help. You want to go hang?"

"Let's go."

We walked back to his shack and hung for a while.

"You know, I didn't even know you knew those people. I mean, you're quiet."

"I know, I'm quiet. Don't have much of a life here, but when I first got here I met a few people and found my way around. I realized there's some sick stuff going on here, just like anywhere else. I listen to junkie rock stars, but I don't want to be one."

"Good to know."

I was relieved, but I was starting to feel restless.

Double Vision

A lot of tourists, including groups of young girls, came down during Spring Break looking for a good time. One night, I met a college girl named Christa from Delaware. She was blond and had metal braces. She was young, but older than Ashley. I poked around about her habits to be sure she wasn't into any bad things.

I brought her back to my aunt Judy's vacation house on Cudjoe Key. The house stuck out on an inlet of a deep blue canal full of fish and crustaceans that stuck to the canal walls. The house was closed up while she was in New York for most of the year, but Annie gave me a key to go check on things once in a while. The house was clean, but a bit warm. I didn't want to run the air conditioner because Judy might notice the electric bill, so I turned on several fans.

I popped open a bottle of white wine I had in the fridge, and the party started. Then we headed into the guest bedroom. When it got too hot in the bed, we resorted to the cooler tile floor in the kitchen. But it was too late. We were soaked. Christa poured the rest of the wine all over us to try and cool us down. We licked the cold white wine and sweat off each other's bodies. She squatted over me to get her aching knees off the hard floor for a while. At the end, she turned over, opened the freezer, and stuck her head in. The frigid air seemed to blow right over her back and hit me in the face as I emptied my spirit out onto the crack in her backside.

It was senseless kitchen-floor passion, and we knew she was going home in a couple of days and never coming back. We used each other. It felt cheap, but we couldn't help it.

☆

Key West was a transient place to be. Always in motion. And it was a small place. The whole island is really two by four. The downtown area is only one mile by one mile. If someone's there, you'll know.

One night the past came to visit. Two girls from that old town showed up at the cart.

"Jack, is that you?"

"Jack, what in the world are you doing here?"

Naomi and Selina were popular girls from my old town in New York. We didn't associate too much in high school, especially at the end when I estranged myself from everyone, but we knew each other well enough and had mutual friends. I told them how I had found my way down here from Paul's place. They laughed, excited to hear Paul's name.

"How is he?" Selina asked.

"Paul's great. What are you two doing here?"

"Vacation. Selina's family comes down like every year."

"We love it. I had to bring Naomi with me."

"It's a small world," I said.

"Hey, what are you doing later?" Naomi asked.

"Good idea, Naomi. Jack, do you want to meet at our hotel later?" asked Selina. "We'll take a dip in the pool and catch up."

"Sure thing. I get off soon. If I run home, I could be there by nine thirty," I said.

"Nine-thirty is perfect. Meet us out front of the Pier House at the end of the block," said Selina.

"I'll bring my suit," I said.

The girls laughed, waved, and walked off.

I asked Freddie if he wanted to join me, but he declined, so I went solo after work. When I got there, the girls were standing there waiting in their bathing suits. Naomi was thin with long straight brown hair and brown eyes. Selina was full bodied with wild curly blonde hair and big blue eyes.

We headed over to the hot tub outside. The girls got right in. I peeled off my shirt, kicked off my shoes, and joined them. We had the whole tub to ourselves.

"So why are you here?" Naomi asked.

"That's a good question. I have some family here and they had a job. I almost stayed with Paul, but..."

"But why did you leave?" Selina asked.

"New York?"

"And our town. What happened last year?" Naomi asked.

"That's a long story. I could write a book about it. Ultimately, I found myself without a home. Paul took me in. I took a break from school, actually dropped out, but then my uncle in Ronkonkoma took me in and Mr. Connolly let me back into school."

"Yeah, we didn't see you around," said Naomi.

"I had to focus on school and work."

"What happened with..."

Selina was going to ask, but I stopped her.

"I don't want to talk about that."

"Okay," she said.

"Are you ever going to come home?" asked Naomi.

"This is home. For now."

"I mean our hometown."

"No, I don't think I'd ever go back."

"Really? Why?" They both asked.

"Too many demons."

Their faces turned to puzzlement.

"Too many memories," I said.

"Not good ones?" asked Selina.

"I don't have anything there anymore. Maybe I'd go back to Long Island, but probably not that town."

No, not probably. I'd never go back to that town.

"So no one will ever find out we were ever here with you in this hotel hot tub?" Naomi asked.

"Not from me."

"Who knows what they'd say," giggled Selina.

Some time passed and we enjoyed the night sky with our eyes closed. When a few other guests were about to join us, Selina suggested going up to their room. We climbed out and threw towels around us.

"Let's go get out of these wet suits," said Selina.

"Oh, I didn't bring..."

They just looked at each other and laughed.

When we got up to their room, Selina went to the bathroom and Naomi handed me a bottle of red wine to open.

"Go ahead, open this. Let's have a glass," she said.

"Nice," I said.

I took the corkscrew and screwed the top off and poured three glasses. Selina came back and we did a salute to the old town. We drank from our glasses. Naomi said she'd be right back and went to the bathroom. Once the door was closed, Selina peeled off her bottom and then her top. I put my glass down and stood there in awe. She pulled me into her sudden nakedness and slipped my bathing suit off. When Naomi came back, we were already in bed under the sheets.

"Couldn't even wait for me?" she asked.

Naomi slid in to join us. They were all over me and in control. I almost couldn't take their beauty. I glimpsed one last look at Naomi as she lowered herself down onto me. Her sharp straight brown hair hung in front, and then all went dark as I found myself lost in the depths of Selina over my face. From here, it was all tasting, hearing the sounds of our bodies, feeling the back and forth wave— a tightening, a letting go. An explosion of ecstasy. Then another. Then another. And then silence.

Recovering the Satellites

On the next day around eleven, I returned to the courtyard for work. I cleaned a bit and set up the cart while a Counting Crows tape played. The spring day was already warm, already feeling like summer. Freddie arrived to open his mother's jewelry shop.

"How was last night?" he asked.

"It was great to see them."

"Will you see them again?"

"No. We said goodbye. They were heading back today."

"You know, they were really foxy."

"Freddie, you should've come along. You missed them in bikinis! Jesus, they were hot."

"No fucking way!" he said.

I thought how unbelievable it would be to tell him the truth, and how many times I had heard wild stories that definitely couldn't be true. There was no reason to ever say anything to anyone about this encounter, and the girls knew it too.

Just then, I spotted someone else I recognized walking up the sidewalk towards me. I excused myself to Freddie. I couldn't believe my eyes. Two run ins with people from that old town within two days. What was going on?

"Mr. Bissell?"

"Jack, my goodness! Call me Rich."

I hugged my twelfth-grade science teacher.

"How are you, Rich? It's great to see you!"

"Good. Things are quite well."

"What in the world are you doing here?"

"My wife and I have been coming down here for years. She's down there shopping. I ran into the girls in the hotel who told me you were down here."

He raised his eyebrows, smiled, and let out a laugh through his bushy beard.

"What's the chances? This is Bermuda Triangle kind of stuff!" he said.

"This place is like that," I said.

"So you're living here?"

"Yeah, crazy right?"

"How do you like it? Big difference from New York?"

"A whole new world. But honestly, I've been thinking about getting back to the mainland. Not sure how I feel all the way down here."

"It sure is nice, but I guess it's a bit isolated to live down here twelve months out of the year. Depends on what you like."

"Yes, it's quite far away."

"Say, have you been out to Benihana yet?"

"You know, it's on my list. I might drive out there this weekend. It'd be nice to get off the main island."

"Great beach. Great fishing."

"I'll be sure to go. How's the school? Mrs. Nelson? Mrs. Graham? Mr. Gongolski?"

"They're all great. I'll be sure to tell them you said hello. Hey, how about a picture together? I'll show it to them."

"I'd be honored."

I called Freddie over and handed him Mr. Bissell's camera so he could snap a photo of us. There we were. He had his fishing hat on and a wild tropical-looking button up. I looked like a tanned island boy. He put his arm around me. We smiled and Freddie snapped a couple of shots.

"It's truly great to see you, Mr. Bissell."

"Rich."

"Rich it is."

"Yes, it was great to see you too. You be well. Come visit us if you ever make it back. Maybe you could come back to talk to the kids sometime. Tell them how you got out!"

"Sure thing."

"You're one of our Hall of Famers!"

"Thanks, Rich. Take care."

We hugged and he was off. I turned back to Freddie.

"What a weekend!"

"That was your teacher? I didn't have teachers that cool! You must have gone to a cool school," Freddie said.

"You don't know half the story."

Good Enough

I spent the night at Freddie's shack smoking from a bong watching old Led Zeppelin and Pink Floyd concerts. I wasn't in danger of anything like I had felt in New York. In fact, I felt rather safe for a time in Key West, but when I got to a certain level of being stoned an odd feeling kicked in— a deep paranoia of something. It wasn't Freddie though. The emotion was almost a fear of place. I wasn't sure if it was a fear of the island or a fear of myself.

When it was a little past two, I thought it was best to hit the road and head home. The road was dark, but the streetlights occasionally blinded me. I glided past a few slow drivers probably creeping their way home from the bars.

Something was growing inside. A restlessness I had felt before. The blackness of the ocean just off the road that led right out into an abyss of nothingness frightened me at night. This place was starting to make me nervous. I felt it in my soul.

I had a dream that night about Uncle Al. I was in his kitchen, and he walked in sweating, red eyes bulging, a look of terror on his face.

"You okay, Albert?"

"Jack. Jack. What are you doing? What are you doing?"

"Nothing. Are you okay? Feeling all right?"

"Where are you? Where are you?" he kept asking.

☆

One afternoon, I sat to take a smoke break during a low point of the day. I had a mixed tape playing in my stereo. On came a song titled "Give In to Me" by Michael Jackson featuring Slash on guitar. I took a hit of the cigarette and strummed the air guitar as Slash hit the chords entering the chorus. Just then down on the sidewalk about ten feet in front of me, I spotted a man in a hat walking by. He was waving and giving me a thumbs up. I presumed it was for the song I was playing because it was the founding rhythm guitarist of Slash's old band, a guy named Izzy Stradlin.

What was this rock legend doing all the way down here? He had walked away from the biggest band in the world at their peak. After putting together his own band, releasing one album, and touring Japan, he disappeared back to Indiana. I ran down after him and then around in front of him. I extended my hand.

"I just wanted to say it's a god damned pleasure."

"Oh, that's cool, man. Thanks."

Izzy was a bit taller than me and his long dark hair was now trimmed shorter, more like my hair. He was still thin, but not unhealthy thin like his old band days when he was messed up on drugs. I heard he had cleaned up before leaving the band.

"Sorry to bother you, but I just had to," I said.

"No, no bother. You have good taste listening to my old bandmate. Slash did mighty good on that one, eh?"

"Yeah, great stuff. Hey, I loved your Ju Ju Hounds album. You have any more of that?" I asked.

"You bet. I'm just doing a little road travelling. It's good to be out on the road when you're clear headed. Nice for a change."

"Funny, I drove down here by myself from up north, and it was a blast. Lot of time to think."

"You know it. Great musical inspiration. Me and Rick got a number of new songs just from this trip alone," he said.

Rick leaned right in for a friendly handshake. I didn't know who he was, but he looked like a musician with his long black hair.

"No way! I can't wait to hear them on the next album!"

"Want to hear a few tonight?" asked Izzy. "Come by the Ocean Key Resort, room 301 around nine. We'll let you listen to a few tracks. You can let us know what you think. Bring a friend."

☆

Freddie and I arrived at the hotel room. It was a fantastic room with a view of the water. I had never been to a hotel room that had its own living room.

"Have a seat. Get comfortable," Izzy said.

"Izzy doesn't drink anymore, but I do. Do you guys want a beer?" asked Rick.

 I turned to look at Izzy.

"Man, this guy's looking out for you!" Rick said.

"See what the magazines do," Izzy said. "It's okay, guys. All cool. Just don't throw up and shit. Or bring any smack around here. Or cause any riots!"

"We'll go to a GNR concert if we want that," Freddie said.

Izzy stopped and looked at Freddie with a sudden seriousness. That's it. We're getting kicked right out of here in the first five minutes.

The two men burst out laughing. I was relieved.

Rick grabbed Freddie a beer. I declined his offer. I wanted to go through this sober.

 Izzy started playing "How Will It Go?" on his acoustic. Rick joined in with his. He was the awesome lead guitarist on the album. After they did another tune from the first album, Izzy said they would do a few new songs.

They laughed their way through a song titled "Here Before You" and then played an incredible song titled "Good Enough" which ended up being my favorite.

They started a chorus to another untitled song and then morphed into the chorus of a song from his old band days. They ended with a big laugh.

"What do you guys think?" Izzy asked.

I was taken back. I looked over to Freddie and he was engulfed in the sofa like a windstorm had blown him into place. The beer and music had leveled him. The three of us knew it and laughed hard. Rick got up to make a drink.

"Man, that was so terrific. 'Good Enough' was my favorite. This is going to be the best album in the world. You have a name yet?" I asked.

"No name yet. We're only just getting started on it. Some songs are still in the early stages," Izzy said.

"When will it be out?" I asked.

"Goodness, a year or two. Not sure. Say, where are you guys from?" Izzy asked.

"I'm from New York," I said.

"I'm from Michigan," Freddie said.

"Oh, we both had our times in New York," said Rick.

"Being from Indiana, I've been up to Michigan a lot too. Great winters," said Izzy.

"Yeah, fun," said Freddie.

 They laughed.

"What brought you guys down here?" Izzy asked.

"My mom came down and I followed," Freddie said.

"I'm just lost looking for myself. I have an aunt and uncle here. Not sure what to do next though."

"I'd hit the road. Travel a bit. See the country. It's a great big place with lots of things to experience," Izzy advised.

"Like Kerouac, *On the Road,*" Rick said with a chuckle.

"Yeah, kind of. One big fucking adventure. Make your own highway, start at zero, and don't look back," Izzy said.

"I have a love hate relationship with New York," I said.

"That happens. Though I have to be honest, I went back to where I came from and it got real again. It was humbling. But pick and choose what feels right," said Izzy.

This rock legend had just given me the advice of my life. We sat around for another hour and occasionally Izzy and Rick would tell us road stories from different states. I told Izzy how cool it was that he was out on his own now exploring. We were respectful enough not to ask him about his old band. It didn't seem like the right thing to do, and he didn't seem interested in talking about the past anyway. He was very much a man in the present.

As hard as it was, after a few hours we didn't want to intrude too long. We got up to leave.

"Thank you. This made my year," I said.

"You betcha, man. Hey Rick, I feel like I've known these guys my whole life," Izzy said.

"You guys take care and keep riding on," said Rick.

"Thanks, guys. Keep rollin' on," said Freddie.

"On down the road!" I added.

"All right, these are all like future song titles and shit," Izzy joked.

We laughed, shook hands, and said goodbye.

Not a single autograph.

Not a single photograph.

Just a moment in the heart.

Izzy made me realize it was time to roll on. Trouble can find you wherever you go. The past can follow. I didn't want to be there when it caught up. You have to make your own path. He knew that. He was a renaissance man. And I was to walk away from all of it too, again and again and again.

Highwayman

I sat Annie down and told her the news. She was still upset about finding out their lawyer had been terribly injured in an accident a couple of weeks earlier. He had been out riding home from the bar on his moped and someone roared right over him on the boulevard. Hit and run. Probably a drunk driver. The man's funny, witty way was gone forever just like that. Now he was in a chair struggling to smile and speak. It was awful, and bad timing for me, but I couldn't wait. I needed to get back to New York.

On July 2, I packed my car up and headed to the post office to ship a few boxes of belongings ahead of my departure to lighten the load. Then I went to say goodbye to some friends.

"So you're out of here already?" Freddie asked.

"Yeah, a whole six months and I'm fried."

"Missing the real world? Are you going to travel?"

"I think so, but I need to get back to start college."

"I'll probably head back north at some point too. Who knows," he said.

"Maybe start a band?" I asked.

We just smiled.

"You have a good heart. Take care, Freddie."

"Thanks, friend. See you around."

Then I walked over and said goodbye to Rodney.

"Is this it for you?" he asked when I walked up.

"Yup. On my way."

"Highwayman!" said Rodney.

"I guess so. Hey, it's been good knowing you," I said.

Rodney brought his big hand down for an arm wrestle handshake and then patted me on the shoulder.

"Same here. Be well. Don't forget us. Visit sometime."

"I'll be back someday, I'm sure."

It was the middle of the day. I took a ride over to Ashley's house. I took the chance that she'd be out, probably getting into trouble. Her mother answered the door.

"Hi, you probably don't remember me from a while back. I came to pick up Ashley..."

"Hi, there. Sorry, she's not here right now."

"Then it might be a good time to talk to you."

"To me? Is there a problem?"

"Yes, I don't say this lightly, but Ashley has a problem."

"What? Who are you?"

"I'm just a guy she met for a week or so. I'm moving back north, but I thought you should know. I'm not looking to get her in trouble or anything, but I think she's going to need help."

"Do you have the right person? Ashley's only in high..."

"Yes, that's her," I said pointing to the picture on the wall.

"I have no doubt with the stuff she's doing that she's going to have a hard time getting off of it."

"What are we talking about here? Coke, meth, heroin?"

"Maybe all of it, but I saw her with heroin."

The woman covered her mouth with her hands.

"I'm sorry. I thought you should know."

"Thank you. Thank you. You did the right thing."

I said goodbye and drove away, a rat without guilt, hoping it made a difference.

We had all driven or been driven to the end of the country, the furthest south you can go, and it might as well have been the edge of the Earth. We all came to that edge for different reasons. Some of us would be okay. Some would leave. Some would never.

Thunder Road

On July 3, I hit the road back to New York. The 1,490-mile trip began at 5:00 pm. By nightfall, I was out of the Keys and passing Lake Worth. I considered stopping to see Paul on the way out, but he was working late, and I was eager to get back to New York and start my life.

I drove through Georgia and the Carolinas in the black of night. I stopped off in Virginia to relax at a rest area as the sun was coming up. I eased the seat down and drifted off.

Only about a half hour later a furious knock on my driver side window tore me from my peaceful nap. It was a big burly state trooper with a round and ridiculous hat.

"Someone says you've been hangin' around here all night," the trooper said as I rolled down the window.

"No, maybe about an hour," I responded groggily.

"Where you comin' from?"

"Florida."

"Where you goin'?"

"New York, Ronkonkoma, New York. Isn't this a rest area?"

"Yes, but it's not meant to sleep and smoke drugs at. Let's slowly get out of the car. I'm goin' to have to inspect your vehicle for drugs and weapons."

"What? What are you talking about?"

"The nature of the call is reasonable cause for a search. Please slowly step out of the car," the trooper said.

"What's going on here?"

"Want to sit and wait for a warrant?" he asked.

"But what's going on here? What are you talking about?"

"I could hold you here all day while we get a warrant and the dogs. That'll take a while."

I got out of the car and the trooper ordered me to go and stand by a tree about ten feet away. The trooper took his clownish hat off and placed it atop the blue roof of my car. Fear surged through my mind as I hoped he wouldn't look inside the dirty sock in the empty shoe inside the red duffel bag, where I had placed the final bag of pot Freddie had given me before I left, which I planned on smoking at the lake.

The trooper searched the inside of the car, picking up items and even smelling them. Coming to the red duffel bag, he took it out of the car and shuffled through it.

Shit. He's going to find it. I'm going to jail.

The state trooper is going to send me to some backwards southern Virginia jail and the local government is surely going to throw away the key on what they'll call a Yankee drug smuggler. But he didn't find the pot.

He put the duffel bag back into the car, and searched around the car one last time. He even opened the gas cap and looked inside hoping to find sacks of heroin or cocaine, but of course he didn't. When his empty search was over, the trooper put his big brown hat back on and told me to get out of his state. I could tell he was disappointed not to have an arrest, but still deeply pleased to disturb me from a nap. I wondered if he would've demanded a search from someone wealthy or someone from a southern state. I doubted it.

I got back on the road, rattled by the shakedown. The closer to New York the safer I felt, but the drivers got more aggressive on the Jersey Turnpike. A red Mazda in front of me hit a large chrome object and its back tires spit it up into the air. A loose truck bumper came flying at me, but it crashed down onto the highway right in front of my path instead of through my unsuspecting windshield. At seventy miles an hour there was no time to dodge it.

It was too late. I drove over the bumper as it shook the Camaro and my seat belt tightened up around my chest. Amazingly, I had escaped destruction. Unfortunately, the red Mazda ahead of me had sprung a leak in the fuel tank and run out of gas less than a mile later. The poor guy in the Mazda with his fuel spilled all over the turnpike was now stranded thanks to someone's garbage.

I refused to let any of the incidents get me down. I popped in an '80s Judas Priest cassette and "Thunder Road" came on. I thought of my metal friend Freddie and smiled. I hit the gas and belted out "I'm coming home..." Cigarette after cigarette, Arizona Iced Tea, a pack of Sunny Doodles cupcakes, and a tray of cassette tapes fueled me all the way through. Other than gas stations and the Virginia rest stop, I had driven straight through to New York. The road was all there in my ridiculously bloodshot eyes.

The George Washington Bridge awaited me. I was delirious and deprived of sleep from hours of being on the road. Colors of cars flew past me. All the memories flew past me. I knew where I had been. I wouldn't forget that. But I had no idea where I was really going.

Ronkonkoma, NY, Fall, 1996

Back at Uncle Al's, I set my things upstairs in the apartment. This time I would be renting the upstairs instead of living with him downstairs. This would give us our own space.

There were still some belongings up there from when my grandfather would visit. Furniture, dishes, pots, basics, all there waiting. I would only need a few things.

I collapsed into the awaiting queen-sized mattress on the floor. What a ride down to Florida. I wasn't sure why it all happened, or what it accomplished, but here I was back at the beginning. Time to sleep it off and start anew.

☆

In late July, I visited the college campus in Brentwood to make the first step toward signing up for classes. I did all the paperwork, grabbed a vanilla cappuccino from the machine, and looked around the campus. This was college. I was going. Not something I really ever planned on.

I called up Cliff to see if he needed any help. He told me to come on down to the station and fill out the paperwork. I was back in the New York groove.

I started back up at the gas station a week later.
"Great to have you back, Jack."
"Same here, Cliff. Thanks for taking me back."
"How did Florida work out?"

"I had a great job, but I really wanted to get college going. It didn't seem realistic down there for me."

"Key West, right?"

"Yeah."

"Wild place. I went in the '70s. It was wild then too."

"Yeah, funny stuff."

"I could see how you felt cut off from the world though."

"It was a strange six months."

"Ah, you'll never forget it."

"True. It's great to be back home though."

Cliff gave me the run down as a reminder, "I never measure the coffee right, but the gasoline tanks— that's what we get paid to measure, so be very careful when you take those measurements at the start and end of each day."

"Will do."

"Well, you know the drill. I'll go make us some coffee before I go."

I helped a few customers as Cliff went to the backroom to put up coffee and get changed into his regular clothes. About ten minutes later, he yelled up to the front.

"Coffee's up, Jack. Might make your hair a little curly!"

I went back and got a cup of his super strong coffee. He had a few mugs we could use and wash and told me I could bring my own if I want. We lit cigarettes.

"So you back at the same house with your uncle?"

"Yes, I've got the upstairs apartment for a few hundred a month."

"Nice deal. You mentioned college. How's that?"

"Yes, all signed up. I went down there the other day and put in my paperwork."

"Sounds like a good plan, Jack."

"Yes, I think so."

"Let me go. My wife's here. Call me if you need anything. See you tomorrow."

"Have a good one, Cliff."

I took over the night shift at the front window. Occasionally, I'd recognize a regular from my previous stint. One guy in a black Cherokee would drop in every Friday like clockwork. He'd linger around the window a little longer than most and tried to make conversation. I started to get the sense he wanted something out of me. The way he stared reminded me of the shirtless guy on the bike in Key West, but then I remembered Rodney and laughed to myself. I politely told the man to have a nice day.

Cruz, a handsome Luke Perry look-alike mechanic at the shop next door, would come over every day for cigarettes and we'd talk for a few minutes about various things. Poor guy had different kids with different women and owed them all child support, but at least he was paying.

"Keep control of the pumps!" he'd say kidding around.

"Speaking from experience?" I asked.

"You know it."

Let Me In

The first day of college was full of butterflies, but I jumped into the pool with confidence. The whole week was exciting, but it had that same mystical feeling I had had in night school the year before when I emersed myself in my education and slowly withdrew from everything I had ever known in my old town. I expected much solitude once again.

My first class was at eight o'clock on a Tuesday morning in September. Professor Kohl opened the class with words of wisdom.

"Look around. We often fail to see the miracles."

The short, older, woman with glasses welcomed us and told us a little about herself before going over the syllabus. We were all deer in the headlights.

"I want to welcome you all to Freshman Composition and college. It's going to be quite an adventure."

She wasn't wrong.

Professor Kohl's first lesson was to contrast the differences among thinking, speaking, and writing.

"Thinking is a natural process. Writing is not; it must be learned. But writing makes us better thinkers."

As she discussed the different parts, from the word to the sentence to the paragraph, she explained, "The whole becomes greater than the sum of its separate parts."

The professor strolled around the classroom and previewed basic paragraph structure for papers.

"10-14 sentences per paragraph, on average... there's a beginning, middle, and an end. You're going to learn the structure and different strategies to integrate your words with credible outside sources."

Then Professor Kohl turned and wrote some quotes on the board. She closed out our first class by previewing our one and only class book, which was a collection titled *Selected Essays* by Ralph Waldo Emerson.

"*Envy is ignorance; imitation is suicide.* What does this mean to us? Really think about this."

Some of this seemed like gibberish to many in the class as they stared off, but the words hit me like a truck full of bricks. I was stunned. No teachers had shared this wisdom in high school. This was my church.

"*Happiness is in the becoming,*" she said.

Indeed, it is.

I was already realizing my love for words in Professor Kohl's class. I had notebooks of cheesy rock lyrics I had written down from the age of twelve, and I had written long narratives for my In-School-Suspension teacher Mr. Kelly, but this was the first time I really considered writing something more substantial on my own.

From English class, I went off to psychology class, which could've been a bit more interesting if it hadn't been for so many formal definitions. After that class, I decided to check out the cafeteria. I walked into a bustling room. Many seemed to already know each other. I was the odd guy out. I got a French vanilla cappuccino and walked deeper into the crowded room. And there to my surprise, smiling, pointing, and waiting for me at a table, were the Kennedy brothers.

"What the..." Jeff said.

"How are you?" Where you been, man?" Andy asked.

"So great to see you guys. What are you doing here?"

"No, what are *you* doing here?" Andy asked.

"This is classic!" said Jeff.

"Yeah, I was down in Florida with Paul for a bit and then went and hid out in the Keys for a while."

"Oh man, how is that guy?" asked Jeff.

"Great. He's doing great. Living the life."

"How were the keys? Crazy place?" asked Andy.

"Yes, quite a different kind of place. I had to get back into the New York groove, if you know what I'm saying."

"Oh yeah!" said Jeff laughing.

"I've been meaning to call you guys since I've been back. It's been too long."

"Yeah, probably that graduation party with...."

I interrupted Andy, "I forgot about that. So what are you guys studying here?"

"Core classes. Basketball. I'm already set to transfer up to Maine in the new year," said Andy.

"Nice. Good deal."

"You'll need to come visit. College life away is going to be different than this place. Not that this is bad."

"Sounds good to me."

"Classes are good and girls are pretty," Andy said.

"Yes, I'd like to transfer too. Not yet sure for what."

"No worries. It's the community college way. I'm probably going to do graphic design after this," said Jeff.

"Nice. You'll do the album covers for our band!"

We all had a laugh at that one.

"Listen, we're going to have a party this Saturday. The fam moved to the next town over. I'll give you the new address. Why don't you come on by?" asked Andy.

"Can't believe your parents left the town."

"Yeah, it's a good move. You should come," added Jeff.

"Man, I haven't partied at all in a long time."

"You know us. I'm not a big drinker. Jeff here isn't even drinking right now," said Andy.

"Oh, really?"

"Yeah, straight edge these days, man. Are you?" asked Jeff.

"No, I don't think so, maybe, but that's cool. I'll see."

"It won't be too big or anything. Just a few of us," said Andy.

Andy handed me his address on a slip of paper.

"All right, where are you guys going next?"

"Math for me," said Andy.

"Acting part one," answered Jeff.

"With Professor Jones?" I asked.

Jeff's head snapped, "Yes, how...?"

 "There's where I'm heading!"

We said goodbye to Andy. Then Jeff and I walked off to acting class, just as we had walked back to school so many years earlier while I was on lunch suspension for ramming a bully's head into the tater tots on his food tray. For a while, Jeff was allowed to go home for lunch for medication, so we had lunch together for two weeks out of school. It was where we talked of music and bonded.

Here we were walking back to school so many years later all grown up. What a trip life is.

Hey Man Nice Shot

When I started back up at the station in August, it was on different shifts on different days. I didn't have to change a thing when college started in September. On Mondays, I would work the middle shift. I had off Tuesdays and Sundays to do homework. On Wednesday and Thursdays, I did the late shift from six to midnight. On Fridays and Saturdays, I worked the morning shift from six to noon. Every other week, I'd do a double on Friday and work from six to six.

We weren't a twenty-four-hour station, so the morning shift responsibility was to open everything up for the day. The last shift would lock up the station. Each shift leader had to do their own measurements, but opening and closing staff had to open and close out the day with a few extra steps in the report. There were locks, flags, and prices we needed to adjust. The day shift was busiest though, which more than made up for the lighter paperwork. The day shift would fly by with customer after customer. I was lucky if I could run to the bathroom.

Cliff worked the morning shifts Monday through Friday, but he'd come in after the start of the opening shift usually between eight and ten a.m. He'd hang around for about four hours into the day shift before his wife would come pick him up. Then I'd be alone for a couple of hours until the next guy showed up. Tony was usually the one who relieved me on the morning and middle shifts. He was a few years older in his final year at Stony Brook, the local state university. He was a smaller guy like me, but confident, athletic, and sharp.

Another guy named Charlie worked mostly morning shifts with Cliff. Unlike Tony's clean-cut look, Charlie had longer hair that would hang below his HESS cap. I appreciated Charlie's taste of alternative music, and I had nothing against him. but we just didn't click well.

Tony and Charlie really didn't like each other. I stayed out of it, but one day as I was taking over a shift from Charlie, Tony appeared to confront him. Cliff had already gone home.

"I hear you're talking shit," Tony said.

"Yeah, I said it. What are you going to do about it?"

Someone had told Tony that Charlie said he was a little man. Charlie had a good four inches on him.

"Let's take it out back and settle it," Tony said calmly.

The two walked back out behind the building. I couldn't help but follow. Business was slow, so I didn't have to worry as long as I kept an eye out. I wanted to make sure no one got killed back there.

Tony got right to it with his fists up. Charlie was a little surprised at his confidence. They went in for each other.

Tony rocked him back with a few good punches and Charlie stumbled back. Tony grabbed Charlie into a side headlock and flipped him over on to the concrete, like I had done during one of my middle school fights to a bigger kid named Jim. Tony got on top and started pounding him.

"Why do you think you're so tough?"

"Fuck you," Charlie replied.

Tony continued to blast him.

"Had enough?" Tony asked.

"Yeah."

"That's what I thought. Now shut your mouth."

That was it. Charlie had had it.

Tony nodded at me and took off on his mountain bike. Charlie struggled up and then silently went his way to his car. His head was down, defeated.

The next day when I saw Charlie, he had a nice shiner and was quiet about the whole thing. It had been settled. Don't mess with the tough small guy.

When Cliff asked me if anything had happened, I told him I was busy on my shift and didn't know anything. That was between them. But I was quietly glad Tony had shut him up— always glad to see the smaller guy teach a lesson to the bigger guy with a big mouth.

The next time I saw Tony, I told him what a shot he had.

"What're you gonna do, right? Some guys."

At the same time, I couldn't believe I was still watching fist fights at this age. I wondered what was wrong with this.

I lit a cigarette and got back to work. "Hey Man Nice Shot" was playing on the alternative rock radio station. I wondered what shot I was going to take at life.

Dark Side of the Moon

Saturday evening rolled around, and I decided to go to the Kennedy party. I hadn't traveled that way towards the old town in a long time. It felt like forever as I passed through a small section of the old town to get to their house in the neighboring village. I parked my freshly washed Camaro out front, the paint as blue as a crayon, and headed on in toward the back gate where Jeff told me to go.

"There he is!" exclaimed Andy.

I gave the brothers a hug. It was good to see them.

"Hey you," said an old familiar voice.

I turned to find my old friend Gil. He was the kind of guy you felt like you knew forever, even if it wasn't for long.

"Man, what are you doing? Nice to see you," I said.

"I heard about your road adventures," he said.

"Is that what they were? More like getting lost for a while."

"It's all cool. You're at the community college now?"

"Yeah, what are you up to?"

"I'm up at Oneonta. Just taking a weekend break."

"Excellent! The real college life."

Gil looked like what I imagined college kids to look like, in his preppy dress and clean-cropped hair. He and I were the same size and build. He had brown eyes and I had blue. We could've been long lost brothers.

I imagined the cool college kids like Gil hanging in the dorms with their baseball caps, pajama pants, red drink cups, and bongs. Of course, the only dorm I'd seen was in the movies.

"Hey, do you still smoke?" asked Gil.

I looked at his cigarette, but he realized and clarified.

"No, I mean weed. I have some if you want to go toke a joint with me."

"Man, it's been a while. I smoked in the Keys, but...."

I was really hoping to stay away from the stuff, and hadn't even smoked the remainder of the bag Freddie had given me, but I was tempted now.

"Mrs. Kennedy is inside, so you want to take a walk?"

"Yeah, all right. I'll have a bit," I agreed.

"Mint!"

"I haven't heard that word in ten years!"

"Bringing it back into fashion, you know."

Gil and I ducked out of the party and took a stroll down the road. The sun hadn't gone down yet. He lit up as we walked. After taking a hit, he passed it to me. There I was at it again, but if this kid up at the big college could do it, why couldn't I? I was going to college too.

We walked a few blocks, passing the joint back and forth. I felt like a kid again, except all the kids I had done this with had graduated to other things and were out of my life.

"Ever watch the *Wizard of Oz* while playing *Dark Side of the Moon?*" Gil asked.

"No, why?"

"The music matches up. It's wicked."

"I'll have to give it a try."

"Just start the movie and CD at the same exact time, and you'll see what I mean. It's a complete bug out."

"Something you learned at college?"

"Yes, the important lessons."

"How is it going up there?" I asked.

"So far so good. I've been meeting a lot of people. I'm thinking of joining the fraternity."

"Fraternity? Like a frat club?"

"Yup."

"I've heard wild stories about those."

"It seems pretty tame."

"They're not going to make you do crazy things just to be a member?" I asked.

"Nah, I don't think so."

"So why did you come back this weekend?"

"I wanted to check on my mother. She's alone."

"That's a good reason."

"I wanted to see the Kennedy brothers too, and good old friends like you. I can't believe we're all grown up."

"Yeah, really. Is it quiet up state?" I asked.

"It is, but not on campus. A little city of our own."

We started to walk back to the party. I was ripped. Gil was even more stoned out. We laughed our heads off once we got back to the party.

The night was young. More people would be arriving—some were distant acquaintances from high school and some I didn't know. The ghosts would be leaving me alone for now.

"Hey, we ought to hang when I get back for break."

"Let's do that, Gil. I'll get your number from Andy. Good luck up there."

A few days later, I dipped into the bag Freddie had given me. Uncle Al was working, so I went out into the backyard to take a few hits from the pipe. Then I went back upstairs, made a small pot of coffee, furiously cleaned my three-room apartment, and then sat down for a snack and a movie. I popped on the *Dark Side of the Moon* compact disc and hit play on the VCR. *The Wizard of Oz* started. Just as Gil had said, the music matched the action of the film. Everything was completely and amazingly in synch, and I was out of this world.

The Pony Express

After a few weeks, it was time to start the big research paper in class. Professor Kohl announced the assignment instructions.

"Sometimes in life, we get selected to do a job. For your research paper, you're going to pick a topic from a hat."

I went up when she called my name, and I picked a slip of paper from the hat. It read *The Pony Express*. I had a vague idea that this had something to do with mail, but I was obviously going to have to look things up.

"How do we know if something is truth or fiction? How do we know the difference? Truth is not always fact.

Research is important in our world. It establishes facts and distinguishes the difference between truth and fact. But we need to use credible sources. Books and scholarly peer-reviewed journals are going to be the best of the best. You'll need them in your paper. Some newspapers will be allowed too.

You are to report the facts like a reporter. So you'll need evidence. There are four types of evidence. Facts. Statistics. First-hand observation. And expert testimony.

You need the three rhetorical appeals. Logos is logic, which includes facts and stats. Pathos is emotion, which is from the testimony of first-hand observation of witnesses and victims. Ethos is ethical appeal and audience awareness."

It was going to be work, but I was determined to do well. Professor Kohl explained the process and told us to get notecards to collect quotes, paraphrases, and page numbers of where the information came from. She told us where to go. The library.

I headed to the campus library. I walked past a group of students who were hanging out smoking in the courtyard, and I entered the grand building. I walked up to the counter and a friendly librarian named David welcomed me.

"Can you help me find sources on The Pony Express?"

"I sure could. Let me look."

David warmly smiled and checked his computer.

"Where are those dusty old cards?" I asked.

"Oh, the card catalogue? This is the new way. Is this a history class or English class?"

"Composition. English. I guess things have changed."

"Yes, they have. Follow me. We'll find your sources."

David led the way. He stopped at a stack of books deep into the rows. Running his finger along the shelf he went up, down, across, and then up again.

"Here we go. There are a few here. Use these numbers. Same thing for the other ones on the list. These will find you books. If you want journal articles, come back to me when you're done here and we'll help you find you some of those."

"Thanks. I will."

After finding books, David helped me find scholarly articles. I checked out some of the books so I could spend time with them, and then David helped me photocopy some of the journal articles.

I took my research with me to work at the station. Early Saturday mornings were a great time for homework because it was incredibly slow for several hours. I finished the four-page research paper. It took hours to write up by hand, organize, and revise. Then I typed it up on a campus computer.

I was amazed that the Pony Express was the first cross country mail delivery from Missouri to Sacramento. The operation started in April 1860 and closed in October 1861. It was quite a feat to travel that far on horse in the 1800s. The ride was 1,900 miles, longer than my trip from New York to Florida, but it would take ten days and ten riders. I wondered what a trip that length would be like with just one rider and a car in the 1900s.

Purple Haze

I blew the pot smoke out my bathroom window and lit an incense stick. I removed the towel at the bottom of the bathroom door and went back into my living room. Uncle Al was at work, but smoking in his house was still risky. After all, he was a cop.

I was working through the rest of the bag Freddie had given me, but it wasn't the same now that I was back in New York. After smoking with Gil at the party, I spent a few weeks taking just a hit or two a day, but it felt like a growing dependency. I would race around and clean the apartment like a madman with Ace Frehley or Van Halen playing on the tape deck. Then I'd plug in the guitar and amp I'd recently bought. I'd crank up the volume and do three to four note solos. I'd play only the three highest strings and let the notes ring as long as I could at top volume. Freedom.

☆

I helped Uncle Al with some lawn work. This wasn't something I always did. He didn't ask, but I volunteered when I could. The autumn leaves had piled up, so I felt compelled to help. I wasn't sure how it came up, but he suddenly started in with how bad he thought abortion was.

"It's bad, Jack. Have you ever seen it or read about it?"

"Seen it? No. I don't care much about it," I said.

"It goes against my church. That's why I'm pro-life."

Church? When does he go to church?

"You go to church?" I asked.

"Yes, I try to get there on Sundays. Your grandmother used to go, but... if you ever want to?

"No, I tried once."

"They've talked about it.... Abortion."

"Yeah, I guess I'm just not that concerned with what other people are doing."

Al just lifted an eyebrow and nodded.

I wondered what his church thought about the 80s video tapes I found in his living room cabinet. Blondes with semen dripping from their lips onto their breast implants. Guys with bushy mustaches and hairy backs busting away at the bush. One man looked like a pro wrestler named Mr. Wonderful. I swore it was him. These tapes made Al's magazine collection in the basement look innocent. I wasn't so sure the church approved of what went on in those wild tapes.

Then I thought about the little diner place we'd get breakfast at. The owner always talked about how criminal the president was, and my uncle nodded in agreeance.

"We have to get that son of a bitch out of office," she said angrily. "He's immoral. A liar."

I generally ignored the chatter, but assuming she was a government protestor I once asked her if she had been to Woodstock. I don't know why but there seemed to be a softness in her that evaporated from her forever when I asked that question. A hardness grew in her eyes. She never looked at me the same.

"Woodstock? Jimi Hendrix and all those druggies? Derelicts. Damned hippies. Sinners. Filth. No, I stand for American values," she said with a stern huff as she cleaned the counter.

I looked around at her restaurant. On the walls were giant portraits of 1950s pride— Marilyn Monroe. Judy Garland. Elvis Presley. All dead from drugs. Just like Hendrix.

Little Man Big Man

In her final lecture, Professor Kohl talked of reality and illusion. We sat and listened, really listened. This was a time for reflection. She mentioned a tale called *The Allegory of the Cave.*

"Read that tale and you'll begin to see the light. But remember that the person who comes out of the cave comes out of the cave alone.

No great man has ever come out of a crowd.

The more we identify as a group, the more we become weak. Those were Emerson's words. He valued individuality. Don't lose yourself out there. Read. Think. Be.

Perhaps the greatest sin is to say one is bored.

No matter what your work is, do your work out of enjoyment. Emerson said, *The true poet does work out of enjoyment not for compensation.*

When you return in two days, I will reveal a prompt on the board for your final exam. Remember what we talked about this semester. Your answers should have depth, as well as precision. It's been a pleasure, everyone. I wish you the best in your future endeavors."

☆

A few days later, we arrived for our final exam. Professor Kohl posted a prompt on the board and gave us a moment to read it and think about it.

The board read:

Many philosophers have concluded that progress and real understanding can only be achieved through pain and suffering. Agree or disagree?

"Any questions?"

She waited and then continued.

"Take your time, but when you're done, please bring up your blue book to me on your way out. Farewell. And remember to see the miracles around us."

Spring 1997

Just like the fall semester, Jeff and I hung together in Acting Part Two every Tuesday and Thursday. But there was also a couple in the class I started to talk to. Dan and Allison were from Islip and had gone to high school together. I thought to myself how they were in for something.

Allison invited me out with them to the car to smoke weed. We fogged out Dan's VW. There was something pretty about her, but she didn't seem happy. Maybe a little happier when she was stoned, but not much. Dan seemed bothered, maybe that I was around, but he tried to be polite.

"Hey, I'm pretty banged out. I have to get to class," I said.

"Shit, what time is it? I have chemistry," Dan said.

"Damn it, we lost track. Good smoking with you, Jack. Let's do it again soon," Allison said.

"Thanks for the smoke. See you two soon."

"Absolutely," Allison replied.

In late February, after a couple of more parking lot sessions after class, Dan and Allison invited me over to her house. We smoked on her back porch and then went and sat inside the living room. She put on a Phish album. No one else seemed to be around. The house was comfortably upper middle class with fine rugs and curtains, paintings, wood trimmings, and classic furniture. The house wasn't far from my grandmother's house by the water.

At some point, Dan took out his coke and started on a binge. He wasn't kidding around with that stuff. He was going through something. I decided to go. Allison looked disappointed that I was leaving. It was her boyfriend. I didn't understand what they wanted out of me. My old town wasn't the only place with trouble, and if I wasn't careful, I'd find my loner-rebel-James Dean-self right back in the same suffocating crowds.

☆

A scene was due in March. I heard some actors would show up stoned, so I said what the helk. I smoked a joint with Dan and Allison before class. I couldn't control myself in the scenes though. Uncontrollable laughter mixed with angry outbursts.

"Grandpa is a self-righteous man."

Louder. "Grandpa is a self-righteous man."

Louder. "Grandpa is a self-righteous man."

Dan looked at me. Get it together, he said with his eyes.

"You're the one who's out of order!"

"What the hell, Jack. That's not even in the script," he whispered.

"Ah, fuck you."

Allison started in, "Let's go to the zoo…"

"Fuck the zoo too…"

I was lashing out on the potheads with amplified Al Pacino-like lines and I had no idea why. Maybe it was my subconscious telling me I was done with these people.

I got back to my lines, and we ended the scene. The professor seemed to lose control of the class, and everyone seemed riled up by my chaos.

"Sorry, guys. I got out of hand."

They just waved me off and left.

"Whoa, man. You're ripped." Jeff said.

"You can tell?"

"Shit, yeah. I don't think the professor did though. Maybe she did, but she probably gets it all the time anyway."

"I just screwed my grade bad. What an embarrassment!"

"No worries, we'll do a kick ass final to make up for it."

Spaceboy

I drove out to the Kennedy house on a Saturday to practice a scene with Jeff and our partner Bryan. We worked at our scene over and over. This was going to be a monumental performance. No one and no drug was going to mess this up.

On the way back from Jeff's place, I stopped into Auto Barn in my old town for some car things. Air fresheners. Gas treatment. Oil additive. As I walked toward the cash registers, a guy got up, turned around, and smiled. It was Judd Reed.

I hadn't seen this guy since we were kids— probably around seven years since he went off to private school.

"Wow, Judd! What are you doing?"

"Jack, it's been so long! My semester just ended, and I'm back for the summer."

He then told me some unimpressive college name and I wondered why he wasn't at Yale or Harvard. What was the point in prep school if he'd just be going to an average university? Had it been to save him from the neighborhood punks like me? Maybe then I couldn't blame his parents, but still why not something bigger? He was a rocket scientist in my mind. He should be interning at NASA or a computer company in California. What the helk was he doing working in a store like I'd done?

"How are you, Jack? Where are you these days?"

"I'm good. I started college in Brentwood. It's going great. I live out in Ronkonkoma. I was just doing some homework with Jeff Kennedy. Remember him?"

"Yes, how are those guys?" he asked.

"They're both doing great. How's your family?"

"They're all well."

"Say hello to your mom. I remember her well," I said.

"Yes, I will," he said.

"Man, I'm so surprised to see you after all these years. I always wondered where you were."

He nodded in agreeance.

I struggled to find anything else to say. He awkwardly smiled, probably also not so sure what to say. Did he judge my college choice? Did he sense the danger or wildness in me that his mother had warned him to stay away from? Had he been conditioned to fear us or look down upon us?

Judd still looked like the rocket scientist I always thought he was, but as we looked at each other in awe, I got the sense he wasn't the same boy I knew. Those train rides to private school in the city had forced him to grow up and change, yet he seemed restrained by something, awkward, broken, I couldn't place it. Maybe he thought the same of me.

"Good to see you, Judd. Really good."

"Yes, you too, Jack. Have a good summer."

"Take care of yourself," I said.

We shook hands like long lost strangers, and I went to go check out. When I finished paying, I looked back before exiting the door. Judd was back to work straightening out brake fluid on the shelf. I was struck by this reality in an odd way and didn't know what to make of it.

When I got home there was an answering machine message from my Aunt Annie. She had a new proposal. No brakes. All accelerator.

Feelings Are Good

"I'm heading back to Florida, Al."

"So soon? What about college?"

"I don't know. The semester ends next week. I have to check out this opportunity with my aunt's business, at least for the season. They moved up to Orlando, so it's a different area. The company's really grown."

He looked surprised but didn't push the issue.

No resistance.

I wasn't going to tell him the truth. That things were getting foggy again. Strangeness had found me at college and work. Strangeness had even crept into our house. Him and I were spending less and less time together, and he had met a new woman. He'd stay at her house several times a week and talked about getting married, which made me question whether he was even going to keep the house. Maybe I was holding him back from restarting his life after his divorce. Maybe he needed to sell the house and move on. This was his chance.

I was disappointed that Al didn't press me to stay, but I assumed that meant he was looking for change.

"I'll miss you, Jack. Stay in touch."

"Thanks for the chance to rent the upstairs. My first apartment!"

"Yes, it's been good. Never even late with your rent! Call your dad while you're down there. Grandpa's getting old too, so maybe this is a chance to see him."

"Will do."

It wasn't at the top of my list to go running to my absentee father, but it would be nice to see my grandfather before it was too late. His heart was getting weaker, so we didn't have much time. He hadn't returned my last couple of calls, but maybe he would if I lived closer.

☆

When I told Cliff, he pressed a bit.

"You sure you want to do that again? What if you're not fulfilled like last time? What about college?" he asked.

"It's just not feeling right."

"Things seem like they're going good though," he offered.

"It's home. It's Long Island. I just don't know anymore."

"Well, I can understand if there are issues at home, and it's none of my business. Just wanted to see if you were really sure. Sometimes things ain't as bad as they seem."

"I'm not sure. Are we really ever? But thank you, Cliff. Thanks for asking. That means a lot. More than you know."

"Enough busting your chops. How about a pot of coffee to put some fur on our backs?"

"Ahh, sure. I'm going to miss it here."

"As long as I'm manager, you're always welcome back. Maybe you'll be back in the fall."

Running with the Night

My final acting class scene with Jeff and Bryan went well. We played three brothers. Bryan had the best of the three roles. He stood between us in the middle. This was his show, and I knew at that moment he could easily go off to Broadway or film, yet he shared the moment with us without upstaging us. I grew up in a neighborhood with racist kids. I grew up hearing stories. I grew up fearing them. Yet there I was at the front of acting class hugging a black man like he was my brother.

Bryan joked around when we talked about it one day.

"You're different, Jack. It was *The Jeffersons*. That show must've saved you."

"What about me, kid?" asked Jeff.

"*Good Times*, right?" Bryan asked.

"You know it, brother," Jeff said.

"Give some credit to Michael and Jimi, right?" I asked.

"I'll allow it. For those two. Yeah," Bryan said.

"God, those two were kings," said Jeff.

"I opened the *Thriller* album on Christmas," I said.

"Imagine all the other white kids who did that in the 80s!" Bryan said.

"Kool and the gang," said Jeff.

We laughed and agreed.

"What about Lionel Ritchie?" I asked. "Running with the Night. Say You Say Me. Hello. Lady. Unbelievable song writer!"

"If you guys start bringing in Grand Master Flash, I'm going to tell you you're not even white anymore," Bryan said.

"Yeah, him too!" Jeff said.

We all had a good laugh.

But Bryan was right. The music and TV had made a difference in our perception for the better.

In our acting scene, I played an emotional wreck of a brother. I said my lines, "What am I going to do now, learn how to play guitar? Start over?"

I was playing the role of a character I completely understood— a guy always seeming like he's on his last breakdown. The utter end or a renaissance. It was either extreme.

We hugged goodbye at the end of class. It was a moment of closure for me.

A few hours later, I was in my Camaro leaving New York for the second time, this time with more confidence. The sun was setting to my right. The Manhattan skyline behind me, fading, as I made my way through the industrial oil hell of northern New Jersey. I headed down I-95 toward the land of the palm trees for a another try. I popped on a mixed tape. On came a song that made me smile and I cranked up the volume.

"Running with the Night"

Orlando, Florida, May, 1997

Annie and Russell met me at the factory in Kissimmee. This time
we had a nice facility. All stainless steel. Multiple batch freezers
lined the back walls filled with pina colada mix and other flavors. I
was going to help manage the place while Russell was busy with
things. I was also going to make deliveries and check on customers.
This was going to be a different experience than the Keys where I
was stationary at a cart.

"Man, pina colada!"

Russell opened a container, scooped some out, filled a small
cup, and handed it to me.

"It's good as a dessert or a drink," he said.

"Yes, it is. Thank you. This is a heavenly creation!"

Russell let out a laugh. He threw on a live Van Halen album
on the CD player and cranked up the volume. Then he showed me
around the place and explained some of the big changes they made.
He pointed out all the new equipment. "Ain't talkin' bout love" with
Sammy Hagar on vocals came on and I was shocked how great it
sounded with him.

"Sammy's the shit, eh?" he said.

"Yeah, great stuff!" I replied.

"So what do you think?"

"I think you and Annie struck it big this time. This is a big
step up from the cart. Even bigger step up from the dry cleaning."

"I don't know if you remember, but we started with food."

"Oh yeah, desserts and cakes?"

"It was okay, but we didn't love it the way we love this."

"How the jump from dry cleaning to this?" I asked.

"We were tired of cleaning stuff for people."

"Exactly what I wondered at the time. All of you, my father, Don too. Always cleaning up."

"How are they? Do you talk to them?" Russell asked.

"My father is the same old. I don't talk to either of them."

"Jack, you know I understand how it is with your father. The same deal with me and my father. We don't talk. He left us too. Did you give it another chance though?"

"Several, I think. He came to my graduation, but then disappeared again. Had me sign off on child support release so he didn't have to send anything to my mother, but never sent anything to me like he said he would. He's the father. He's supposed to check on me, right?"

"You'd think. He's probably feeling too sorry for himself. Give him another chance. At least you can say you tried."

Sammy doing "Panama" came on the CD next and we both looked at each other in awe.

"You would've loved the karaoke studio we had for a few months. We bought it from Cousin Alonso."

"That would've been awesome. What happened to that?"

"That asshole sold us a sinking ship. He had already ruined the reputation by yelling at people and falling asleep on a few. There was a lot he didn't tell us. Totally scammed us."

"You think we had bad dads? Poor cousin Courtney. What a mess," I said.

"Yeah really. Hey, we have lots of great ideas with this business and we're glad you're here with us."

"Thanks, Russell. I appreciate the opportunity."

I went back to my one-bedroom apartment and unpacked. It was a two-story complex. I lived on the first floor. There was an apartment upstairs and another one across from me. On the other side was a lake. I couldn't see it from my porch, but I could hear the fountain at night.

I finally had my own place. But it was an odd space. My closet was filled with sweatshirts and a couple of winter coats, which seemed bizarre for Florida. A refrigerator packed with Yoo-Hoos, boxed cereal, milk, and a few apples was even stranger. I had a small stereo, a rack of cassette tapes, and a rack of CDs on the floor next to my bed, which was a one-hundred-dollar mattress I slapped down on the carpet. The only furniture I had was a small metal folding table and a couple of beat-up chairs Annie had found for me.

It was my first day and yet I couldn't help but already think this was all so temporary. I loved the product. I enjoyed being around Annie and Russell. They were fun and good wholesome people. But when I thought about the business, I had trouble seeing a vision of my future. I really had no idea where I was supposed to be.

Higher Love

Weeks of uneventful work passed. 9-5. Monday through Friday. I'd go food shopping on the weekend. On Saturday nights I'd cruise around downtown Orlando bored out of my mind. Not yet twenty-one, I couldn't get into the bars, and the dance clubs never appealed to me. I always ended up back home alone to watch TV on an old set I picked up. I had a VCR and would pop in some of my favorite videos to imitate the actors. Here I was saying lines from early Alec Baldwin and Eric Roberts movies in a state of mania. I had no more marijuana and no connections. No friends. I told myself I wanted the time to clear my head with a new beginning, but I was losing my mind in a lonely apartment jacked up on Frosted Flakes and coffee. It didn't take long to figure out that I had screwed myself into a strange existence once again. I should've thought about what Cliff said.

My phone rang, which was a rare occasion now.

"Oh, hi Al. How's things?"

"Okay here, but your grandpa died. I'm heading down to the funeral. I'll see you there. Just call your dad and make the arrangements."

It wasn't a question; it was an expectation, and I owed my uncle. I would go for him.

"Sorry about your dad, Al. I'll see you there."

☆

I took off for a few days to go to my father's place. I hopped on I-4 and crossed Florida to the west coast and drove down I-75 to Naples, an upper-class city where my grandfather had spent his final years waxing his car and taking his boat out past the mangroves into the Gulf of Mexico. He had just died of heart failure.

My grandfather hadn't returned my calls. Maybe he was sick, but a goodbye would have been nice. I suspected his new wife was not telling him about the calls, but who knows. It's not like he reached out to spend time with me when I was a boy when he still lived on Long Island. Like father, like son with these guys.

I knocked on the door. Al opened up and half hugged me. Something was distant about him. Where was he? I chalked it up to the loss of his father. I entered the cold house.

My father meandered over to the foyer. He looked worn. My father had lost his buddy, the one he had followed, even left his own son for. What could I say to make him feel better? Nothing. I had only come for the funeral because it was the right thing to do.

"Hey, Jack. Thanks for coming," he said.

My father shook my hand. And I had thought my uncle's half hug was cold.

"Sorry to hear about your father," I said.

"Yes, your grandfather too. Sorry."

"Yeah, I wish I had been able to talk to him."

He looked at me oddly.

"I tried but I always got the answering machine," I said.

"Did you leave messages?" he asked.

"Yes, I did. But he never called back."

"I also had a problem with his bitch of a wife not letting him know I was calling. I had to go over there and tell him in person and had it out with her," he said.

Al intervened, "Let's not start anything here, okay."

"Yeah, yeah, Al. It's the truth though. Jack was calling him too and never got a call back."

Here was the guy who never called his son now playing phone police.

The next day, we went to the funeral. My grandfather had served in the Korean War, so he had a military service in the funeral hall. There would be no churches because he wasn't religious, but the pleasant service was run by a reverend. A soldier handed my grandfather's sniffling fourth wife a meticulously folded American flag to take home with her, though it might as well have been the whole bunch of loot she would now inherit.

I looked around as the reverend said his final words. One, two, three, eight people. Eight people at a funeral. That was it.

A business. A bank account. A house. A boat. A Mercedes Benz. A portfolio of investments.

And just eight people at your funeral.

It seemed like a sad ending— an epic failure actually.

I still loved the good in him, somewhere deep down in there. He was genetically a part of me. I knew I had to reach for the good and remember him for that.

The next day, my father asked if I wanted to take a ride to the water. I figured I'd go for an hour and then leave. I said goodbye to Al who was heading to the airport, and then I jumped in with my father. He drove a pick-up truck as he had always done. We stopped at a gas station just like we used to when he'd pick me up on Sundays. He told me to wait and ran in.

I curiously opened the glovebox to see what kind of junk he kept in it. I didn't think I'd find a gun and an ounce of marijuana.

My father jumped back in the driver's seat and started the truck up. He passed me a Coke and Kit Kat, like he had done years earlier. Then he popped the truck into first gear, and we carried on.

"So you drive around with weapons and drugs?"

He laughed.

"You're searching my vehicle now? Al is growing on you."

"A glovebox is in front of you. Most people would open it if they're waiting in your car for you. Pretty normal, I think."

"What were you looking for?"

"Nothing, but I didn't think I'd find that."

"Just a little pot and protection. The pot's not even mine."

Sure, yeah right, I thought.

"Just like the Aerosmith concert you took me to when I was thirteen. Not that it's a big deal. Just don't lie."

"So why make a big deal out of it?"

"Not sure how I feel about driving around with a gun."

"You wouldn't be in trouble. It's really fine."

"Is it licensed?"

"Of course."

"You leave it in there unlocked though? I mean, that's the kind of thing that Al has to worry about. Someone leaves a gun in a glovebox. A criminal steals it. Uses it on a cop."

"You watch too much TV."

"Cops get shot all the time. Sometimes with stolen guns."

"And what about the pot? You don't smoke it?"

"I've been trying to steer clear."

"Good. It messes up your brain anyway. I saw too many people I grew up with get freaked out on drugs and it starts with pot. One guy overdosed after becoming a heroin junkie. One guy ended up on acid and jumped out the window of my school."

This must have been early on before he dropped out.

"Your Uncle Al used to smoke. He and his buddy drove across the country in a van. Straight Arrow Al. He was like all of us back then. Maybe more lost. Mowed lawns until he was twenty-five. Anyway, I don't smoke much anymore, but I'm dropping it off for a friend."

"So you're a drug dealer?" I asked.

"I can't win with you," he said.

Al had already told me of his travels. Yes, he had been a wandering hippy for a little while. Yes, he had mowed lawns, which is why the police department was a big deal for him. But he had also gone to community college as he prepared for his career in law enforcement. He took his job seriously.

My father turned on the radio and Steve Winwood's "Higher Love" came on. It was 1987 all over again, maybe in my father's mind too. He lit a cigarette and blew the smoke out the window. I lit one too as we drove in silence to the beach.

When we arrived, we got out and he set some chairs up by the water. He took out two poles and put the bait on the hooks, then handed me one. We whizzed the lines out and sat down to wait.

After a while, he turned to me.

"I know you're probably mad at me. I really tried though. Your mom..."

"Let's not do this again with your stories. Leave her out of this."

"It really wasn't fair, but I'm trying now."

"Trying what?" I asked.

"To be a dad. I'm your dad. I love you, Jack."

I couldn't believe this— my very own afterschool-special.

"It's hard to be a dad so far away."

"You're my son. I love you."

"Those are words. You have to show it."

"Maybe one day you'll understand," he said.

"Maybe someday I'll understand even less."

Neither of us caught anything as we sat there smoking and drinking Coke for the next couple of hours. We packed it up and headed back to his house. On the way back he started to explain how his father had changed the will and all the money would be going to the kids, but no grandkids. He said his father figured they'd take care of their kids. He said he'd set up something for me. He was also sure to mention how he wasn't sure he'd get through the week with all the funeral expenses and all. I wasn't sure what those expenses really were since my grandfather's wife would be paying for the funeral. Maybe it was the time off where he was losing money. He'd be fine soon enough. He was sure to tell me there would be at least a few hundred thousand coming in from the will in a few months. When we parked the car back at his house, I handed him five twenties and told him not to worry about it.

"Don't be a stranger," he said.

"You know where to find me," I replied.

"Thanks, Jack. I'll send you the cash back."

"Sorry again about your dad," I said and got out.

I jumped in the Camaro to head back to Orlando. I popped in a Queensryche tape and a song titled "Bridge" came on about a father not building a bridge. Mine never built one.

☆

After some Frosted Flakes, I went out on the patio and drank some hot coffee. It was June and already blistering in Florida. I sat there and looked out at the parking lot like some kind of lunatic in a catatonic state. I guess this was it. I wasn't going to get in trouble. I wasn't going to get killed. I wasn't even going to get hurt being here. So why did I already feel like I was dying inside?

Long Way to Love

One Friday night in late June, I went out to Orlando by myself to a club called Jani Lane's Sunset Strip. I supposed it was owned by the '80s rock star Jani Lane, but I really had no idea. I dressed up in all black and felt compelled to wear black cowboy boots under my jeans. I bought the things on sale a year earlier probably thinking of some old 80s rock video. I hobbled into this place, ordered a soda, sat down by myself for fifteen minutes, looked around at the crowd, got up, and walked right out the door in my stupid boots. What was I trying to do? I realized the scene was nowhere near the one I had seen years earlier in rock videos. It wasn't the real world.

What was I thinking? What was I doing in this club in Florida anyway? What was I doing in this town, in this job? Suddenly everything seemed wrong again. I knew the feeling well. It was an urge that boiled deep down inside, but it seemed like everything changed in a moment, maybe because the realization takes just a moment to wake you up.

I got home and put the boots in the dumpster, and then I started to pack. Then I dug through my books and papers, found what I needed, sat down, and started looking at the map.

Heading Out to the Highway

Breaking it to Annie and Russell a second time was difficult. Annie was visibly devastated. Russell looked confused. I told them it just didn't feel right. I needed to get on with my life.

"But what are you going to do?" she asked.

"I don't know. College. I have to find my purpose."

"You know you could stay here and do college and work part time for us," she said.

"I know, that's generous. But I don't think Orlando is for me. It's damn hot here!"

"I understand, it isn't for everyone," Russell said.

"Wherever you end up, you could drive taxis and make a lot of money," Annie said. "I could totally see you doing that."

I didn't know what to say to that. It reminded me of Uncle Al's porter suggestion. I was willing to work whatever job while I figured out my future and took classes, but I didn't want to be known or seen as anything in particular or get stuck doing something. My desire to drive wasn't just about driving around, especially driving people around. I wanted to go somewhere.

"When are you heading back to New York?" she asked.

"I'm not."

"Where are you going?"

"I'm shipping my things to New York, so I'll probably end up back there, but I'm going to California first. I want to get out and see the country."

"You're going to drive around the country?" asked Russell.

I nodded and remembered what Izzy had told me about getting out to see things. Hit the highway, as he put it.

"See, you're like a pro driver already," Annie said.

"I guess so. That's the plan. Drive. See the world. Take it all in," I said.

"Road trip warrior!" Russell said.

"Be careful out there. It's a crazy world," Annie said and hugged me tight, holding in the tears. She wanted family near, but she'd be starting her own family now. I wasn't a part of that. I needed to find my own way.

"Best wishes with the business. You have a really great product. Keep at it. And thank you for the opportunity again. It was a great experience."

I shook Russell's hand. He was a warm genuine man who had had a distant father just like me. I admired how he held it together and then walked away from a regular job to take a risk to be an entrepreneur. They would do fine without me.

E-Bow the Letter

I drove down to the east coast to Lake Worth to meet Paul for dinner at a steakhouse before my departure. He ordered a ribeye steak and I ordered chicken. Then he told me he was gay.

"I'm gay, Jack."

"Oh, yeah. Okay."

"No, really. I'm gay."

"Okay."

"Really. I am."

"Yeah, I know."

"You know?"

"Yeah, I figured."

"And what do you think about that?"

"It's fine, man. It's fine. Whatever you're into. No big deal."

"I didn't know how you'd respond," he said.

"Why? No big deal."

"Well, we used to say stuff and call each other...."

"No, you used to use that word. It always gave me the shivers just like the N word. Especially the way they say it, with some heat to it," I said.

"I'm pretty sure you used it too," he said.

"Yeah, maybe after you did, but I always remembered being bothered by it... the word."

"That's great to know," said Paul.

"You would've appreciated the Keys."

"I'll be visiting soon."

"Just be careful," I said.

"What do you mean?" asked Paul.

"You know, HIV and..."

"Would you say that to a straight guy?"

I didn't know what to say to that.

"Ah, no, but you know, it's...I'm sorry..."

Paul interrupted, "Just kidding, buddy. I know. It's true, we have to be careful."

"Always."

"Cheers," said Paul as he held his glass up.

I lifted my glass to his.

"To a whole new world!" I said.

"Hell yeah! So tell me, where are you heading?"

"I'm hitting the road in three days. Heading west. I'm going to explore California. Maybe stay out there."

"Just be careful. You know, HIV and such."

"Ah, you got me back!"

"But in all seriousness, be careful out there on the road. There are all kinds of things that could happen out there."

"Yes, I've read horror stories about the road."

"Where are you going to stay?"

"Motels. The driver's seat. Who knows?"

"You're one brave dude," he said.

After dinner, we walked out to the parking lot. I hugged my good old friend goodbye.

"We're both going to be all right," he said.

"I hope so."

"We will. We got out of there."

"Thanks, pal," I said.

"Let me know where you end up!"

America, Summer, 1997

The Camaro was packed and ready, freshly inspected with brand new tires and a full tank of gas. I took a final nap before I carried the mattress out, almost doing an airplane spin with the thing on my back. I dropped it in front of Annie and Russell's place so they could get rid of it for me. I knocked and said goodbye to them.

Then I said goodbye to the apartment. This was a strange stay. Who was I? What was the purpose of this? I didn't figure out anything in that apartment, but it pushed me out and I thought maybe I'd figure it out now on the road. I had only made it three months, less than last time. Both times, I had kept my New York plates on the car, maybe knowing deep down inside I would be going back. My real destination was a mystery.

I set out at nine 'o clock. The July Florida sun had just gone down. I was off to see America.

My very own Pony Express.

I took I-75 north for the first time up to I-10. This interstate highway was the beginning of the western stretch all the way across the country straight into Los Angeles. I passed the exit sign that read Panama City and popped in my Van Halen mixed tape with the live Sammy version of the song "Panama" that I copied from Russell's CD.

I soon said goodbye to Florida and crossed the state line into Alabama. I had delegated Alabama and Mississippi to the middle of the night. A quick drive through Mobile in the middle of the night was all I could muster. This got me to New Orleans in the morning for breakfast.

I had driven all night and was already worn. I stopped to refuel the car and my stomach. I walked around Orleans Street and Bourbon Street in the morning as the sun came up. I ate at a café on the sidewalk. This was a charming city that reminded me of bits of Key West, but a bigger version with its own personality. I knew I could have fun if I checked into a motel and stayed the day to hit the night life in the evening, but I knew I had serious driving ahead of me. I was determined to get to my destination, and I was not yet at the halfway point to California.

By one o'clock, I was back out on the interstate in the hot summer sun cruising towards Texas at an even seventy-five miles an hour in the Camaro. I made it to Houston in time for a late evening dinner. I was fried and needed a motel. After a tour of the city, I retreated to the motel room for a long sleep.

I awoke late the next morning well rested and ready to fight the rest of my way through Texas. It was the first place I had felt hostility. They didn't like my blue Camaro with New York plates. A few cars pushed up behind me at high speeds. A few cut me off. I pulled to the right. I didn't want trouble. Driving through Texas was like a fulltime job. It took all day but felt like three days.

Singing along to cassette tapes helped pass time. I felt like I was giving a concert. I'd push my voice to its limit. There was no one around to stare at me, judge me, or tell me to turn it down. I put the music loud and shouted to the heavens. It was beautiful.

I was wiped by the time I made it to New Mexico around eleven p.m. I collapsed in a motel bed in some small New Mexico town along I-10. It felt like I was coming out of something and heading back into civilization. I fell asleep after watching a film on TV called *Fire in the Sky* about a guy abducted by aliens.

In the morning I continued west. The day was already starting out hot. New Mexico still had palm trees and what looked like smaller palm bushes, but the entry into Arizona was an almost immediate transition into desert terrain full of cacti and brown hills in the distance. It looked like inhabitable territory, yet I knew I was getting closer to something.

Closer into Tucson, I stopped along I-10 and rested at a park. The heat was dry and hot, unlike the humid east coast of Florida and New York. But it was still hot as hell. I ate a sandwich and then noticed people swimming in a pool. The clear water looked refreshing, so I got changed into my suit and took a dip to cool off.

After a swim, I got back into my car and drove downtown to the city. I wandered around the city of Tucson. I didn't know what I was looking for. The city was strangely familiar. My grandmother Rosa told me she had run away from home to this place with my grandfather when they were just teens. They stayed for six months and then headed back to New York. I imagined if they had stayed and had my mother in Arizona instead of Queens. I certainly wouldn't be the Jack I was.

I decided to stay for the night, so I found a cheap motel and checked in around four o'clock. I lay in the motel bed and stared at the ceiling as I drifted to sleep. I might as well have been outside. It felt like I was right under the Tucson sky with stars overhead and the sound of desert life all around. I could smell it. I could taste it. Something was there. And I slept on.

Tucson was a vibrant city full of spirit, but it was time to go on to California. Phoenix was my next stop for an early lunch. It seemed like such a clean and modern city. I wanted to come back sometime. I knew the majestic Grand Canyon was only three to four hours north from here, but I needed to get on to LA. I knew I'd be back. Next time I'd spend more time in Arizona. In my head, I was already making plans for a second road trip.

I continued west on I-10 singing along to a new Gin Blossoms tape. It was the perfect road trip album. The song "As Long as it Matters" came on as I left Arizona and entered the Golden State. This was it. I was getting close. But first I'd drive through what looked like another alien planet. I stopped at Joshua Tree, got out and walked around to look at the beautiful scene. After taking some pictures with my Kodak, I jumped back into the car, and popped in the *Joshua Tree* tape by U2. "With or Without You" pumped through the speakers of my soul.

California

I was going to make it to the Pacific Ocean by sundown. I arrived in LA on a huge four lane freeway. Traffic. Smog. An instant sore throat. I gulped down several Arizona iced teas. All around me were slick looking people in their cars with California plates. It was right out of a movie. I turned off my music just to take in all the sounds. Rock music drowned out the horns and motors, hitting the air from the convertible sports cars, probably from a few real rock stars, and the hopeful.

I got off on Eleventh Street and Olympic, turned down Lincoln heading towards the water. The small one-level stores in Santa Monica reminded me of my old town, but this was a different world. This city was flatter than New York and stretched out wider. The energy was amazing. The return of palm trees made me happy.

I turned left on Santa Monica Blvd. I couldn't believe I had finally arrived. The road led right to the water. A golden sun was setting over the great Pacific. I parked and walked down off the sidewalk onto the sandy beach. All those videos and movies. But this was a real place. It wasn't just a set after all.

After the sun went down, I grabbed something to eat from a food cart and stared out at the dark ocean. Tomorrow I would go into that ocean for a full swim. That first night I just stared at it for hours, like some kind of foreign treasure. I wondered if Jane had ever walked the very beach I was standing on. I knew she was near, closer than we'd ever been in many years. I found a parking lot along Ocean Avenue and pulled into a spot to rest a bit. I reclined my seat and fell off to sleep sometime around three.

The light of the morning woke me a few hours later. I drove up the coastal highway to Malibu and then got out at a cliff to look over. The view was stunning. I pondered all the explorers who had moved west for a better life. Here I was at the edge of civilization.

I drove back down the coast a few miles to Santa Monica and prepared to stay awhile. I could sleep here. I could eat here. I could even meet people here if I wanted.

I spent the day on the beach. The ocean was my bathtub. I ate out of a beach shack that sold fried fish, chicken, and fries. I smoked Marlboro Lights and put them out in the sand before filling half a cup of old soda. Time stood still. I was so young and alive.

Some beachy young hobos pestered me with questions, eventually trying to shake me for money. I could smell their neediness, and I could tell they were into stuff. I slipped away and tried to stay to myself. It was a matter of survival.

I slept in my car the next two nights with the windows mostly rolled up. I rolled them down a little more each night. On the third evening, I walked down to the end of the pier and stared out at the ocean. A young lady walked up to the rail a few feet away and started to chat with me.

"It's beautiful, eh?" she asked.

"Sure is."

"You look lost."

"I am. Can you help?" I replied.

"What are you looking for?"

"Home," I said.

"Oh, another homeless runaway?" she asked with a smile.

"Another? Do you take them in? I'm no runaway or homeless. I'm just doing a cross country adventure."

"Like *On the Road*?"

I just looked at her.

"You know, the book?"

"Oh yeah, kind of like that," I said.

I hadn't read it, but Izzy's guitarist Rick mentioned it back in Florida. I put it on my list of things to do this week.

"Where are you staying?" she asked.

"You're looking at it."

"You have to be careful out here. There are some rough and tough characters out here."

"I'm starting to feel grungy. I'm going to find a motel in Hollywood for a few nights."

"You have to be careful there too," she laughed.

"Anywhere where I don't need to be careful?"

"Welcome to the jungle," she said.

"The song was about New York though, where I'm from."

"So you're an 80s fan too?" she asked.

"Sure. Love rock and roll."

"What are you doing out here from New York?" she asked.

"Just exploring. Getting to know my country. Getting to know myself. Los Angeles always seemed so exciting."

"I live around here. It is fun."

"Maybe you can be my tour guide," I said.

She let out a big laugh and then turned serious.

"Sure. Why don't we meet tomorrow? I'm Sarah."

We shook hands. She was confident, short with dark curly hair and overwhelming brown eyes.

"I was kidding, but I could use a tour guide. But don't you want to know who you're meeting up with?"

"I'm a good judge of character, but yes, this is the point where you tell me your name."

"Sorry, I'm Jack."

"Like the author? Come on."

I remembered *On the Road.*

"No really. It is. Like the author. But I'm Jack Tortis."

"Tortoise? Like a turtle?"

"Me and you, you and me..."

"No matter how they..."

We erupted into laughter. This girl was fun and witty.

We walked down to the beach and strolled along the water for a little while.

"I was in Key West right after high school. Went back to New York to start a year of college. Then my aunt and uncle pulled me back to Florida to work for their business."

"What do they do?" Sarah asked.

"Frozen drinks."

"Oh fun. Why did you leave?"

"I just didn't love it. It's a great product. But it just wasn't mine. It wasn't home."

"I totally understand. I'm from Sacramento. It'll always be home, but I didn't want to stay. I was lucky to have a cousin here. He took care of me and helped me move down here."

"How are you liking it?"

"It's great. It's been six months. I may go home eventually though. I do miss my parents."

"You have two normal parents. Still together?"

"Yes, I do."

"Wow, that's rare. You like your dad?"

"Of course. Love the man."

"No dad issues! You might be the first one I've ever met."

"Those poor girls. Poor you!"

"Yeah, one of them..."

I was about to tell her how Jane also lived in southern California, but then decided not to open that up.

"I might just end up here. Who knows? I'm staying open."

"Where are you really staying tonight?" she asked.

The nine o'clock sun was now down and the dark California night had begun.

"I was thinking about camping out tonight right here."

"Crazy. How about you stay at my place? We have a comfy sofa you can use."

"I'm not sure I can trust you," I said.

She laughed and waved me toward her car.

"Funny how we both trust each other so quickly. I mean you don't really know me either. I'm only five one but I could be a killer," she said.

"Ah, you could for sure. I could end up in a bad situation. But I don't think so," I said.

We got into our cars, and I followed her back to her apartment. She drove for fifteen minutes and then pulled up in front of a peach-colored house. I grabbed my travel bag and locked the car. She opened the front door, and we headed inside.

"You have a nice place. It's peachy."

"Credit to my cousin and rent control!" she said leading the way inside the rounded front door.

"It must have been improved with your touch."

"Maybe. Have a seat. My cousin is up in San Jose this week, by the way. Still trust me?"

"I didn't know if he'd be sitting here waiting with an axe."

"Ah, a set up!" she laughed.

I dropped my bag by the sofa and had a seat. Over a glass of iced tea, we talked about all the fun of southern California. All the mythology. The rock bands and legendary actors. Traffic and earthquakes. Fires and fame. Beaches and sunshine.

After a while, I took a shower and cleaned up. It was nice to have a shower and then a clean sofa to sleep on.

I awoke the next day and Sarah was standing over me.

"Didn't mean to scare you. Do you want breakfast?"

"No fear. Breakfast would be terrific."

By ten a.m., Sarah and I were out exploring Hollywood. We walked up and down Hollywood and Sunset Boulevards. It was quieter at this time of the day and the sun wasn't so hot yet. I took pictures of the sidewalk stars like a tourist, which made her laugh. We ended up in an old-style theater where we watched two movies back-to-back for five dollars. Then we walked through the wax museum. In a souvenir shop, I took a picture next to a cardboard cutout of Britney Spears for a ten-dollar laugh.

We ended up at a place called Pig 'n Whistle for dinner.

"Wow, it feels like we're on a date," I blurted.

"You wish," she joked.

"Ohhh," I said, turning red.

"I'm kidding with you."

"No, really. I had a good time with you today," I said.

"That's not you trying to move in with me?" she asked.

"Yes, that's the plan, but…"

She froze.

"Got you now," I said.

We laughed and then the waiter arrived. We said hello, put our order in, and then resumed our conversation.

"To be honest, my heart's all messed up inside. I wouldn't want to drag you into something," I said.

"Me too. Just getting over someone. I guess we can use each other," she said.

"There you go again! I'll leave the using up to you."

"So you've been in love?" she asked.

"That's an abrupt way to change the subject." I laughed.

"Sorry. Isn't it the same subject?"

"I guess you're right. And yes, I have. In fact, an old girlfriend lives right here in southern California."

"Really! Get out! Are you going to see her?"

"No, it's been years. Back in New York."

"Let's look her up. What's the last name?"

"Martelli. Jane Martelli."

"We'll look her up in the phone book at my place."

"Not sure I want to talk on the phone."

"So what? Just go see her in person then."

"We'll talk about it later."

We ate a fine Hollywood meal. When we got back to her apartment, Sarah pressed me again on looking up the old flame.

"So let's look her up," she said holding a phone book.

"She's not going to be in the Los Angeles book. She's in Ventura. I'd have to go…"

"I just happen to have a Ventura phonebook. It's only the next county up. I remember my cousin popped it out one night. Let me get it," she said and pulled the book out of a cabinet.

"Um. I don't know, Sarah. It's been a long time."

"Let's see. Here's M. Maebel. Marbell. Martell."

"Damn, you're persistent."

"It's just up the coast. Take a ride. Stop along the way."

"She's probably not even in the book."

"Martelli. Here it is," she said pointing to the white page.

"Holy shit," I said, shocked to be looking at her name.

"Give her some shit for years ago. Or just kiss her."

"Whoa, we're getting carried away."

"In all seriousness, just go say hello. It's innocent. Old childhood friends. It doesn't have to be more than that."

"You're working tomorrow, right? Maybe I'll take a ride."

"You should. We can meet up tomorrow night and you can tell me all about it, unless there's a big magical reunion."

"Ha. Funny."

☆

The next day I took a drive up the coastal highway. On the way, I took a right up a long winding road. I read the address written down on a scrap of paper and checked my pocket mapbook. Then I popped on the Izzy Stradlin cassette and cranked it loud. "Somebody's Knockin'" came on as I arrived at the gate on the left. I stopped, got out, and looked up at the hill into the trees that shielded the rock star's home.

"You in the jungle..." I yelled at Axl Rose's gate.

I didn't expect him to come out, of course. But it was cool knowing he might just be in there hiding from the world. I hoped he heard my tape playing his old guitarist.

At seven p.m. I met up with Sarah at her house.

"You didn't see her, did you?"

"No, I didn't have the guts. I drove there and looked around Ventura. I wanted to know where she lived. It's nice there. Nice choice. But that was it. I felt too stalky to drive past her house. It's bad enough I did that back home to make myself feel better."

"Why not just say hi?"

"It's been a long time. There was someone after her. And then I heard she was in bad shape. Someone I knew had travelled out here and bumped into her."

"Bad shape? Sounds like excuses. You're still thinking about her though. That's a reason to go."

"Drugs."

"Oh. I'm sorry. That makes it complicated. But maybe she needs you."

I put my hands on my head in agony.

"She didn't need me back then, but then again maybe I didn't push hard enough. I feel like a quitter."

"Listen, you're not responsible for anyone. No one is going to judge you either way. She'll never even know you were here. I understand now why you wouldn't want to open up old wounds."

"What's the chances...?" I started to ask.

"It's never too late, but you're leaving soon anyway, right?"

"Yes, I probably should," I said.

"I mean, I don't want to rush you out. Stay here longer if you want. My cousin's gone for another week."

"That's generous. I was actually thinking of staying on the strip somewhere for a couple of nights for fun."

"Dangerous! Going to get a hooker and some cocaine?"

"Not quite, what do you think I..."

"Hoo hoo. I'm kidding! But listen, stay tonight and come back in a couple of nights if you want. Unless I bore you and you're done with me."

"Not a chance."

☆

I stayed another night. Sarah and I stayed up until two a.m. talking, listening to records, and drinking white wine. Like the night before, I stayed on the sofa.

Sarah went to work the next day, and I drove over to Sunset Blvd. I spent the whole day wandering around Hollywood and ate lunch at Canter's Deli on Fairfax Blvd. I got a kick out of all the rock band photos, especially the ones of Izzy and his old band.

Around four p.m., I turned the corner on Hollywood and LaBrea and checked into a cheap motel only steps from the Walk of Fame. The LaBrea Inn was about a hundred dollars a night, more expensive than Motel 6 and Motel 8, but a bit more raw. I entered my room. The air was warm. The decorations were plain, not the zebra-striped, red-satin-sheeted wild room I expected. There was a motel back in New York called The Hollywood far wilder inside than the one in Hollywood.

But there was history in this room. I was sure of it. Future Hollywood actors and rock stars on their way up. Junkies and prostitutes on their way down. Whacky tourists like myself. All kinds of people passed through this place.

I showered, dressed, hid my bags in the closet, locked the room, and headed out onto the strip. I ate something at a café and then went to The Roxy to see a music show. I didn't know who was playing, but I didn't care. The place had history and I wanted to feel it. A band called Ednaswap started their show. The lead singer was a cool woman who belted out some wild songs. She slowed it down for a deep track titled "Torn" right in the middle of the set.

I sat at a table and watched the show all alone. This was the real deal, not like the one in Florida I had walked out of after five minutes. I didn't care if I was alone here. How did anyone know I wasn't some hotshot music reviewer or record producer or talent scout? I sat and imagined all the greats who played in this historic venue. I had read so many legendary stories.

But then I wondered what Sarah was doing. Maybe I should've invited her. I guess I needed this time alone to soak in the city and think about what I was going to do with my life. There I was on my first cross-country adventure in the great summer of 1997 with endless opportunities. But the little money I had wouldn't last. I needed to get a job and stay somewhere, start my new life, or get back on the road.

☆

Sarah had asked me to come over the next day. We walked over to a café for dinner. A guy was playing an acoustic guitar in the corner. I wasn't alone in a crowd anymore. We enjoyed each other's company and talked about all kinds of great things, but we also knew it was all right to sit quietly and listen to the music.

We strolled back to her place after dinner. She lit a candle and poured us some white wine.

"You like Tracy Chapman?"

"Yeah, like 'Fast Car'? I love that song."

Sarah put an album on her turntable.

"Her debut from '88 was great, but this is her latest one. I know we both love 80s music, but how about TV shows? Which ones did you watch?" she asked.

"*All in the family,*" I said.

"Archie Bunker!"

"Yeah, and then *The Jeffersons.*"

"Loved that show too!"

"I watched a lot of cop shows, like *Miami Vice, Knight Rider, TJ Hooker,* and a show called *Hunter.*"

"I don't know that last one," she said.

"It was this super cool cop named Hunter with a smart, hot woman partner and they went around and solved crimes. It was on Saturday night at ten 'o clock. Then I'd watch Saturday Night Live, or once a month Saturday Night's Main Event."

"I like that she was smart and hot. Wrestling too?"

"Liked it, yeah. Haven't seen it in a long time."

"I watched some with my dad," she said.

"Oh, and I have to admit one show I loved that was on earlier in the night on Saturday was *The Golden Girls.*"

"Love it!" Sarah reached over for a high five for that one.

"What else did you watch?" I asked.

"*Facts of life* was great. *Family Ties.*"

"Both classics! I loved those too. They just don't make TV shows like that anymore. The golden age is over."

"I'd agree. It was quite a time to be alive."

"I wonder what TV is going to look like in another ten years from now," I said putting my hands in the air.

"Who knows! But I just thought how cool it would be to bring back the stars of *Facts of Life* in a *Golden Girls* reboot when they're all older," said Sarah.

"I'd watch it!"

"Right?"

"You're a lot of fun, Sarah."

"You too, Jack."

"Not sure I want to leave on Friday."

"Let's enjoy tonight," she said.

I got up to get a drink and she got up at the same time. We stood close face to face. I looked into her big brown eyes.

We kissed passionately. My lips got lost within hers. My hands got lost in her thick black hair. We pulled each other close, and then she stopped for a moment.

"I need you to know right now. I'm a virgin and I intend to stay that way for a while. So no matter what we do, we're not doing that okay."

"Yeah...I don't..."

She silenced me with her lips.

Off He Goes

"I'm heading north next."

"Seattle?" asked Sarah.

"Maybe. I don't know. No real plans. But I guess I have to get back to college. Not sure I want to leave here."

"Think about it while you're out there on the road. You have to go where it's right for you. No matter who is there. You'll come back here if it's meant to be."

"Thanks, Sarah. You're thoughtful and unselfish. We'll see each other again. I'll call when I get to my final destination."

I did my best *I'll be back* followed by "Damn, I'm corny."

"You sure are! Hit the road, Jack!" she said and laughed.

We hugged and gently kissed goodbye.

When I was pulling away, she blew me a kiss. I was off to head north on I-5 for a day of driving.

I-5 in California was uneventful, yet it was magical to be out on this road. I burned through eight or nine cassettes. It was just me and the music. I lit cigarettes, sipped Yoo-Hoo, and sang along to my favorite tracks. Ten hours of driving, thinking, observing, listening, and belting out tunes.

It was still dark when I hit the end of California. The smell of pine trees and a wood burning chimney lit up my nose. The summer air here was cool and fresh, a relief from the heat of southern California.

I came to a welcome sign and then a sign that read *Free Coffee.* I pulled into the rest area where some people were standing under a light at a table with paper cups and large thermoses.

"Welcome to Oregon," said a woman with short hair.

"Thank you. Free coffee?"

"Yes, come on over."

"That's very kind. Thank you."

"Where are you heading?"

"I'm heading north. Just exploring America."

"Where did you leave from?"

"Florida, but I'm from New York. Probably heading back."

"That's quite a journey!"

"Yes, it's been. Just me and my music tapes and coffee!"

"You should check out Seattle if you like music."

"Oh yeah? That's where I'm going."

"The whole grunge movement was born up there. A bit different from the LA scene."

"Very true."

"You'll like it. It's a great city. Portland is fantastic too."

"Portland?"

"Yes, it's not our capitol but it's our biggest city."

"Maybe I'll stop in there."

"You should. You'll feel quite at home. It's only four hours north. You could make it there for breakfast. But take your time in Oregon. There's beauty all along the path."

I thanked the woman and liked what I saw so far. Fresh air. Nice people. Good free coffee. It all seemed too good.

At twenty to five, the sun started to rise to the east along my path on I-5. Overwhelming trees surrounded the sides of the Oregon highway. The terpenes of the pine trees seemed to dominate the air all around. Such a strong sensory overload boggled my mind. The place was a land of déjà vu, but I had never been there. I wondered why I was there.

Around nine, I pulled off a Portland exit. From I-5 to 405, I then meandered through the downtown city streets. What was this place? I had to get out and see. I parked the Camaro and walked for blocks. The city seemed to be in the trees. I noticed a university. I looked around and was baffled at this accidental discovery.

After only a couple of hours, I had to carry on. I knew time was essential if I wanted to see enough of Seattle. I also knew I didn't have enough money at this point to push my trip much further. I had at most three cheap motel stays, a little bit of food, and enough to make it back to New York on about ten fill ups. I vowed to return to Portland.

I popped in a Pearl Jam cassette, and it was on to the home of grunge rock music. The trees seemed to get bigger the further north I got. Canada was getting closer. This was truly another world to me, a boy from a bubble in the backyard of New York City. My sheltered existence embarrassed me.

I pulled into Seattle around two o'clock. I didn't even know where to go. I had no idea what or where the major attractions were. The Space Needle. Okay. That was easy enough. But then I just found myself at Pike Place roaming around.

It was a beautiful sunny day. Really just perfect weather. I noticed the people were hippier up here than in California. It was the '90s with a strong touch of the '60s. Many of the men had beards and goatees. The girls were pretty, but I thought of Sarah. I wondered what she was up to, whether I'd ever see her again, and why it was both so easy yet so difficult to leave her behind.

Seattle was great, but it was big and overwhelming like Los Angeles, even for a New York boy like me. I wasn't going to stay there, so there was no point in spending more time. I didn't have the energy or passion to hunt down the music history spots the way I had in LA. And if I hadn't stayed in that magical sister city two hours south, then I wasn't going to waste any more time anywhere else. I had a meal at a café on Pike Street and then walked back to the Camaro to take off to head east for the first time on my trip.

I took I-90 back down to I-84 in Oregon to head east and then south into Idaho, where I collapsed into a motel bed at two thirty in the morning in Twin Falls. That night I dreamt of the Pacific Northwest forests, their piney smell and vibrant green.

Running on Empty

At eight a.m. I jumped back on the road. The smell of the great Salt Lake was nauseating, but thankfully it didn't last long, and I was impressed with the sights in Utah. It was a strange world.

I-84 connected to I-80, which could have brought me all the way home. At a truck stop I bought a magazine called *Hometown Girls.* Then I went through southern Wyoming in what seemed like the middle of nowhere. I stopped at a desolate rest stop. There wasn't a soul in sight. Me, a dirty mag, and the Wyoming sky.

At I-25 in Cheyenne, I decided to head south to Denver. I would hit the Mile High City as night approached. Once there, I stretched, walked around, ate something, and then got back in the car. Denver seemed like a fun place, but I was exhausted and had to get a bit further. Tonight, I would be camping out in the car to save a motel for the next day.

Somewhere along I-70 East, I stopped at a rest area and slept for about four good hours. It was an invigorating nap. I needed the time before embarking on a fourteen-hour stretch, perhaps the most difficult leg of the trip. I needed a variety of tapes playing and plenty of caffeinated drinks to keep me going through my first encounter with Kansas, straight through Missouri, all the way past Illinois into Indiana.

From Indianapolis, I headed north on I-65. I popped in a tape and cranked up a song called "Dust N Bones"— I was heading to the songwriter's hometown. The man I had met in Key West, Izzy Stradlin, and the lead singer of his former band, were both from Lafayette. I read that Izzy had returned there to live a quieter, simpler life. He mentioned returning, but I hadn't asked him if he still lived there. It was a very small town. If he did live there again, he lived on a secluded estate, with plenty of space for a racetrack, as I read in one magazine. I went into a deli and as I waited on a short line, I looked at the people, and I wondered if they knew what kind of greatness had once walked the streets of this town.

After eating a meal in a local park, I took 26 East, a small, slow road that led straight to the hometown of another famous Indiana-born star, James Dean. A few miles in, there was a big red sign that read Fairmount with a white arrow pointing toward town. The arrow pointed to a full body illustration of James Dean with his blue jeans and red coat. His left arm hung around the top of the sign and his right-hand rested on his belt buckle. At the base of the arrow was an illustration of Garfield. The cartoonist Jim Davis was also from Fairmount, but he was still alive.

I drove to Dean's gravesite, got out, and stared at his tombstone like some kind of idiot. I recited some movie lines like a million other lost souls before me.

"You're tearing me..."

His gravestone was simple. Under the stone were two white flowers and one set of yellow flowers in the middle, all planted in the dirt in front. There was a worm patch of dirt around the stone, probably from the occasional lunatic who came to sit by his grave and talk to him.

On the way back to I-70 East, there was another Portland. This one was a small rural town on the way out of Indiana into Ohio, and a world away from the state of Oregon, but it reminded me of where I had been. I popped in a tape called *Accident of Birth* and a song titled "The Road to Hell" kicked on. The singer echoed the words of Blake— "the road to hell is full of good intentions."

I-70 ran through Ohio, and the world seemed to finally awaken again in western Ohio. After a good one thousand miles of nothingness, I was back in civilization. I could feel the heartbeat of the country as I rolled into Pennsylvania. It was onto I-76 straight to New York on the final day of July.

Sayville, New York, Fall/Winter, 1997

The house on Lincoln Avenue had been abandoned for a couple of years since my great grandfather had passed. The family didn't know what to do with it because it needed tons of work. But it was a livable house with working electric, water, and heat. That was what mattered. Basic shelter. My mother would need it now that she had left Don.

Sayville was the perfect place for my mother and I to regroup. It was back to Sayville where she had grown up, where she had met my father, where we had lived for several years together before moving to Patchogue. From there, we moved to that other place, the wicked west. Everything went downhill for both of us there. So we were back to our roots, back to where we belong. Me and my mother. And JP this time.

The house had a flood of memories of legendary family members and gatherings. My aunt Gloria had bought the house for her parents to live in, and she would come out to the island from Manhattan on the weekends. We would visit her there.

I hadn't been in the old house since after Aunt Gloria died. They had had a family get together there after the funeral, and then her father, my great grandfather, lived out his time there with a nurse. The house still looked like I remembered it in the 1980s when my great grandmother was still alive. The decades old furniture was now accented with a blanket or a pillow from my mother's touch. After entering the big old wooden door with a giant gold knocker, Gloria's old bedroom was to the right. That was now my mother's room.

A hallway opened up to the living room. In the center of the furthest wall was a big stone fireplace with white bookshelves on each side. The shelves were still filled with my great grandfather Romeo's dusty, old, science and philosophy books. Religion killers as he called them. I would have fun going through them all.

I brought my bags in. I was delirious from the road. My body was used to the constant state of movement. You never feel the tiredness until you stop moving.

"That's where you'll be sleeping. Sorry," my mother said as she pointed to the living room sofa, which was in the shadow of the towering bookshelves.

"No, it's all right. It's only for a bit."

"Hopefully, we're only here a bit too," she said.

"How's JP?"

My mother gave a nervous laugh. "I'm never sure. He's happy to be out, but he's found trouble here again."

"Even in the new town?" I asked.

"Yup. You guys could share the room upstairs, but..."

"No, that's all right. I'll give him his space— he's twelve. I remember that. But what's wrong with the room?"

"Take a look. He'll be home any minute."

I put my things down in the corner and then climbed the most ridiculous and steepest stairs I'd ever climbed— like a doll house. At the top, I turned into Romeo's old bedroom. I gasped.

A punctured up queen-sized mattress lay on the floor with one dirty sheet hanging off. No curtains on the windows. Cigarette butts put out on the wood floor. Empty bottles. Graffiti scratched into the wall. It looked like an exorcism had occurred in the room, or needed to.

I went downstairs and asked, "What the hell is that?"

"I told you."

"You didn't say it was a horror movie."

I started to unpack a few things, but decided it was best to keep most of my things in the hall closet out of sight. I closed the bathroom door and opened my travel bag. An unbelievable lady with adorable feet lay on the pink tile floor of her bathroom a million miles away in the magazine centerfold I'd picked up at the truck stop in Wyoming. It made me want to head right back out onto the road in search of her. But here I was in this old house with pink tiles under my feet. I got in the shower and washed off the road. When you're on the road, showers are a relief, but they're not home. This felt more like home, even if it was temporary.

When JP got home, he ran up and gave me a hug. He seemed genuinely happy, but he also seemed burned out again.

"Hey kiddo, what's happening? You're getting big!"

"All good, man. Good to see you. You know they had me locked up a while. It was shit, man."

"How are things now?" I asked.

"A lot of bullshit, but keeping it cool. Trying to hang low."

"Well, you stay out of trouble. It's good to see you again."

"It's been a long time," he said pulling at his hat.

"Sure has. Things have really changed now that you two moved out of that town. You still talk to your dad?"

"Fuck that shit, man."

"I know how it is."

"Where'd you just come from?" he asked.

"California. I was on a big cross-country trip after working in Florida for Aunt Annie and Uncle Russell in Florida."

"What's that song about the asshole brother in LA?"

"Bush "Everything Zen"? You know that?"

"Yeah, I heard it the other day," he laughed.

I assumed he only knew rap music by the way he dressed. His pants were falling off his waist. His t-shirt was two sizes too big. His baseball hat tipped to the side. He was straight out of a '90s rap video, yet he knew a song I listened to often.

"Hope that brother's not me!"

"Nah, man. Just don't go straight shit on me," he said.

"What do you mean? Straight like not doing drugs?"

"No, man. Playing police or dad."

"That's the last thing I want to do."

Mind of My Own

When a few weeks had passed, I finally called Jeff.

"Hey Jeff, I'm back."

"Oh man. Really?"

I could hear the 'it didn't work out, did it?' in his voice.

"Yes, it was quite a summer. I hit the open road, went out to California, just me and my tapes."

I sang into the phone, "losing my mind!"

Jeff laughed hard.

"Man, let's hang. I can't wait to hear about it," he said.

I drove out to the Kennedy house on the weekend. Andy was out working. I hung out with Jeff and told him the gist of the road stories. Then he told me all he had been up to. He too was growing away from Long Island and all we had known. He just didn't know it yet. He invited me to a punk show.

"It's not really my thing, but let me give it a try," I said.

"Cool. You'll dig these guys."

We walked out to his living room for me to leave. His mother was standing there. I hadn't seen Mrs. Kennedy in years, and she had been sleeping earlier when I arrived. She had grown frail and gray, and an oxygen tank stood at her side connected to her by a plastic tube that ran up into her nose. I remembered her smoking her long 100s in the car. She was a woman of the 1950s, a darling right out of an Elvis film where he'd fall for her and sing her a love song.

"Hello, Jack. So nice to see you," she said.

"Great to see you too, Mrs. Kennedy."

The air tank was hard to keep my eyes off, but I tried.

"What are you doing these days?" she asked.

"I'm getting ready to go back to college. I started classes, but then took some time off to work and travel. I just got back to New York a few weeks ago."

"Nice to hear you're finding your way. You know..." she said and stopped to take a breath. "...I wasn't very hopeful for your future when you were younger, though I did pray for you. It's a miracle. I'm very glad."

"Thank you. That means a lot."

"Are you still smoking cigarettes, Jack?"

I looked away, then back at her, "I have to cut down."

"Quit. Take it from me," she said holding up the tube.

"I will."

"Promise you will," she said, and I nodded.

"I'd hug you goodbye, but I can't get too close to people these days with my immune system," she said and blew a kiss.

I sent one back and waved goodnight.

The following weekend, I drove out to Jeff's and parked my car out front. We jumped into his Jetta and drove into the city for the show. It was at a little place called Coney Island High. The September breeze had already started in, and it was a beautiful night. We went into the place, and it was packed with pink and green haired punk fans. The ceiling seemed low in some places. Exposed pipes ran up and down around the dimly lit room. The music kicked in and he led me through the crowd up toward the front. Strung Out was the name of the band, but they were far from that. Full of energy, the singer jumped around and the guitarist jumped up and down nailing the guitar. The drummer pounded the drums. Only the bass player drifted around the stage cool and calm as he plucked at the bass. They had a few melodic pop punk songs mixed in with some harder ones. It was an exhilarating set, and we both stood there in awe. The music was alive, and we were enjoying it with nothing but water bottles in our hands.

You Not Me

JP was out of control. Just as I arrived back at the house one day after looking for work, I could see JP running off with a friend. My mother was crying in the hall.

"What happened?"

"He hit me. Cursed at me. He's so angry at me for putting him away. I just wanted to help. The school...the truancy..."

She pointed at her bed and then put her face in her hands.

There was a glob of excrement on her bedspread.

"Is that what I think it is?"

I made her some tea and tried to calm her down. But I was angry too. How could he do this? How could he blame her when he damned well knew the school was to blame for the lock up. What about his actions? What about his father? Our mother was doing her best with what she had.

When JP got home, I popped out of the bathroom and grabbed him by the throat.

"What are you doing?"

"No, what are you doing?" I roared back.

"The shit was my friend. This kid..."

"Bullshit. Even if it was, why'd you let him?"

"I didn't know until we left. He told me down the block."

JP started to fight back. I grabbed him in a headlock and brought him down to the living room floor. My mother came out and started screaming to stop. I grabbed him by his feet and dragged him to the back door. He was crying, and I had lost control. I grabbed him by the face and looked him in the eyes.

"You have to stop this. Get control," I yelled.

Who was I talking to? Him or me?

"I'm sorry," he said.

"Cut it out. Okay. Respect your mother. She's the only one in this world we have who wouldn't sell us down the river."

"I've already been sent down..."

"You peed on a kid on the bus and started skipping school at eight. What is the state supposed to do?"

"Sorry."

"Clean the shit up."

I pointed at him furiously.

The next day I hugged him and said sorry for getting rough. I felt bad. I knew he'd had enough of that kind of thing.

"We have to stick together, brother. And be healthy."

"Yeah, I know. I know, bro," he replied.

There I was lecturing my brother, and I was just as lost. I was sleeping on my mother's couch, stoned out, watching late night space documentaries and music videos. The Camaro was now in the driveway with expired plates, and I had no money to renew the registration. I needed a job. I felt too stupid to go back to Cliff at the station, and it was too far from where I was living now anyway.

Al had stopped by one day. I hadn't called him, but I had called my grandmother. I hadn't told her too much, but she must have told him. When I didn't answer the door, he walked around the outside of the house like it was some kind of investigation. Al called my name, but never spotted me up in the corner window. I couldn't face him. I felt naked. I felt broken. I needed time.

I took care of the house while my mother was out at nursing school. JP came and went. When she got home, I went outside to sit in my car. I smoked a joint to a heavy metal tape, and when it finished, I went to go inside the house. I was stopped by a new song playing on the radio— "You Not Me" by Dream Theater. I sat back and listened, new music once more reminding me of the importance of newness.

Devil Inside

I was reading Kerouac's book when Andy called. I had grabbed a paperback in California, but hadn't had the chance to read while I was traveling. Any time I wasn't behind the wheel was time reserved for serious rest. I finally cracked the book open after settling in. I found the pioneering road trip novel to be amusing. I couldn't help but think about how much had changed in America, and how different his road trips had been from mine, yet we were both out looking for something.

Andy was home from college and wanted to get together. Jeff was out with a girl, so it would just be us. He offered to pick me up, but I decided to borrow my mother's car for the night. She had offered. I didn't want to make it a habit, but I needed to get out for a few hours. I made the twenty-five-minute drive to his house.

"You want to go to a club to meet some girls I know?" he asked as he got into my mother's Toyota Corolla.

"Sure, let's go. Tell me where," I said.

"Head to Queens."

"Queens?"

"Yeah, they said they'd be there," Andy said.

"All right. Let's do this."

Thirty minutes later, I pulled into the back lot of some brick building. It was dark. There weren't many people outside. We got out and walked inside after the doorman gave us a pat down.

"The door man looked at us a little funny," Andy said.

"Well, he looked a little sinister. See the devil beard?"

"Yeah, and the horns coming out of his head!"

We walked into a dimly lit bar. We grabbed beers at the bar right away before looking for the girls. The bartender was a bit off, like the doorman. I couldn't place it, but I started to look around as we drank our lousy beers.

Something seemed off. My vision started to adjust to the scene. My gosh, I said to myself. Everyone was dressed in dark, but not just black club clothes; these people had black shirts with purple and red collars. Their hair was dyed black. They wore black eyeliner and lipstick. Fingernails were painted black. Some had piercings and devil tattoos. A man made a grand entrance and whipped a big black cape around his shoulder.

"Fucking Dracula," I said.

"Ah, what's going on here?" Andy asked.

I looked at Andy and then down at myself at what I was wearing. He had on blue jeans and a Mets jersey. His blonde hair was gelled back. My sandy sun-stained brown hair was messy. I had on blue jeans and a green plaid shirt. We looked ridiculous in this place.

"I don't know. You brought us here. Where are the girls?"

"I don't know," he said.

We walked around the place, but he didn't see them anywhere.

"Let me call them."

"Good idea," I said.

I sat at the bar and watched the scene while he called them on the payphone. A woman came up and ordered a drink nearby. She had high black boots, a short tight mini skirt, and a tight dark top. Her hair was black. Her lips were black. Her green eyes pierced through black eyeliner and looked at me. I turned away, almost recognizing her. I turned back, and she was lifting her drink. It was a tall glass filled with red like blood. She held it up in front of her pale white skin and the glass glowed in front of her chest like an extension of her heart. She brought the glass to her lips to drink and then licked the red from her lips like a serpent. I shuddered. Andy tapped me on the back telling me it was time to go.

"What happened?" I asked.

"They decided on something else."

"Not in the mood for vampires tonight?"

A guy next to me heard me and bent his nose at us, the jock and the rocker who stumbled into a New York Goth club.

Andy and I drove back out to Long Island and met our old friends Jason and Rob at a bar. They had taken a cab there so they could drink liberally. Since I was driving, I had one beer when we arrived and then stopped. I had a water and fries, while they drank for another couple of hours. Afterwards, I took them for a ride through a few towns in my mother's car. We cruised around like we had done in high school.

I popped in Billy Joel's *Greatest Hits Volume I and II* on cassette, and we had a massively fun singalong right from the top of the album. To my surprise, we all kept singing along all the way through to "It's Still Rock and Roll to Me" and all of us knew every single word of these anthems by our Long Island musical hero. None of us had laughed that hard in a long time. Once we were good and tired, I dropped them off at home one by one. I listened to the rest of the tape on the way back out to the reality of Sayville.

Until It Sleeps

I needed to get my car back on the road soon. I thought I'd make some great money being a bartender, so I threw down a hundred bucks on bartender school and took a job at a restaurant as a barback. After a few days, I hated popping beers and grew bored with learning drinks, and I never went back.

I took a job at a vitamin factory. I boxed up crates of vitamins all day. I was bored, but it wasn't terrible. I wouldn't have to shake people's drinks and listen to their madness.

My mother's nursing school at night was doing well. During the day she studied and worked a part-time job. Some days she was able to drive me to the factory. Other days I walked or called a guy named Greg to pick me up on his way.

One day, my mother mentioned Win from the old house. She wondered if he had ever done anything to me or JP.

"No, not that I know of. Certainly, never with me. I mean, he put his hand on my leg once, but I think it was his way of trying to be a big brother or father or whatever he was trying to do. It wasn't deviant. Why, do you think he did something to JP?"

"No, I was just wondering what you thought all these years later. Don and I were pretty careless and wrapped up with things back then."

"Yeah, I know."

"I heard Win was having a tough time," she said.

"How do you know?"

"Don told me."

"How's Don?" I asked.

"Good. We talk here and there. He checks in on JP."

"Good. What happened to Win?" I asked.

"His sister died recently. He was living with her family."

I felt bad for the man. I was curious to know how he was.

When my mother left for school, I looked up his sister in the phonebook and gave him a call.

"Win? Wow, it's been a long time. It's Jack Tortis."

"Jack? Ages! Good to hear from you. How are you?"

"Good. My mother, JP, and I live out in Sayville now."

"Yes, I heard."

"Sorry to hear about your sister. How are you?"

"Thanks, Jack. I'm just all right. Each day is better."

"Well, I just wanted to check in with you. It's good to know you're holding up well. Things didn't really end well."

"No, they didn't. And after you, that crazy kid, and troubles with your stepfather."

"Yeah, what a mess. I'm surprised Don even talks to you."

"He was very forgiving actually."

"Really?"

"Yeah. Hey listen, how about getting together? Can I buy you a steak and a beer?"

"Sure. I'm off any night this week."

"All right, how about Wednesday?"

"That works."

I gave him the address and hung up. Right away, I had second thoughts. Why was he interested in seeing me? What would we talk about? Did I really want to open this weird thing back up? He was there during a rough time. He fed me cigarettes and drugs. It felt almost controlling. I was just a kid then, and now I was twenty-one years old. I was trying to go forward and get back into college, not go backwards.

On Wednesday he arrived at 6:30. I opened the door.

"Listen, Win. I'm sorry you drove all the way out here. I'm not feeling up to it."

"You should've called me. I drove all the way over."

"I wanted to tell you in person. I'm not interested in opening anything back up."

"Just have a steak and a beer, Jack."

"I haven't eaten a steak in years. I don't think it's a good idea. But I'm glad I got to see you again and know you're well."

"I appreciate that, Jack. Glad to know you're good too. Going to college?"

"Yes. On a break right now. Can I ask you something?"

"Yeah?"

"Did you ever hurt JP in any way?"

"How is he? Did you ask him? Did I ever hurt you?"

"You probably got a little weird and interfered too much, but no. I can't say you hurt me."

"There's your answer. I was just trying to help the same way someone helped me. Nothing evil."

"You know what I'd do if I found out you did?"

"I can imagine. But we won't have to find out. What did you think? No, I don't even want to know. As long as no one is making up things about me."

"No one has said anything. I was just curious."

"All right then. Feel better?"

"I do. Thanks, Win. Take care of yourself."

"Good then. You take care, Jack."

Win drove off. Maybe we both needed closure.

I went out and sat in the Camaro, put on some Metallica, and puffed a few hits of a joint. A final goodbye to Win. Another notch forward.

Sayville, NY, Spring/Summer, 1998

Al managed to get the house phone number and called. My mother talked to him for a few minutes before handing it over.

"Hey, Al. Great to hear from you. Thanks for calling. I've been meaning to reach out."

"How's everything going, Jack?"

"Oh, okay. Trying to get back into school."

"You've been back a year, right?" he asked.

"God, has it been that long? I guess so. Almost. This August will be a year. I had car problems. Had to get a new job."

"Why didn't you call? I stopped by a couple of months ago."

"Oh, I figured you were busy getting on with your life, and I just got caught up with things. I've been helping my mother out."

"Your mother mentioned they're selling the house soon."

"Yes, my grandmother and her siblings are looking to sell it, so we'll be needing to leave. My mother's finishing up nursing school and then planning to go to Florida."

"Yes, she mentioned that too. What will you do? You know, I'm not sure about my house since I'll be getting married soon. But grandma mentioned her apartment."

"I talked to Grandma a few weeks ago and she mentioned that her tenant might be moving up state," I said.

"It's definite now. This summer. You should take it. It'll make her feel good. And it's right there in Sayville."

"I think I'll do that. It's good timing."

"And listen, I heard Roberto is needing some help."

"You mean at grandpa's office?" I asked.

"Yes, it's got a little life left in it. Roberto's running it until AT&T takes over the whole operation. Go down and talk to him."

"Will do, Al. Thanks. Are you good?"

"Yes, can't complain. I miss my dad, but that's life. Haven't talked to yours, have you?" Al asked.

"No, not since the funeral. I tried but left a voicemail."

"You two are bad."

"Yeah, I guess so."

"We'll have to talk about your travels sometime soon. Give Roberto a call. All right?"

"Sure thing. Thanks, Al."

Al seemed to be passing me off to his mother now, but I understood and expected it. I had left him twice for two failed endeavors in Florida. He couldn't keep me happy there. He was moving on now and getting married. I couldn't intrude.

I finally got the Camaro back on the road, so on Monday I stopped over at the office on my lunch break from the factory. Roberto was a short Italian man married to my father's sister. He welcomed me in and confirmed that he indeed needed help. He showed me around the place.

The office had two columns of drafting tables. The four rows had two people on each side of the room. A space went right down the middle that led to the back manager's office, which no one used anymore since my grandfather's retirement to Florida. I wondered why Roberto didn't use the office since he had essentially taken over the business. He suggested I take the back office to do my paperwork, since I wouldn't need a drafting table. He needed me to do filing, payroll, and check over paperwork. I'd also come in on Saturday and clean the office. This was fine with me. It would work well when I started back up with college in September and was only minutes from my grandmother's house in the next town over.

I went back to the vitamin factory after my lunch break and gave my notice at the end of the day. They told me just to finish up the week. I looked around and found it difficult to imagine working in this same place my whole life. People needed work though, and

I guess they were content. It wasn't that bad of a place, but I was restless. This was why I needed to get back to school and figure things out. College was my way out of a life that I just wasn't going to be satisfied with.

☆

Work at the office went well for the rest of the summer. Every morning at ten, a snack truck they called the roach coach would roll up, and we'd take a coffee break. Lunch was at 12:30.

There were a few old crochety men. They were quiet and kept to themselves, as did everyone. This was a laid-back introverted crowd.

One of the older guys would break out into laughs. Who knows what he was laughing at in his twisted mind. Another one a few seats away would occasionally fart on his chair. The guy in the back of the room across from Roberto would laugh at all of it.

"Shit, man. Shit. That's some real shit," he'd say to me.

One guy was in a rock band at night.

One guy named Pete was an army veteran who often gripped his legs from gout.

Another guy listened to Sarah McLachlan all day on his headphones. Her video for "Building a Mystery" repeatedly played on the cable music channel every night and I never tired of it. But this guy had a framed picture of her on his desk. I guess I couldn't blame him.

Nice folks, but pieces of work.

☆

I finally got my hands on the new Izzy Stradlin album *117°* and sat in my car by the marina to listen to it. Tears of joy slipped from my eyes as I heard the final studio songs he had performed for Freddie and I in Key West a couple of years earlier. A part of my soul lived in those fourteen songs, and maybe the future too.

Not For You

The Camaro grew ill on me. It had sat in the driveway for months, perhaps too long. The paint began to fade, parts began to rattle, and the engine began to squeak. On the third day I had it back on the road, a man in a van came along and smashed off the passenger side mirror as he pulled into a parking spot. He had the decency to come into the bank and tell me. He decided to pay me three hundred dollars on the spot instead of reporting it to the insurance.

Then just a couple of weeks later, I was combing my hair in the mirror, getting ready to go out to the bars with Andy, when I heard a giant crash out front. I froze in place. It sounded like someone had hit a telephone pole. It sounded bad. Rushing outside to look for a dangling powerline, I was struck with the realization that my car had been hit. I ran out into the street. The front fender was wrecked and the driver side front wheel twisted in a manner I could not have imagined. I looked out into the street and down the block. A gray car was making a left, metal grinding as it crawled around the corner.

With desperation to find the attacker, I jumped into my mother's car with JP. A block and half away, we found the suspect's vehicle. The gray car had a cracked-up fender and a smashed window— it was the one. But the suspect was nowhere to be found. He had surely taken off on foot in a hurry.

Gathering the plate number and insurance information from the glovebox, I drove back to wait for the police. As we waited on the front lawn, I occasionally let out a war cry. As the neighbors looked on, a disheveled man came staggering up.

"That's him, that's the guy," the neighbor said.

The man stumbled over to us.

"Yeah, I crashed. I'm sorry," he confessed in a drawl.

"Sorry?" I screamed as I approached the slurring man "You fucking ran. Hit and run! I should kick your ass right now."

"I'm sorry, man. You can hit me if you want," he offered. But I didn't strike him. Instead, I waited for the police to haul him off to jail. This drunken man had blasted into my parked car just minutes before I was about to set out for the night. I felt like I was becoming a target. It was time to turn the page.

Two weeks later, I received a check to fix the Camaro. Another two weeks later, it was repaired. A week later, I sold the car to Pete from the office. He bought it for three hundred dollars and said he'd "fix her up" and take good care of her.

I was half filled with sorrow. An era was over. The Camaro had been there with me through my twelfth-grade dropout, brief homelessness, locked out nights when I was staying with Paul, my return to school, my uncle's house, my Florida escapades, the start of college, and my first cross-country trip. But the other half of me was filled with excitement to move on to something new. To remember the car, I ripped off the silver Camaro emblem from the damaged fender— I vowed to get it dipped in gold someday.

I got a deal on a white '91 Civic hatchback. The car had high mileage, just over 100,000 miles, but it was a Honda. I had heard they go forever. I drove home to pick up my belongings. I was moving out, and my mother and JP were moving to Florida to start over. I helped them pack the truck. I was hopeful this new beginning would be healthy for both of them.

"You're going to have to come down and visit," Mom said.

"Yeah, definitely."

But I knew it would be difficult to do now that I was getting more dedicated to college. And of course, I'd be heading back out onto the highway in less than a year's time, even though I didn't know it yet.

Sayville, NY, Fall, 1998

I dropped my bags downstairs in my grandmother's apartment. Her long-time tenant had just moved up state to be closer to his family. This was a studio apartment with a large closet. The gay man slept in the closet, which was just big enough to fit nothing more than a single size mattress. There was also an open space where he hung his clothes. A locked door that led up to my grandmother's house was in the closet room. He was free now.

Around the back of the house, two concrete steps descended to the main apartment door and led into a small living room area. The man was kind enough to leave a cedar coffee table, an old television on a stand, and an old blue sofa, which would make as my bed for now. One of the best features was the shelf area that wrapped around the wall on two sides where I could display my favorite books. To the left was a narrow hallway with a kitchen area along the wall. It had a small counter, electric stove, sink, and a half-sized refrigerator at the end next to the bathroom door. The two windows looked out on a view of a forest that stretched for miles into a county park.

The birds woke me most mornings. I'd open my eyes and from the sofa I could see the tops of the pine trees. The first morning was unusually serene, a connection with nature I hadn't felt since my road trip. Other than a faint sound of her TV in the afternoon and evening, I could barely hear my grandmother going about her business.

The small green house was on a tree-lined suburban block in Sayville. A village of stores was a quick drive away. So were the apartments where my mother and I lived when I was younger. The Lincoln Avenue house too. I couldn't help wonder why my mother had ever left the town, and now again to Florida. Maybe she felt the same way as I did about my old town.

One night, I heard voices upstairs. It was Grandma and Al. He had apparently stopped over. He was talking louder than usual, almost shouting. I went over to the door to listen out of curiosity.

"He's a good president," she said.

"Shut up. You don't know what you're talking about."

"Why are you getting so upset?" she asked.

"Shut up, Mom. Now. Just shup up."

"Well, I like him."

"You're being stupid. He's against family values."

Al was being nasty, and I felt bad for my grandmother. I really hadn't seen this side of him. I felt like running up there to defend her, but she was fending him off just fine.

"Oh, stop with that. No one's perfect. Like your father knew anything about family values?" she said.

Moments later, I heard the front door close. He had left.

☆

I was back at the community college, but this time at a campus farther out east where no one would know who I am. Andy had gone off to the University of Maine to play basketball and Jeff had gone to tech college. There was little possibility of running into someone I knew. I was a new person in a new world again.

Although some students talked about how they felt like it was thirteenth grade, I felt like I was in a serious place, a real college, a world away from my hellish high school experience.

My first class back to college was Introduction to Literature with Professor Tony Donovan. He was a wise middle-aged man with glasses, graying dark hair, and a Mister Rogers persona— except on the second day of class when kids in the back of the room tried to talk about their own thing, he interrupted them abruptly.

"Excuse me, you'll need to stop or leave."
The kids were surprised at his bite and never said another word.

Professor Donovan had great personal stories about travelling Europe, and he selected literature that spoke to me. Literature hadn't spoken to me in Mrs. Lumbrera's high school class when we went around the room reading various stories out loud. The experiences were night and day. Professor Donovan read passages and then let them hang in the air for a moment. I hadn't felt this way about the written word before, but I knew I always loved a good story. I appreciated all the moral tales from childhood. I loved movies. And I loved to write. But I was finding myself now.

Another favorite class was Introduction to Sociology. Dr. Freeman was a big jolly man with a gray beard and ponytail— a real hippy survivor of the '60s. Professor Freeman confessed his deep philosophies of life through stories he told. He always posed questions to us. How many of us live in our living rooms? Or even spend time in them? Why are we so competitive and obsessed with sports? His class wasn't persuading me of anything new, but it did reinforce questions I already had.

In between classes, I walked around on the trails through tall pine trees that reminded me of Oregon.

☆

On a Saturday in October, I got a call from Gil. He was home and wanted to see if I was up for coming over to hang at his house. He said there was no need to wait until nightfall if I was free. I had cleaned the office that morning, so I was free to enjoy my weekend. I cruised out to Gil's house, which was in the town to the west of my own town. I followed the directions he had read off to me over the phone and pulled up to a white house. I followed a path around to the side and knocked.

"Hey you!" Gil exclaimed and hugged me like we were old lost friends. I guess we were in a way.

"Gil, what's going on, man? Great to see you."

"Same here. Come in and let's catch up."

He closed the door behind us, and I followed him down to a dark basement apartment. The bottom of the stairs opened up into a white tiled kitchen. Ahead was a living room. His older mother sat on a chair watching television, much the way my grandmother did at home upstairs. I couldn't help thinking about how old his mother looked. The sweet woman turned around and said hello and then returned to her show.

We slipped into his bedroom, which was like his own studio apartment. He threw a blanket down on the floor against the door. The place was a bit of a mess and a big ashtray sat on the floor between two chairs. He sat and motioned for me to grab the other chair. I popped open my soda for a sip and then he asked if I wanted to get into smoking.

"You mind the glass pipe?" he asked.

"Eh, I guess. No papers?"

"I could roll up a couple of doobies if you want."

"Sure, if you got them. I don't mean to be picky."

"Not a problem, Jack. How are you these days? Andy said you were back at college after another trip out of New York."

"Yes, I took off to Florida again and then hit the road on a cross country adventure to California."

I went on to explain my trip as Gil rolled two fat joints with great precision. It was like an art. At this moment, he reminded me of an older kid named Randy McKinney from high school who used to pick us up and drive us around for kicks. The dedication to his pot was amazing.

"Anyway, I'm back in the New York groove again," I said.

"That sounds like the adventure of a lifetime."

"You should do it sometime."

Gil laughed and sparked up the first joint, took one quick hit and handed it over to me.

"Take your time with that," he said.

"So what's going on with you?" I asked just before ripping on the joint and letting out a big cough.

"Whoa there, killer!"

"Yeah, I better take it easy with this," I said handing it back. I took a sip from my bottle of Mountain Dew.

"I had to withdraw from college up state. I'll be starting the local state university in January," said Gil. He took a hit and blew a giant puff of smoke out into the space between us.

"What happened? You were pretty excited to get back up there to the fraternity and everything."

"Man, things kind of fell apart. The pressure. It was big. The kegstands where they feed the beer through a tube upside down. The wake and bake. The constant flow of drugs. The acid. The acid is what really screwed me up."

"Man, sounds like you partied like a rock star."

He took a hit and handed the joint back to me.

"Too much, man. I had a breakdown. Couldn't handle it."

"I'm sorry to hear this, bud," I said and then took a puff.

"No, you know what? It's better off. My mother is older, as you can see. She's happy to have me back home. I have to be here for her."

"Any siblings?"

"No, it's just me. My father died when I was ten."

"Sorry to hear that, bud."

"Thanks. You know he used to call me bud, actually."

"Oh, man. Sorry again."

"No, no, it's really okay. I like it. I use it all the time too."

After a few more puffs, we put out the stub of the joint and lit cigarettes. He got up and put a CD on.

"You like Dylan?" he asked.

"Sure, classic stuff."

He pressed play.

"It's *Greatest Hits, Volume Two*. Good stuff on here."

We listened for a while, just smoking our cigarettes and drinking our soda. I was in love with the album by the second track "Don't Think Twice, It's All Right," which seemed to capture my feelings about all the girls I'd ever loved. I felt empowered. Once in a while, Gil would sing along to a wise lyric, which would get us laughing. By the time we got to "All I Really Want to Do" we were both cracking up. Gil was singing along and I joined in on the chorus as soon as I learned the words.

"Hear that shit?" Gil asked.

"It's healing," I said.

"You bet it is."

I was amazed with the poetry. A whole new world had opened up. I'd be going back to Gil's house soon for sure.

☆

My grandmother and I bumped into each other coming out of the house one afternoon in late October. We didn't see each other much, but I always knew she was home and when she was awake or asleep. I also knew her hearing was terrible, so she didn't know as much about my activity.

"Hi, Jack. I was just going to take a walk."

"Could I join you?" I asked.

"Why, of course!"

We strolled down the street, and she told me about what neighbors lived in the houses, and who had kids who grew up with my father and his siblings. Then I brought it up.

"I heard Al over a few weeks ago."

"Oh, you did?"

"Yeah, he didn't sound very happy about the president."

"Your uncle gets upset about politics."

"I'd say so. Not sure what his issue is."

"It's a divided world in some ways. Some people are never going to be open to change. It makes me sad, but you just have to try to love everyone the way they are, no matter what they believe."

"You take the high road, Grandma. That's admirable."

She took my hand, held it, and then awkwardly shook it, not knowing what to do with it next. We walked back, and she pointed to a few birds on the way.

Echo

Gil's room was becoming the new place to hang. His mother didn't hear me come and go most of the time. The TV was too loud. We disappeared into his room and got right to the joints. This time he cranked on some newer Tom Petty music I hadn't heard. We played the entire *Echo* CD to the end.

"Man, you listen to some fantastic tunes! Great stuff."

"Thanks, man."

"Got any Pink Floyd for the next listen?"

He stiffened up.

"I wish I could, but I can't do it anymore."

"Why?"

"The acid. I had a bad trip on it. Can't even hear it."

"Oh, that's too bad. The Gilmour albums, after Waters left, are just so full of light and hope."

"Yeah, it all freaks me out, but here, let me give you these since you're a fan."

He dug into a notebook and then handed me four Pink Floyd postcards of four album covers.

"Send me a postcard with them one day."

"Will do."

"How about some Bob Dylan next?" he asked.

"Sounds good."

We sat and smoked weed for a while listening to *Bringing It All Back Home* by Bob Dylan. So many of the songs made me smile and brought happiness. After a few songs, I turned and asked him if he wanted to go out for a change.

"Gil, you feel like taking a ride today?"

"Ah, I don't know, man. What's there to do? You want to go eat something? We could order in."

"No, it's not that. I just feel like getting some air. Hitting the town a bit. Well, not our old town."

"You don't go back there much?"

"Not at all," I answered.

"I don't much either. Did you know our old town was known as "forsaken land" by the Native Americans who lived there four hundred years ago?"

"That sounds accurate," I said.

"Let's take a ride somewhere else if you want."

I could tell he was nervous and didn't really mean it.

"No, it's all right. I'll have my ride home tonight. Let's just chill and finish this album."

☆

On December 31, Andy managed to get Gil to come out. We all met at Andy's. Jeff was already out with his girlfriend, so he wouldn't be joining us. Our other friend Jason was driving tonight, and we headed out to a pub called Mulcahy's. We drove thirty minutes and got there around ten o'clock. The lot was packed. This was a big and full place.

The place was wild. Girls in short skirts and tight low shirts were going around feeding us booze. The bar area was packed, so we filled up and headed to the corner.

Around eleven o'clock, we bumped into Michelle Muraco, an old friend's older sister. She knew all of us, but she was particularly surprised to see me.

"How have you been, stranger?"

"Hi Michelle. Decent. How about you?"

"Things are well. Good to see you guys. It's been a while."

We raised and clinked our beer bottles.

"How's your brother?" I asked.

"He's good. He went through a little bit of a rough patch right after he graduated, and he had a little bit of a scare, but it was good for him. Really turned him around."

"Geez, is he all right?" I asked.

"He is now. Really finding his way. Wouldn't even be caught at a place like this."

"Too good for a bar?"

"Too healthy. Too disciplined."

"Are we talking about the same guy? Is he in bootcamp?"

"People change. I'm proud of him," she said.

"Wow, that's truly good to hear."

"Give him a call sometime. He'd love to talk to you again. He was pretty ripped up when you guys parted."

"Yes, I should call."

"Well, it's almost midnight. I'd better get back over to my friends. You all have a good night. Happy New Year."

"You too, Michelle. Take care."

The clock was nearing the end of the year. Andy, Jason, and I were drinking some lousy beers with some girls. Gil was arguing with a girl over to the side, which made things tense and awkward. We didn't care to get involved.

Prince's "1999" song came on and the party kicked into gear. 1998 was ending and the final year of the century was about to begin.

Ants Marching

In the middle of January, Gil and I hung at his house and ordered a pay per view boxing match. We smoked, drank beers, and watched Mike Tyson sink a white dude after a few rounds. The guy looked like he had a chance at one point, but all Tyson needed was one shot. He waited for the opportunity. I was waiting for mine. We're all waiting for that moment.

My spring semester started a couple of weeks later. On Tuesday and Thursdays, I'd go to four classes in a row. They were long days, but I'd rather get everything done in two days. Western Civilization was first from 9:30-10:45. Next, it was onto Abnormal Psychology from 11:10-12:25. Then, Screenwriting at 12:40-1:55. Creative writing ended my day from 2:10-3:25. On Thursdays, I'd return in the evening for a theater class. This all worked well with my days at the office, which were Monday, Wednesday, and Friday. I'd finish up paperwork and clean the office on Saturdays.

For what would've been James Dean's 68th birthday in February, I stayed in and watched *East of Eden* after taking a few hits of a joint out my window. On my road trip, I had seen where he had lived and died. There was something about him that made young guys like me see themselves in him. It was the confusion and struggle of being young. He wore it on his face.

The following weekend I met with Gil and Jeff at a bar called Rockwells. Gil and I had drinks. Jeff had a soda. I told them I would be going to see Andy in Maine at college in a few weeks during the March break.

"Are you going to party like a rock star?" asked Jeff.

"Maybe like a college student," I said.

"Same thing," said Gil.

"Yeah, I guess so. You guys want to come with me?"

"Wish I could. I have plans with the girl," Jeff said.

"Understood."

"I'll think about it, man," Gil offered.

"You do that, Gil. Let me know. It would be a trip."

☆

In mid-March, Gil and I drove up to visit Andy at college. The drive to Maine took five and a half hours, enough time to listen to about seven albums. We took my Honda, and I did all the driving. It reminded me of my road trip in 1997. It had been a while since I had been on the road. Gil had hardly been anywhere, except the tri-state area and to his college town in upstate New York. He was scarred by his trip to college, so this was a chance for redemption.

We got to Andy's apartment. He met us outside and pointed to a pile of snow in the corner of the parking lot.

"That's my car," he said.

"You mean under the snow?" I asked.

"Man, you're not going anywhere until April," said Gil.

"Probably May, but I don't need to anyway during the semester. Everything's walkable."

The inside of his furnished apartment was bare bones, a step away from a drug house, but without the drugs. Andy barely drank. He stayed away from bad stuff. But his living conditions were horrendous.

"This place looks like a crack house," I whispered to Gil as Andy stepped into the bathroom.

"No joke," Gil said. He pointed to Andy's small mattress on the floor. "I like the pad. It looks like a dog bed!"

Andy had some things going on the first day with his girlfriend, who we never got to meet, but we kept ourselves busy.

135

We walked over to the village and checked out the shops. I bought some vinyl records in a record shop, and we had lunch at a café. Then we got together with Andy for a party that night. We walked a few minutes and arrived at someone's apartment, which was loaded with drinking college kids. Gil and I stayed to ourselves, observing from the side.

Gil pointed to a piece of paper on the kitchen counter.

"Open your mind, open your ass," the paper read in marker.

"That's college life for you," he said.

"I just dig the tunes they're playing. What is that?"

Gil chuckled and told me it was a song called "Ants Marching" by the Dave Matthews Band.

"Fun stuff," I said.

"Yes, very college," said Gil.

"It's different. I like it."

"I have *Under the Table and Dreaming* at home. I'll give you the CD. You'll dig it."

We drank a bit and observed the crowd. I spotted a beauty. She was dressed warmly in a thick sweater. Her dark brown curly hair spiraled down on each side of her white sweater. There was a look that reminded me of Jane. A good thing or a curse? I didn't know, so I kept my mouth shut, staring at her from across the room wondering what she was like and knowing I'd never see her again.

What were we doing here? I wondered. I wanted to visit Andy. I wanted to see the college life. I guess this was it. But it wasn't ours. Gil had his and walked away from it. I hadn't experienced it yet. There was no point in engaging with these kids. They were mostly friendly but seemed closed off. This was Andy's new world. I would hold out for my own.

On the way home from Maine, I stopped the Tom Petty tape and asked Gil if Maine reminded him of his college days.

"No, not at all. Those guys were tame. My college was a madhouse. I have to say I was a little nervous going up here this weekend. Didn't want any flashbacks," said Gil.

"Geez. Yeah, Andy's a laid-back guy, so I had a feeling it wouldn't get too crazy," I said.

"You'd be surprised. Some of the calmest are party tyrants. But you're right. We know Andy well enough to know he stays out of trouble," said Gil.

"Man, you'll have to tell me about your time upstate someday," I said.

"My war scars. You don't want to hear them. But maybe someday, maybe on a cross country road trip."

"You'd do one?" I asked.

"Yes, yours sounded good. You going to do another one?"

"Maybe. Probably."

I turned the Tom Petty tape back on and thought of my 1997 trip. It was almost two years since I'd been out to California. I thought of Sarah and wondered what she was up to. We wrote post cards from time to time, but not enough to keep up with each other's lives. I thought of Portland. The wide-open road. Maybe.

Busted

In April, I helped Professor Donovan with his film casting. One of his stories was being made into an independent film, and he would be directing it. I took the train into the city and found the address of a small studio space he had rented for auditions. He welcomed me in and gave me the scripts. I would be the reader who actors auditioned with. He was careful not to get my hopes up, warning me that the male roles were all too old for me, but it was still a great experience to read with serious actors. I went through the lines with a dozen men and women for different roles as the professor looked on taking notes with an assistant. It gave me a taste for the profession that went beyond my acting class, but it all seemed so competitive. All the work these actors would do for little or no pay. It seemed like you already needed to be wealthy for that kind of work.

☆

A few days later, I drove over to Sound Beach on the north shore of Long Island. I liked driving up there once in a while. The beach was rockier up there, yet some people still used the beaches there in the summer. It was quiet in the off seasons though. I liked to sit in my car and look out at the Long Island Sound. You couldn't see Connecticut, but you knew it was there across the way.

The semester was almost over. I needed to think about what I was going to do in the fall. Things were going all right, but I wasn't fitting in, and it was hard to meet new friends at a community college. I had Gil, but he was back over near the old town.

I went out with a couple of girls, but they seemed very into where they were. One bubbly blue-eyed blonde girl named Keri baked me cookies. I met her at the diner to eat lunch and she gave me the cookies in a tin. We were in Professor Donovan's class together, so we talked about people in our class. Then we talked about ourselves. She said she wanted a big family full of kids, so they could all get into a station wagon and go for rides to the water park. A nice plan for some, but it scared the helk out of me. I didn't even know where I'd be next month. She told me all this with a distracting low-cut shirt, giant breasts hanging in front of me. At some point she invited me back to her house. I knew she'd be happy with someone, but I couldn't get into that kind of situation.

I went out with a girl named Louisa from another class. She was the opposite of Keri. Thin, dark hair, brown eyes. I picked her up at home and went in to meet her family. It all reminded me too much of the past. We went out to a restaurant. Once we got halfway through the meal, I realized there was nothing there. No magic. No real connection. She talked of Long Island things in her Long Island accent, as I sat there and dreamed of walking in the woods, living in a faraway city, meeting all new people from a different culture. What was there to talk about? We were already bored with each other, and we both knew it.

☆

On my way home from the office one Friday, I was sitting at a red light when I saw a car swerve off the road and head right towards the front of my car. The car swiped the bumper enough to give me a jolt, and then crashed up the road a bit. I got out to check on her, but there were already people pulling her out. Someone said she had had a seizure. The police arrived quickly. I filled out a report and watched them take the woman away in an ambulance. Within an hour, I started to feel my sore neck. By the time I awoke the next morning, I was all locked up.

I found a chiropractor and went in for an evaluation. He took x-rays and scans, and then he cracked my back and neck into alignment. He said it would be a couple of months' worth of treatment. He wanted me there every day of the week. But after four days in a row, I dropped it down to three days a week. He recommended a lawyer, whom I called and met with. The guy gave me some papers and said these kinds of injuries could be lifelong and that I should get some kind of small compensation for all the treatment in the future once the insurance ran out. I signed the papers and didn't see him again.

On the final night of theater class, I performed excerpts of a play titled *American Buffalo* with one other guy. I played the character of Donny Dubrow, and we did the first ten or so pages of Act I. At the new campus and without Jeff or our partner Bryan, I could no longer rely on someone familiar. But I did well. The performance was fun. It was a good way to close out the semester and my time at this college. I didn't know where I'd go next, but the feeling was certain that I would be moving on.

Long Island, Summer, 1999

I stood outside smoking a cigarette on a warm day in early June with the door open to let fresh air into the apartment. I took a few steps away from the entrance and turned to look up at the trees. When I turned back toward the house, I froze. A large cat was walking down my steps into my apartment. Had the beast not seen me standing there smoking? Did it not care? What was this and where did it come from? This was no normal cat. It was bigger, wilder looking, with pointy ears and some black spotting on its fur.

The wildcat disappeared into my apartment. I knew not to get too close, but I needed to get a picture. My Kodak was right on the ledge, so I inched down the steps, peeked in and saw the cat sniffing around my kitchen. I quietly grabbed the camera and exited back out the door. A few moments later the cat returned to view. I could see it sniffing around my sofa now. It had surveyed the entire apartment and then proceeded to make an exit. This cat could strike at any moment if it felt threatened, so I backed away as it came up the steps. I raised the camera to my eye and the cat stopped to turn back at me. Snap. Got my picture. The cat wandered off into the neighbor's yard and then presumably back into the county park where it lived. I went up to ask my grandmother.

"Yes, that was a bobcat. They live out there in the park woods. It's been a long time since I've seen one. Very rare sighting. That means something. You're one of the lucky ones."

☆

I arrived at Gil's around 7p.m. when it was still light out. He had worked until 5:00 at his part-time job at a store stocking shelves. I had spent the afternoon cleaning up the office. Gil looked like he had already hit the bong by the time I arrived. Music was already playing. He sparked up the pipe and passed it to me.

"I'm all out of papers, man. Sorry. You mind the pipe?"

"No, it's all right," I said.

"What did you think of running into Steven the other night? Andy told me you guys saw him at the bar."

"He looked a little worn, but not as bad as expected considering the rumors. He was truly happy to see us, as I was to see him. My god, he was the very first friend I had in this town. He saved me from some bad stuff. We were just little kids."

"Do you think he has a problem?" asked Gil.

"I don't know, but I asked him to ditch his friends and take a long drive with me. He wasn't going anywhere though."

"He said no?"

"He said he just couldn't. Then I saw him in the alleyway out back when we were leaving. Not sure if he saw us, but we pretended we didn't see him."

"Sorry, man."

"What do we do, right?"

"So, what are you going to do in the fall? You mentioned something about transferring."

"Yeah, it's time to move on, Gil. I have a pretty good idea, but I have to apply."

"Where to?" he asked.

"I'm thinking of New Hampshire or Vermont."

"Did visiting Andy inspire you?"

"I guess so, but I'm also thinking about the west coast."

"The west coast?"

"Yeah, I'm thinking about it."

"Wow, no one does that. That would be pretty far out."

"I'll let you know. I'm a little late in the process to get in somewhere for September, but I'm going to try."

Gil and I smoked and listened to music for the rest of the night. He wanted to keep smoking, but at some point I told him I'd had enough. Around 2 a.m., I went to leave.

Gil walked me upstairs, said goodbye, and closed the door. I started down the steps and froze. There at the bottom was a growling big black dog. First a bobcat, now a wolf? I knew it wasn't a wolf, but it sure looked like one. This was one bothered dog. I backed up the steps, which put me higher than the animal. The dog growled louder staring up at me. I reached back, opened the screen door, and jiggled the knob. It was locked. I had nowhere to go. I thought of knocking. I thought of making a run to the car, but I knew it would trigger a chase. I wasn't sure I could outrun the dog to the street. If it caught me, I'd have to fight. I stood still. The dog growled louder, took a step forward, and then I spoke to it.

"Go home. Good boy. Go home, boy. Leave."

The dog took another step forward and then pivoted away and took off. There was a breeze in the trees. The dog was spooked by something.

I cautiously made my way to the street and slipped into my car. I lit a cigarette and made my way home away from this place. Maybe Gil was too close to the old town. Something was telling me I didn't belong there. I was spooked, but I knew it was this all-too-common slip to the void that always happened just as the change was coming.

The Best of What's Around

The drive up to Massachusetts went smooth in the middle of the night. I was restless one night in late June and decided to get away and see something new. I don't know why I chose it, but I had never seen Plymouth Rock in person. It didn't seem right that I was from the northeast and had never seen this. I wanted to walk on the land that the pilgrims had walked on. I wanted to imagine them getting out of the boats in knee deep water to make those first steps onto the North America mainland. I imagined their fear of the unknown. I sat there on the shoreline in the dark and watched the sun rise.

When the sun was finished with its ascent, I looked at the rock with 1620 engraved in it. I wasn't even sure it was the real thing, but a sign said so. A historical symbol of the past. I had to get away from mine. I had made the escape twice before. I had travelled the country and caught a glimpse of the possibilities out there. Even my mother was gone from this place now. What was holding me back?

As I got up to leave, I imagined the natives watching from the distance as the pilgrims looked around at the new land they would take. Did even a single man consider the people who already lived there, or were they just hungry desperate dogs sniffing territory?

I drove home and popped in the Dave Matthews Band CD Gil gave me. For over an hour, my entire life and everyone I've ever known flashed before my eyes on the road. The album brought me to a place that reminded me where I'd been on the great American road trip of summer '97. The plan was born. I was going home.

The Sound of Silence

The next day after my voyage to Plymouth, I decided to stay in a while to catch up on some chores. I suddenly heard a light knocking. I ignored it, but then it happened again. I froze to listen. There it was again. I went over to the door that led upstairs and opened it.

"Hello. Grandma?"

She didn't answer. I waited a few seconds. Nothing. I went back to the kitchen where I heard the knocking and it happened again. I rushed back over to the door and went up the stairs.

"Grandma? Hello. Everything all right?"

I got up the stairs and she wasn't in the kitchen or living room. I went up one more set of steps. Nothing to my left, but there to my right was my grandmother lying on the floor in the hallway. I rushed over. She could barely move, so I didn't know how she managed to knock. It must have been the echo of a finger tap I was hearing two floors down.

I put my arm around her head and she looked up at me. She was still here. Her eyes were glassy but not of fear. On her face was a half-smile.

"Let me get help," I said.

She wasn't able to speak, but she nodded.

"I'll be right back. Hang on, okay."

I ran down to her kitchen phone and called 911.

"Send an ambulance. I found my grandmother on the floor."

I gave them the address and then rushed back up to her. She was weaker now.

"They're on their way. Hold on, Grandma."

I leaned over and held her hand and rested her head on my lap. She had a smile of a child. It felt like I was looking at the five-year-old version of her. She wasn't crying. She wasn't afraid anymore. She looked into my eyes once more, and then her eyes closed.

☆

The funeral was on the Fourth of July. Dozens of friends from the town pub where she had worked for years hanging coats came to the church. I was surprised she had known so many people. She lived such a quiet life, but she was well loved. Everyone seemed genuinely upset.

I felt rotten. I felt like if I had found her sooner, maybe the stroke wouldn't have been as bad. But the doctor at the hospital assured me there wasn't much that could've been done.

Only two of her kids were at the funeral. Al and Hillary were both crying. My own father hadn't even come to his own mother's funeral.

"You're not going to come on Sunday?" I asked him over the phone.

"Nah, I was just on the road for work. I won't make it. Not like she's going to be there to see me."

"Yeah, sure, all right. Well, sorry about your mother. I'll let you know how it goes."

After the ceremony, just the family went over to the gravesite to watch them lower her into the ground. Tears ran from Al's red face. He held Hillary's hand as she gushed with tears for her mother, certainly the greatest person they'd both ever known.

When I got back to my grandmother's house by myself. I saw her other daughter Marjorie leaving in a car. I saw her through the window and recognized her. Instead of going to the funeral, she gathered up the last of her childhood belongings. Marjorie was estranged from everyone for some reason. I had no idea what had happened, but it must have been bad to be completely disconnected from three siblings and your only remaining parent. Her estranged son Michael was also missing from the funeral, and I couldn't understand because he had grown up around his grandmother in his early years.

A week after the funeral, Al and Hillary came over to start clearing out the house. I helped them clean and sort things out. Al and I sat down at my grandmother's kitchen table for a cigarette and a soda.

"Listen, Jack. We're going to put the house up for sale, but we'll do some work. It won't be until the fall. Do you have any plans?"

"Yes, I have a pretty good idea what I'm going to do next."

"If Diane hadn't moved in, you could have..."

"No problem, Uncle Al. I won't be staying in New York."

☆

On the Monday after the weekend of July 22, I watched the news about Woodstock 1999 on TV. It was a shitshow. People had torn apart the venue and set fires. It was the opposite vibe of the 1969 show. The country had changed, and it wasn't pretty. I was glad Gil and I decided to back out based on the ticket prices. I certainly wouldn't have wanted to get stuck in the rain and mud.

On July 30, I went to a far more peaceful show at Jones Beach, a small outdoor place where I'd seen many shows. I took a friend named Sue and we arrived in the parking lot just in time to hear Paul Simon singing "The Sound of Silence" all the way as we walked to our seats. It was a grand entry. After a show of historic hits, Paul Simon shared the stage for three songs with Bob Dylan before the second legend closed out the night with his own classics. It'll always be how I remember New York, just before I left again.

Don't Fade

September was my final month to prepare and save money. I did some odd jobs cleaning windows to save up more cash for the big voyage. During my time off, I used the computer at the public library to research my new destination and apply to college.

After selling off most of my cassette collection to a record store for a few bucks, I paid Gil a visit.

"You finally did it? All five hundred tapes?" he asked.

"Yeah, I had to. Too much weight. I have CDs now. I don't even have a tape deck in the car anymore."

"It's a new era. I can't believe you're really doing this."

"The change will be good. Do you think you'll ever leave New York?" I asked.

"Maybe. Definitely to see the country."

"Hope you'll come visit."

"You can count on that!"

I hadn't told Gil about the dog outside. I felt bad. I didn't want him to think he had anything to do with my leaving New York. The big cat, the big dog, my grandmother's death, they were all signs that I wasn't supposed to be there anymore.

I gave Gil some belongings I didn't want to bring, and then I hugged him goodbye. It felt like I was leaving him behind wounded. But there was nothing I could do to convince him. He had his own path to follow.

☆

I called Jeff and went over to say goodbye one last time. We called Andy at college to say goodbye.

"See you guys on the west coast next time."

"Oh yeah?" Jeff asked.

"I think so."

I hugged Jeff goodbye, my good old friend, the one who befriended me without judgement. I waved goodbye to Mrs. Kennedy, careful not to get too close to her in her condition, remembering what she said to me about quitting smoking as she pointed to the oxygen tube that dangled from her. This would be the last time I'd see that wonderful woman.

☆

I had one more wonderful person to say goodbye to. On October 2, I drove over to her house. I rang the big old bell at the front. The yard and the house were as I remembered it. A courtyard of red bricks led up to a screened-in porch that wrapped around the front of the house. On the porch was a white wicker rocking lounge chair I always loved sitting on. All kinds of potted plants lived on that porch. It was an ecosystem.

"Hello, you."

"Hi, Grandma Rosa. How have you been?"

"Oh, good. It's been too long. Come in. You want something to eat? Let's eat something."

"Sure, why not."

She made us turkey sandwiches as I looked through her books on the kitchen shelf. There were books all over the house, even in the bathroom. I realized how much we had in common.

"I'm sorry again to hear about your other grandmother. I remember her from so long ago. She was sweet."

"Yes, thanks. It was her time."

"So you're leaving in a few days?" she asked.

"Yes, hitting the road. I'm heading to Oregon to start college in January. I'm finally transferring to a university."

I needed to stress the college plans so no one thought I was just wandering around again or running away.

"I'm proud that you're going to continue your schooling. Remember that ridiculous poster I got you?"

"Yes, Justification for Higher Education? I wish!"

I remembered the poster of a mansion with high-end sports cars parked out front. We both laughed.

We ate our lunch and looked out at the bay for a while.

"And you're sure you don't want to try Virginia or Florida or North Carolina, somewhere on the east coast?"

"No, maybe someday. I need to do this now. It's a calling."

"I know how that is as a writer. I'm glad you decided to study literature," she said.

"Yes, I finally declared a major."

"We'll have to write letters. And call me once in a while, damn it," she said with a smile.

"I promise. I'll tell you all about the writers I study. We'll compare notes."

"You're going to look at a number of writers I never even got to," she said.

"I look forward to your book too. When is it out?" I asked.

"Next year. It's taken me twenty-five years of writing stories and poems to finally put out a novel. I'll be close to seventy, but it's never too late to do anything in this life. You remember that."

"I will. I will."

After a while, it was time to head out. I looked around and took it all in for one last time before I ventured into the unknown.

"I love you, Jack. Be safe."

"I love you too, Grandma."

I could smell the Sicilian lemons as I hugged her goodbye.

"Now, you get going. Oregon awaits," she said.

America, Fall, 1999

I was back on the road. The interstate grew quieter and quieter the further you got from the cities. Eventually, you find yourself in a place of solitude. I longed for this. There I was again finding that place out on the road, all alone, not a car or soul in sight.

The drive started on a Wednesday night in early October. By 10:30 I was on the expressway speeding towards the city with my bags packed in the hatch. I left behind a few boxes for Gil to ship to me once I got there. I was through New Jersey by midnight on my way through the night of Pennsylvania. It was a long night through the "key" state. I played a CD by David Gray and cranked up the song "Late Night Radio" and sang along as I drove west. Then I sang along to the entire *Boggy Depot* album by Jerry Cantrell. The song "Between" was pure road trip bliss.

I hit Youngstown, Ohio at 5:30 a.m. with "One Headlight" playing by the Wallflowers. I slid in a Springsteen CD to play an appropriate song called "Youngstown" as I drove through what appeared to be a beaten city. But I thought the place had a good chance for revival.

I continued on to Columbus and then Dayton by mid-morning only stopping for fill ups and a gas station breakfast. I blasted right through the middle of Indiana on I-70 this time. By 2:30 in the afternoon, I was in Illinois. A half hour into the state, I decided to get out and look around Champaign. It seemed like a cool place, but I had to keep moving. I slid in a CD by Bad Religion, a going away gift from Jeff, and I carried on down the road with the first song "Modern Man" blasting me out of the gate.

By dinner time, I was in Davenport, Iowa on the Mississippi River. I walked along the river and found a restaurant for a sandwich. This would be my only meal for a while. After this, I'd make it to central Iowa for a cheap motel in some rural town. It was already dark, but I could tell I was going to wake up to see cornfields and great open farmland for miles.

On Friday morning, I woke up and hit the road. I landed in Lincoln, Nebraska about three hours later and stopped for my first meal of the day at a Denny's. After walking around a bit, I got back in my Honda for a day's worth of driving. I made it my job and took few breaks. At 8:00, I stopped at a cheap motel in Laramie, Wyoming. The place was right off the road by the university. I'd be a university student soon too.

On Saturday morning, I woke early and hit the road for a four-hour trip to Bear River on the border of Wyoming and Utah. It was a small town of four hundred or so. I couldn't believe this small of a place existed. I thought of the American contrast between this and a place like New York. These people had the same number of senators. I filled the tank and carried on with some snacks.

Another grueling seven hours and I arrived in Ontario, Oregon, a small eastern town of ten thousand people. It was now dark, so I couldn't see much, but the cheap motel would do. In the morning, I stepped out of my room and looked around. The air was weird. Once I got back on the road, I got a better feel for the place. The town looked like it was still in the 1970s. A real time machine.

I carried on out of town and the land grew desolate again. Things get weird when you don't talk to anyone for hours, when the only people you talk to for days are motel and gas station clerks with small pleasantries, if lucky. To kill the loneliness, I lit a cigarette and put on "One More Day, One More Night" by Tom Petty.

The sandy hills of eastern Oregon seemed to stretch on forever. But soon the dirt turned to grass and giant open fields. From the road, I saw horses. I stopped and got out to look at them. They noticed and turned to look at me. I snapped a few photos with the Kodak and waved goodbye to them.

In another two hours on Route 20, I was in another small farm town called Burns. The town was quaint. I grabbed a Pepsi and sat and watched a few town folks go about their business. I felt like Cal Trask in *East of Eden.*

I drove on and then stopped at a rest area just shy of the next town. A big brown wood sign read:

Ages ago a river flowed across the high desert country in the rocky canyon several hundred yards beyond this marker...During periods of high water the lake spilled over a low pass at the eastern edge of horse ridge—The ridge seen behind you...

I drove another two hours to a small town called Bend. There didn't seem like much was happening there either, but it was livelier than Burns. I suspected this place could be something big someday. Nature wrapped all around Bend, and it was a safe, beautiful town with a view of the mountains in the distance. One day, the yuppie investors in their khakis and boat shoes would arrive to build their castles, just like everywhere else. I just knew it.

Instead of continuing north toward Portland, I decided to turn back south down Highway 97. I looked at the map and realized this would take me down to California if I kept going too far. I wondered about Sarah. I needed to call her when I got to Portland. There was so much to tell her about my journey. Maybe she'd visit in the spring.

There was a national volcano monument along the road. I had no idea what that meant so I pulled into the side road entrance. There was a sign in the parking lot that read:

Squirrels Beware

Human Food is Bad for You.

I didn't notice any squirrels, but tons of chipmunks scurried all around me. I'd never seen so many little critters. These amazing chipmunks were brave and social. This was their neighborhood.

A path led to the beginning of something. The trail wound around the rocky landscape, a barren, dead land of six-thousand-year-old lava. I looked up at the top.

Along the way to the top viewpoint, a tree poked out from a rocky hill. I stopped to stare at this anomaly, the beginning of something. Life was starting over.

At the top of the path, I sat, ate a snack, smoked a cigarette, dreamt of a hot cup of coffee, and took in the bizarre landscape. I took a small volcano rock with me, said goodbye to the chipmunks, and got back into the Honda to continue south.

Soon I was in the part of Oregon I had fallen in love with. The huge trees overhead. The pine smell mixing with the mountain air. The beauty of the Upper Klamath Lake. Blue purple sky, the color of heaven all around. I could breathe again. It was time to make my way home.

Realizing I had gone too far south, I needed to cut across to I-5 on a small road, route 66. It was only 60 miles, so how bad could it be? After twenty minutes of twists and turns in the dark, I was cursing the road, calling it route 666. I gripped the wheel tight, and my body tensed up, just like when I left New York in the snow a few years earlier on my first voyage. I shouted along to a song titled "Wrong Way" by Creed. Then I blew my voice out on "Highway to Hell" by AC/DC. This demonic road went on for an hour and a half. My eyes strained. I cursed at the night. This was the darkest road in America yet.

I gasped for air at the end of the road. 66 finally ended, and I spilled into a town called Ashland. It was the literal light at the end of the tunnel. Even at night, the place was lovely. I drove around the small city and softened my mood with a song titled "Nightblindness" by David Gray. Then I headed up to Medford to eat at a Denny's. This gave me the power to push on another few hours north to grab a motel for the night. It was eleven o'clock, but it felt later. I was worn from the road, especially after 66. I checked into a Motel 6 in a mall parking lot in Springfield. Tomorrow, I'd be going home to a new city.

Portland, Oregon, Fall, 1999

The sky was gray. A mist hovered in the air. The greenery all around was brighter than usual. I arrived at the apartment and parked at the top of a big hill. From my car, I looked down on the roof of the three-story building. I took the long stairs down and knocked on the door with a bag over my shoulder.

Mark opened the door and greeted me. I would be staying on the couch there for a couple of months before my room on campus opened up. They were okay with the short-term situation, willing to help out a fellow New Yorker. I found them in a local ad looking for an extra roommate to share the rent. They had moved out to Oregon a couple of months before me.

The living room floor had a little shake to it that reminded me of that noise from the middle of a wrestling ring. They let me sleep on the couch the first few days to get some good rest after the long trip, but then I'd have to split the floor in the bedroom or camp out on the living room floor. It was a three-bedroom apartment, but there were no beds. It wouldn't be fair if someone used the couch every night. Not that it was that comfortable anyway.

The next morning, I looked out on the porch. A pumpkin was carved and had a used cigar sticking out of its mouth. Fresh smelling pine trees stood grand all around the property. Out in the distance was the tip of Mount Hood, the tallest mountain in Oregon. I had never been this close to a real mountain, and I was taken by the brief view before the clouds moved back into place.

I started a job search that day for part-time work. I applied to be a loss prevention agent at Fred Myers, which was a west coast store I hadn't been to. It reminded me of TSS and Caldor back in New York, but it had food. Then I drove over to The Benson and put in as a night associate at the fancy hotel. Toby and Magnus were valets at the W, but I didn't want to get too mixed up with them, so I didn't apply there. Next, I applied as a campus dispatcher at the state university where I'd be going to school. Lastly, I stopped at the Pioneer Square Mall and applied to the bookstore. I was sure one of the applications would come through.

Mark freaked out one day. Claiming his back was broken, he woke in the middle of the night, packed his bags, wrote us a note, which Toby referred to as the suicide note, and hopped on a bus to Nevada to go stay in a motel. He was really going to say goodbye to a girl he had supposedly fallen in love with who was about to fly out to North Carolina to her new home on an army base with her husband. We didn't know what to think.

Mark arrived back home a few days later with a broken nose but fortunate enough not to have had anything else broken by the girl's army husband who answered the door.

Toby was toying around with a local Portland girl named Mally, who we met one night at a coffee shop. One morning, I woke to find the two of them naked under a blanket, sprawled out on the living room floor with her pretty little feet hanging out of the bottom. I asked myself how such a pretty girl like Mally could choose a guy like Toby. She seemed too good to be sleeping on the floor with that creature, who had a fiancé back in New York and a dancer girl on the other side of town. He was a cheating juggler.

Magnus and Aldo shared a room. They went to art school together. Aldo, Toby, and Mark were from the same central Long Island town. Magnus was the only one of us not from New York. He was an all-around good guy from Fairbanks, Alaska. Aldo didn't bother me at all, but I sensed he didn't like me around. Maybe he was jealous that Magnus and I got along.

Just as things started to get tight in the apartment, I found Ginny. Or so she found me. Here comes the rain.

Meet Virginia

On a cold rainy night in late November, the telephone rang and it was Ginny. She had met Mark a couple of months back. She had been by the place a couple of times and I'd seen her in passing. I was unsure of her relationship with Mark. He claimed she had attacked him and that he didn't want anything to do with a dirty girl like her. I didn't quite believe him, both about her attacking him and about her being a dirty girl, so when she called that night for a favor I didn't hesitate. I was the only one around with a car since Aldo and Magnus didn't drive, and Mark and Toby were out.

Ginny needed to go visit her cousin Vince who was in prison right outside of the city.

"Prison?" I asked, "for what reason is he there?"

"Oh, just minor robberies and stuff. He really is a nice guy. Please, I'll pay you and fill up your gas tank."

"Why not, I could use a ride out of the city and as long as I don't have to go in and see him, I'll do it."

I hung up the phone, showered, and cleaned myself up a bit with a subtle realization of my attraction to her. All I could do was tell myself that Mark wouldn't really care, and if he did it would be his own fault for talking about her the way he did.

At six o'clock, I picked her up in the Safeway parking lot. She was dressed casually in a loose sweatsuit.

"I'm Virginia Glass. Call me Ginny," she said and winked as I opened the door for her.

I left the city to take her to see her cousin in a Beaverton jail. On the way, we talked about Portland and about our goals in college and such forth. She said she worked at a children's center and was majoring in elementary education and expressed her love for children. I told her my plans to teach English at a community college. We seemed to get along.

I waited in the parking lot of the lousy jail. It reminded me of going to see JP. Ginny returned after about forty minutes. I didn't ask any questions other than how the visit went. She said good and told me to drive back to Portland so we could drive around the city.

We returned to Portland and ended up in some strange part of northeast. In the midst of a hard rain, the Honda's clutch blew. We rolled into an industrial parking lot and wondered what to do next. We looked at each other nervously and laughed at our misfortune. As we sat there, the windows began to fog. She slyly changed my rock station to her country station and somewhere in the middle of me saying something, she suggested we fuck in the parking lot. I started to respond, but she cut me off.

"I see the way you look at me," she said moving closer.

"Oh yeah?" I asked moving closer.

"Yeah. How long has it been for you?"

"Too long."

Ginny slipped her pants right off and then got on top of me. I couldn't resist. I was about to suggest protection, but she was already into something I wasn't going to interfere with. Ginny had brown hair with blond highlights, and deep brown eyes that entranced me as she looked into my mine. Her petite but ravishing body was smooth everywhere. When she was done, I got up and she stretched out in my driver's seat. All she had on now were black roll up tights on her legs that seemed to wrap me like a web. We went at it in the fogged-out Honda with the rain falling all around us. Everything about her was fresh, just like Portland, just like my new life away from home.

When I finished, she rubbed the mess all over the bareness between her legs.

"You didn't have to do that. Put it right inside next time."

I didn't know what to say to that, so I just chuckled.

We dressed and sometime later I started the car up and managed to get it going in a low gear. We putted back to her place at a dangerous average of ten miles per hour with cars beeping and swerving around us. When we finally made it, she took me upstairs to her campus apartment in a tall building. We retired to a comfortable night's sleep on the living room futon in the apartment she shared with a student named Tara. The next morning, after meeting Tara and talking to her for a bit, Ginny and I took a peaceful walk through the park to a Starbucks.

On a park bench, Ginny opened up to me about her recent past. She told me she had regrettably been with a good number of guys. I liked her honesty. For a nineteen-year-old girl, she had one hell of a quick past, one that I was not so fond of, but oddly sympathized with. My acceptance is I think what she appreciated in me. We enjoyed each other, so we decided to be with one another and take it slow, but we were really jumping right in.

I said goodbye after walking her back upstairs, and then I attempted to get back to the off-campus apartment. I drove through the streets of downtown Portland in first gear with the hazards flashing and a line of frustrated people behind me. Just as I reached the complex in southwest Portland, the car died for good on a hilly road. Another part of me was gone. Rolling it to the side, I removed all my belongings and then walked the rest of the way up the hill.

Two days later, the Honda sold for $250. I thought about how much further the Camaro had gotten me. I knew I wouldn't need a car now since I would soon be relocating to campus and could still use a bus to get in and out of downtown. Finally, I'd be a university student.

Hurricane

Ginny and I had grown close very quickly, and I lived with her while waiting to get into my dorm, which would be ready in late December. I didn't want to deal with the guys, so I stopped going back to the apartment at night. I'd slip back in to get my things and check the mail. I felt alienated from the guys. I knew they were talking about me, and I knew how Mark felt about Ginny. The way I figured it though is that they should've appreciated one less body around. Either way, I paid them my share for December and appreciated not being crammed up with them.

One day I stopped in and Mark was home. He laughed in my face and asked, "What the hell are you doing to yourself? Craziness, craziness!"

"Chill out, man. I have it covered," I said.

"Sure about that?"

I walked away and didn't want to deal with him.

Magnus did not have much to say when I saw him, but I think he was disappointed in my quick exit. Aldo seemed to grow even colder towards me. Toby was a mixed feel. At first, he made snappy wisecracks. But then he made an effort once he knew I was staying there with her and getting into something. I felt like maybe he only kept in touch with us to feed his own curiosity and serve as a means of getting gossip for the guys.

One night, Toby and Mally stopped over the apartment with two bottles of wine. We drank, talked, and laughed for a few hours. As we were saying good-bye, Toby cracked a joke about Ginny and I going to get it on right away after they left. Why ruin a good night with a wisecrack? With that, Ginny gave Toby a knee to the groin that left him on the brink of tears. Mally scolded him as they left. He couldn't look at me.

☆

With her roommate Tara gone on the fourth of December to spend the holidays at home, Ginny and I had several weeks to ourselves. We had gone from not knowing each other to living with each other in less than a few days. During the day, Ginny went to work at the children's center, and I would spend my time looking for work and taking care of the necessary paperwork for the upcoming semester. Dalton bookstore in the mall had finally called and I worked there for three weeks, but it was miserable. I grew tired of the mall and fast-food Chinese for lunch.

At night, we came home to each other like newlywed husband and wife. She would cook up a pasta dinner or we'd order a cheap pizza, and then we'd eat while watching a movie or listening to her country music. Ginny loved her baths, letting the water run to replenish a fresh and warm supply as she'd lie there soaking up the suds in candlelight. I would join her after my kitchen cleanup. On the weekends, we'd spend half the day in bed.

Christmas closed in on us. Ginny and I exchanged gifts, and then said goodbye as she headed up north to her hometown of Tacoma for the week.

Aldo and Toby went back to New York first. I never said goodbye to them. Magnus was home alone at the apartment enjoying solitude, and I made plans with him to visit and pick up mail. On the day he was to leave for New York, Mark helped me move my belongings into my new dorm room. Relying on people was the only downfall of not having a car anymore. But we got it done and Mark was helpful. In two trips, we packed his car with my belongings and got everything up to the fourth-floor room, leaving it all in a pile. Then I bought him breakfast at the diner across the street, and we talked for a while, avoiding Ginny's name.

Mark had all kinds of gossip about Toby. He said that Mally had stumped him with an interrogation visit the night Toby departed. She was onto to him. Mark told her exactly what she wanted to hear. Early the next morning, Mark got a call from Toby asking him what he had said to her.

"Damn, why'd you tell her? The bitch broke up with me," he said and then added "ah, she was trash anyway."

Mark denied the accusations and that was that for now. There he was telling me all of this. I simply laughed it off and wished Mark good luck. I thanked him for his help and told him to keep in touch.

Back in my new room, I was relieved to have my own private space back, but also felt odd about where Ginny and I would be heading now. I opened a letter she had left for me.

Dear Jack,

It is Christmas break, and I can't wait until I get to come home to you. I can't wait to see you. I am so sorry that you had to spend the holiday alone, I wish I could have been there with you. I am so lucky that I found you. You accept me for who I am and the choices I have made and continue to make. I chose to make myself a better person, one worthy of you! We started off quick. I have jumped into relationships quickly before with people who I thought I cared about, and it has been thrown back in my face. I don't want that to happen with us. I have made many mistakes in the past, especially with relationships, but I am ready now to be loving, caring, and loyal to you. I will do my best to make you happy, because you make me so incredibly happy. I appreciate everything that you do for me. Not always the physical things... though I do thank you for what you do... but more than that how you make me feel. You make me feel so loved by the way you touch me and how you look at me. You make me feel so beautiful, all the compliments that you give me, the way that you hold me. I love being around you and love every second I spend with you. I think about you continuously while we are apart. I have so many thoughts and feelings that I can't remember all of them at once. I am not as good at expressing myself in words as you are, but I hope that when you're with me you know how much I love you and want to be with you forever.

Love,
Ginny

Damn, she was serious. I closed the letter with relief, but still I wondered how having my own space would change things.

I now had a week to myself to unpack, settle into my own private space, prepare for the winter term to begin, and relax until Ginny returned. We agreed to only a few phone calls, so she could spend time with her family. We figured when I met her at the train station we'd have so much more to talk about.

☆

Toward the end of the week, I paid Magnus a visit. I sorted through my mail as he threw on some coffee.

"How you been, man? Feels like a long time," I asked.

"Pretty decent, I guess. Spending time with the girlfriend, busy with schoolwork. Let me show you some new pieces I did."

Magnus walked over to the desk in the living room and lifted up some of his drawings. I was surprised to hear about a girlfriend. I considered the possibility of him and Aldo, two artists sharing a room. He continued to talk while showing me his drawings.

"These guys are getting me crazy. You know what I mean?"

"They'll do that. Believe me, not everyone from New York is like us," I said as he held up a drawing of a futuristic skyline.

"Man, I really hate Toby, and I hate him even more every day. He is such a dick. I don't know, I'm glad for you that you got out. I think I'll have to do the same."

"I'm relieved to be out," I replied as he held up a drawing of a medieval beast holding a torn-out heart in its hands.

"How's your new place?" he asked as he walked back over to the kitchen table where I was sitting.

"It's comfortable, especially after these rough floors."

"How's Ginny?" Magnus asked.

"Ah, good, she's home up north until the twenty-ninth."

His facial expression froze into an odd frown.

"What? Are you going to give me shit like the other guys?"

"No, no, just making sure you're okay."

"What would make you think I'm not?" I inquired.

"It was something Mark told me."

"What did he say?"

Magnus hesitated.

"What?" I asked again.

"He just told me how she was with him and that's all."

"That's it?" I asked.

Magnus lit the pipe and took a small hit.

"Yup, nothing else really, probably things you've heard already. It's not that I dislike her or anything. I'm no judge," he said coughing out his smoke.

"Thanks for your concern and all, but I'm a big boy."

We both smiled pleasantly, and he passed the pipe.

Hours passed. Magnus and I hung out as we had months earlier when I first met him. We drank a few pale ales as he showed me some more of his recent work, and I talked about the literature I'd been reading. I told him how excited I was to get into a collection of Hemingway's stories the week between Christmas and New Year's. I planned on writing a few of my own stories.

At nightfall, I departed the three-bedroom apartment after making plans with the Alaskan for the following week.

"What are you doing for New Years?" he asked.

"No plans yet, but it's a big one. 2000."

"Why don't we get together with the girlfriends?"

"Sounds like a plan. I'll let Ginny know."

Room at the Top

I opened the door. A closet was immediately to the left. Just past that, there was a sink and medicine cabinet on the wall, a dresser, and then the steps leading up to the bunk bed. It was seven steps to the top. Seven steps to heaven. Below the bed was a desk and chair. On the other side of the room was a mini refrigerator with an attached microwave above it. I looked around the room. I had slept in my car, on a friend's floor, on a couple of old couches, and now here I was in a room that was one hundred twenty square feet, smaller than a typical jail cell. For $290 a month, this shoebox of a room would be my new home. And it made me perfectly happy to know I had my own door to close and my very own bed to finally sleep in. I had everything I needed right there in my cell.

The old brick building was constructed in 1917 as a hotel for working women in Portland. It wasn't bought by the university until 1969. There were a lot of ghosts in this building for sure. I thought about all the heartbreaks. I wondered how many had died in the building. As I zipped up the plastic mattress cover and put my own sheet on the bed, I wondered how many had slept or made love in my new bed.

My side of the building faced a sports field away from the city and park blocks. From my window, I looked out at the world. Other campus residential buildings were across in the distance. Beyond was the West Hills neighborhood that wrapped around the top of the valley. Ritzy homes looked down on us. I blew smoke out the window at that world. House lights came on as the sun went down. As the night went on, the lights would go off one by one.

There was a tree outside my window with birds always chirping at me. I sat there with a cup of coffee, filling ashtray after ashtray, burning through the book of Hemingway stories.

There was a trolly that would come around a few blocks away. I got on one day to see what it was like, but ultimately preferred to walk.

I'd walk for miles exploring my new city, and I usually ended up at the Djangos music store. I was a kid in a candy store. On my first visit, I bought five used CDs and a poster of Jack Torrance sticking his head through the broken door in *The Shining*. I put the poster on the back of my door, so it looked like he was busting right into my room.

"Here's Johnny!" it read along the bottom.

On Christmas morning, I woke up to my first holiday completely alone. The building had emptied out. Students had gone home to their families. I was probably the only person in the entire building, It was eerily quiet as I walked down the hall and out of the building into the empty city park. When I returned from my walk, I called my mother in Florida and wished her and JP a happy Christmas. They seemed well and would be getting together with Annie and Russell later that day.

I read, smoked, drank coffee, and even wrote a couple of stories. It was a strange Christmas, but I reminded myself this was a choice I made. I knew many didn't have any family to see or call. They were all alone every day all of the time. I was fortunate.

For dinner, I went out to the Chinese place and grabbed take out. The place was quiet, as were the streets. I took my food back to the building. Instead of my usual walk up to the fourth floor, I rode the elevator this time. I didn't see a soul in the building until I reached the fourth floor. I got out and walked around to the left toward my wing. My door was at the end on the right. I heard something back toward the elevator and turned to look up the hall. A large man with long hair was opening his door on the other end.

"Cheers. Merry Christmas," I shouted down the long hall.

I heard him grunt and saw him disappear into his doorway.

My whole life I had the joy of being around family. It was chaos on Christmas every year. A chaos some would die for. It was nice for a change to just disappear into my little box, eat Chinese food, and stare out a window while listening to music. Everyone needs to spend a holiday away, all alone. It's good for the soul.

☆

The night before I was to pick up Ginny at the train station, I got a knock at the door. Just having moved in, I didn't really know anyone other than Magnus. Turkey sandwich in hand, I answered my door and there she stood. She appeared happy despite her recent breakup.

"Happy Christmas. What a surprise! How have you been?" I asked.

"Hello, Jack. Good to see you. How about you?"

"I survived. It was a quiet one, you know."

Tears bulged from Mally's eyes, and she fell into my arms. We hugged each other until it grew to be too much. Stepping back, we looked at each other and comfortably smiled.

"This place is a mess. Want to go for a walk?" I asked.

"Sure. I found you through the directory, by the way."

With that, we strolled out down the hallway, down the stairs, and out the front doors.

"So what happened?" I asked.

"That dirtbag. Are all those things Mark told me true, you know all those things that Toby has been saying about me the whole time while he's been wining and dining me?"

"Well, yes but what did Mark tell you?"

"How he's been talking trash about me and dating two other girls, one in Portland and some other young girl back in New York by the name of Darcy."

"Wow, Mark even told you the fiancé's name?"

"He was engaged to her? Jesus. Anything he didn't tell me?"

"I know. I know. At least it didn't go any further."

"It's not so hard for me to see now how big of a bastard he is when his own friends are giving him up. I just wish I had seen it a little sooner," she said.

"I wasn't actually his friend, just a temporary roomie from the same state."

"Yeah really. Hey, how's Ginny doing?"

"Good, she's in Tacoma now, I'm picking her up from the train station tomorrow morning."

"That's good. She left you here all alone?"

"Just me, my cigarettes, and a room at the top."

Mally smiled.

"You know, I really trusted Toby."

I just looked at her.

"I'm sorry, I'll shut up about him, it's just so frustrating that I didn't have the chance to break up with him in person."

"Well, maybe you can again when he gets back."

"Yes, that might be fun, but then again, I don't even want to see his face. I might throw up."

"I can't blame you, and don't worry about talking about it, if you need to talk about it…"

She stopped and grabbed me.

"He really hurt me, that asshole."

I held her in my arms in the middle of the park for a while. When her spirits finally lifted, we went and had a cappuccino at the Parklawn Café. Mally and I were both glad to be out of our situations at the three-bedroom apartment. We had a mutual feeling of relief that bonded us. I wondered what would've happened if I had made a more aggressive move on her the night we all met back in late October at a coffee shop. But then again, I had flirted with her, only for her to choose Toby, the tall blond stud. I wasn't going to tell her any of this, but after she said goodbye, Mally turned back to me.

"I made the wrong choice. I hope you know that."

☆

On the twenty ninth, I met my girl at the train station with a rose in hand. We talked all the way home, as I filled her in on all the recent news. Ginny was all about getting together with Magnus and his girlfriend on New Year's Eve. We dropped her luggage off at her apartment and then headed to a local hotel restaurant to enjoy a fine overly expensive meal, which she didn't even finish. But it wasn't her fault— sometimes those expensive meals are the most upsetting. She suddenly started to cry for some reason during our meal. When I asked her what was wrong, she didn't know. That was when I knew things were going to change. Something now felt wrong. My head got wavy with nausea, but I fought it. My head cleared once she stopped crying and I brushed off my fears of change. We went back to her room, tore each other's clothes off, and had mad sex all over the apartment. Everything seemed better.

☆

One morning, a couple of weeks into our relationship, Ginny had told me more of the details. Of course, I knew there was plenty she was leaving out, either purposely or subconsciously. She sat me on a bench in the cold park on a December day in front of the Parklawn Café and explained.

"I never had sex until about two years ago, but some guys were rough, some guys used me, and many talked about me and spread rumors around my high school. I've been with eleven guys in a very short amount of time and fooled around with others."

"What do you mean, eleven?"

"I've slept with eleven guys, but don't worry. I promise I used protection."

HIV registered in my mind. We had not used a condom. I was older and had nowhere near that number. What had I done here? I had no idea the number was so high.

"All right, I trust you," I said, trying to reassure myself.

"Do you think badly of me?" she asked now on the verge of an enormous breakdown.

"We all make mistakes. That's the way we learn, right?"

☆

A few mornings after she told me about the eleven boys, I awoke to a burning sensation like I had never felt before. This was not a normal friction burn. This I knew. Peering down in fear of what I might see, with memories of the pictures they'd show us in health class, I found my penis was oozing a white fluid.

"What have you done? Have you been with anyone else?"

"No, I swear, I haven't. It might be from right before you. These things take weeks sometimes. I'm so embarrassed."

"As long as I'm the only one now," I warned her.

We marched hand in hand over to the downtown clinic to get tested. She became nervous, and this made me nervous after she had just expressed to me a no-need-to-worry-story. We were both called in at the same time, but she was waiting there when I came out. Ginny stepped up to the counter to pay our small fees, and I started to walk towards the restroom. The restroom sign seemed high above. I was moving slower and slower. I was dizzy, losing consciousness as I walked. The blood rushed through my head, thinking of the needle moments earlier, then the feeling of the long Q-tip being inserted up my burning penis. I began to fall. Knocking into a row of chairs, I stumbled into a wall. Ginny and a nurse rushed over to me. Nobody could give me back life. All was black. Just when life seemed to slip away, the lights went back on. I looked up as Ginny leaned over me holding me in her arms, like I held my dying grandmother. I expected to see her, but all I saw were the lights above.

We started the medication, and I was better in a few days. The test results came back days later, and we returned to the location of my collapse at the clinic. Both tests were HIV negative, but both were positive for chlamydia. The doctor gave us a fair warning and a bag of condoms. I told Ginny it was no big deal because she'd probably had it for weeks and had not even known it when she met me. The doctor confirmed this when I asked him.

"It's actually pretty standard to feel the effects weeks later. If that wasn't the case, I'd let you know," he said.

☆

There we were weeks later, disease free, yet now things seemed diseased between us. After that episode, how could one expect to survive in a relationship? We were ruined, but we continued to live a lie. We were caught up. But now the time away for the holiday seemed to wake something in her. There was a distance, but we tried to hang on.

On New Year's Eve, Ginny and I met with Magnus and his girlfriend Pia at a restaurant. We had dinner and then walked down to Pioneer Courthouse Square for the celebration.

The rain had vanished for the big day, but it was in the thirties. We huddled with hundreds of others like penguins, bundled up in our coats, shivering off the cold as the festivities began. Big white pillars stood over us like guards. The threat loomed of all the computers in the world crashing and the ensuing chaos. New York had already brought in the new year on the east coast, so our west coast midnight was the final test.

Somewhere in the middle of it all, a sign showed the distance to all kinds of other places in all directions. Vancouver. Walden Pond. Times Square. Pacific Ocean. A dozen other random places. We were in the middle of the world.

The ball dropped in the final seconds of 11:59 and we all hugged each other like long lost friends, though we barely knew each other, but we'd never forget. No one forgets where and who they were with on New Year's Eve 1999 as the new decade and millennium began. There were no acts of violence, no attacks, no bombs, no prophetic ending, no failures in civilization. We had survived, and it was the year 2000.

How's it Going to Be?

Ginny's schedule had grown busier between her job at the children's center and her four full time classes. My classes also started up, so we saw less of each other. I no longer stayed at her place, except for on weekends. Her roommate Tara was back, and I now had a place to call home. But now that I had my new independence, I felt more confident as a boyfriend. And I was still excited to see her at the end of the day.

Although it was cold, it wasn't cold enough to snow. In fact, the city of Portland hardly saw much snow at all due to its location in the low altitude of the Willamette Valley. Instead, it rained and it rained, and when it wasn't raining it was getting ready to rain. The skies were generally gray and foggy from late October through May. As the locals spoke of a lighter season, there I was in the middle of my first rain season and beginning to feel it.

It was a frosty Friday in late January. Ginny and I had no big plans for the night, just the usual movie rental, or homework, or dinner, or something of that extent. Knowing she didn't get home until 5 p.m. from work on the weekdays, I usually gave her some time to wind down and settle in before I came over.

I had been out at the city center doing some window-shopping in the cold, and I was beat tired as I made my way back home. It was still early, but I figured I would set out for Ginny's and wait for her there, instead of going back to my building. I decided to wait in front of her apartment and maybe her roommate would be home. I stood in the elevator trying to warm up as it climbed to the ninth floor, and then it dawned on me that her roommate Tara would still be at work. Since I was already there, I decided to wait in the hall. It would be better than having to walk back to my place in the cold.

Arriving at her door, I heard music coming from the apartment. I wondered if she must've come home early. I curiously put an ear to the door and vaguely heard the distant sound of country music over the sound of splashing and running bath water. Not a surprise. Then I heard her voice. Like a cough. No, a moan? Was she masturbating? It sounded like she was saying something. I leaned against the door and my forearm turned the doorknob. The door was open.

I slowly crept through the front door and made my way toward the bathroom. The bathroom door was cracked, and I could just barely see inside, and how I wish the front door had been locked, and how I wish I would've never peaked in that bathroom door to see my end with Ginny and another battle with trust. There she was moving on top of a man in the tub. Her bareness gave me the shudders. His big hands over her precious breasts rubbed in the foam of the suds. She was getting louder. Her eyes rolled in pleasure until she opened them to my face peering down at her. Even the big man was startled and maybe feared for his life. Ginny gasped, but she had nothing to say. None of us said anything. What does anyone say in this kind of moment? With a look of disgust, I turned and left, grabbing the few things I had at her place on my way out.

I shouldn't have been surprised, but the anxiety of the proof stirred me up. I went back to my room to listen to music. Then I went out for coffee. After walking it off, I was fine. Barely two months of my life wasn't enough to shake me. Not yet anyway.

The Bends

My first ten-week term of classes was under way. It was glorious to finally be at a state university. When I wasn't in class or reading in my room, I was roaming the city. I had no need for a car. My feet took me everywhere I needed to go— Plaid Pantry around the corner, Safeway up the block, Powell's Books and Fred Myer on Burnside, Djangos record store on 10th Avenue, a Chinese smoke shop, the coffee shops, and work at the campus computer lab.

An awesome person I met while using a computer in the lab got me the job. Candace and I bonded over our love for Bon Jovi. We compared songs and debated the ranking of albums. I had no experience with computers, but she told me to act like I did. After I got hired, our shifts didn't really line up, but I still went in to visit.

☆

Just as the dreary skies of Portland had begun to work on the destruction of my mind, a savior showed up at my door.

"Hi Mally. What in the world? Looks great."

She had cut her long black hair into a bob haircut.

"Thank you," she said flipping the front over. "I was in the neighborhood, but I'm surprised you're not out at Ginny's."

"We broke up. I was hanging around doing homework."

"Ah, what happened?"

"I found her in the tub with some goon."

"Oh, you poor thing. Are you alright?" she asked wiping her hand across my face. Her Asian eyes widened and her smile lit up.

"Want to get a drink across the street?" she asked.

"Why not, let's do it," I said.

We crossed the street to the campus bar called The Last Act. It was a low-lit, smoky, lounge type of place with red leather furniture from the seventies. A big circular fireplace roared in the middle of the room. To the side was another room with pool tables where some derelicts hung out.

"What kind of place is this?" she asked.

"It's the seventies!"

We laughed and she swung a hip into mine and danced around me like it was '70s disco. We sat down at a table in the corner and the waitress came over to take our order.

"How can I help this marvelous looking couple tonight?" asked the tall masculine waitress.

We looked at each and smiled.

"What's tonight's special?" Mally asked.

"Greyhounds."

"I'll have one of them," she said.

"Make that two," I said.

The waitress returned some minutes later with our drinks. In what seemed like slow motion, Mally dipped her index finger in the drink and then in her mouth to taste it. She slowly pulled the finger out of her dark red lips and smirked. She knew it was a sexy act. Soon the waitress returned with another two, and then another two. By one o'clock, Mally and I were smashed on Greyhounds. We both knew she wouldn't be able to drive home in her condition.

"Just stay with me," I told her as we walked out of the bar.

"Yes, I definitely can't drive."

We held onto to each and rode the elevator to the fourth floor. We clumsily used the restrooms and then retreated to my room. Mally opened up her purse and took out a CD.

"You like Radiohead?"

"Sure, pop it in. What is it?"

"Radiohead, *The Bends* album," she replied as she placed the disc into the player and pressed play.

"Don't know them, but they sound pretty good. Oh wait, 'Karma Police' right?"

I remembered seeing the artsy video playing every night as I slept on the couch at the house on Lincoln Avenue.

"Exactly, but this is the best stuff. Their second album from 1995. Prepare yourself."

Mally lit a candle and then got comfortable on the floor. I flipped off the lights. Lying down next to her, I questioned my intentions. Could I really sleep with her after she had been with Toby, especially since I'd been with Ginny and she'd probably been with the whole apartment? I feared if anyone found out they'd think I was the cleanup man taking sloppy seconds, as they called it.

But I did it anyway. I couldn't help it. Our faces moved closer to one another and our lips interlocked in a fiery passion. Mally pulled me on top of her. The song "Fake Plastic Trees" took us somewhere far away. Before I knew it, we were into something and coming together. She cried for me to stay in her, which seemed crazy to me. Here I was fucking up again. More STDs? Maybe a baby this time? We lay there a while on the floor naked zoning out to the Radiohead album, smiling, getting lost in each other's souls.

☆

On Valentine's Day, Mally and I took an hour and a half drive to the Oregon coast in her Chevy. It was stormy, but we got out and walked the shoreline anyway. I wanted to touch the Pacific. We ran out into the breaking waves holding hands. We got down onto the wet sand and kissed. There wasn't another soul in sight. Drenched from the ocean and rain, we walked up to a motel and checked in. We stripped out of our clothes for the night. The wind outside blew violently against the windows of our room.

Mally and I fit so perfectly. Yet, I had the feeling we were doomed from the start of our relationship. I did not want to be dragged down again by another girl, and I was afraid she had her own reasons of vengeance for starting something with me. Even if this was all real, I couldn't help resenting that she had chosen Toby over me. If only she hadn't.

One morning, Mally found a copy of the *New York Times* on the windshield of her car parked down the block from my building. Toby had somehow found out. Whether he was angry or just horsing around was another question.

We decided to spend more time at her place in northwest. Mally had a cozy one-bedroom apartment over a restaurant. We'd read together, listen to music, and watch movies. She had an incredible knowledge of the music and movies I somehow missed along the way, despite my own vast knowledge.

"You've never seen *Spinal Tap*?" she asked.

"No, I don't know how."

She grabbed her car keys, and we took a quick drive to Blockbuster Video. Then we went back to her place and watched it right away. I laughed my head off at the comedy that poked fun of the '80s rock period I had loved so much.

We always got into it on her couch, but she never invited me into her bed. I didn't push it. I was beginning to wonder if she was using me as vengeance against Toby. Yet, she seemed so into spending time with me. I was confused by the mixed messages.

One day, she took me to her parent's house in Milwaukie, a suburb of Portland. No one was home, but she wanted to show me where she grew up. The house was beautiful with a pleasant feel. She sat down at a baby grand and started to play "Moonlight Sonata." I fell into a state of relaxation.

"What the..." I was taken back in shock.

When she finished, she turned and asked if it was good.

"Are you kidding? I could listen to you all day! Please, play more! Any other secret talents I don't know about?"

"Guess you're going to have to find out later," she flirted.

I thought to myself how I had just fallen in love with this young woman, and I was about to tell her, but the words curled back inside and never came out of my mouth.

Later that week, Mally took me to a diner to meet her parents. We all sat and had a meal. They were pleasant people. Her mother was American and her father was Japanese. I envisioned them as my in-laws. I was relieved that they seemed to like me. The pieces were coming together.

And then everything just collapsed.

I don't know why it fell apart. Was it her or me? Did she not feel for me? Was she turned off by her sense of my slipping confidence as I wondered if I was good enough?

Were we both just cowards of love?

But I do know exactly when and where it ended. We ventured up to a rooftop one night in mid-March to look at the cloudy, starless sky. On the way down in the elevator, the fatality of our relationship was sealed with each floor number down.

"What's wrong?" she asked.

"I was going to ask you the same thing."

"No, I see you're pre-occupied with something," she said.

"I'm not sure what you're talking about, but you seem different. Distant. Is this just not going to work?"

"If you really feel that way," she responded without a fight.

"Do you?" I asked.

"But there's no going back," she replied.

I stayed quiet.

By the time the elevator landed on the first floor, I was a free man. Free of Mally, free of Ginny, free of Toby and all the guys in the old apartment, free of New York too. Free I was, for now.

Warm Machine

The rainy winter lasted from October to the beginning of June, a month longer than I expected, and a month later than the rest of the nation. May was a real teaser, instead of one occasional day of sun light, the sun would rise and stay for three or four days before sinking back into the blackness. Thankfully, I received a surprise settlement check for the neck injury I sustained in the Honda before leaving New York. With that money, I went and bought a new car. I was now able to venture out of the foggy valley to clear my head, and I appreciated this new luxury, one I certainly hadn't counted on.

I found my next car by overhearing a conversation. As I walked into my apartment building, I overheard a young woman named Marion telling another neighbor Michael how she knew of someone who gets quality cars for cheap.

"What's that you say," I butted in. "I'm looking for a car."

"Really, perfect then. I'll give you his number," she said.

"Can I trust this guy?"

"Totally."

Marion gave me the phone number of a man named Naveen. I called him minutes later. I told the man how I'd heard of him and then what type of car I was looking for. Naveen and I arranged to meet the next day.

"I have the perfect one already. You'll love it," he said.

At 2:00 the next day, Naveen picked me up at the corner of 10th and Jefferson. He drove us towards the upscale neighborhood of Lake Oswego. Pulling up to the dealership lot, he pointed out the car he had in mind for me. A teal-colored Toyota Celica— sporty looking and economically superior. It was love at first sight, but I didn't let him know this. We got out of his car, and he went to retrieve the keys. I was skeptical of car salesmen, since my first car, a Thunderbird of a lemon, had been purchased at a bloodsucking dealership. But this time I felt more confident. After all, I was now dealing with the dealer's dealer. Naveen bought cars at auctions in Minnesota, Michigan, and North Dakota and shipped them off to dealerships in Oregon and Washington. Why such a far distance? Why not just buy from a local auction instead of crossing the continent? I didn't want to know.

"Have a seat in her, we'll take her for a test," said Naveen. I sat down and the seat seemed to wrap itself around every curve of my back. My hands gripped the steering wheel so compatibly. The interior was gray, which I always wanted. The speedometer read 40,000 miles.

After the test drive, Naveen showed me all the records. A twenty-six-year-old female named Diana had owned it in Minnesota. She was meticulous, with receipts for everything ever done: 155 car washes, 13 oil changes, 1 tune up, 4 fuel and air filters, 2 brake jobs, and a new battery. Other than a little hail damage on the roof with scattered dings, the car was immaculate. And so I bought it on the spot.

Two weeks later, I departed Portland with my New York friend, Gil.

Even Flow

It was not my intention to leave Portland for good. I had just gotten started, but I needed a reset button. I was frustrated. The spoiled relationships with the girlfriends and the few guys at the apartment had turned me inward. I didn't want to meet anyone new. I kept a distance from people. The spring was dark and lonely. I found solace in a local rock radio station. They'd play Godsmack's song "Voodoo" over and over again. The lyrics reminded me of how far away I'd gone. I needed something familiar. Gil was up for a visit. So I figured I'd drive him home to New York, go for a visit, and then drive back by myself. Another round-trip cross-country adventure.

Gil didn't want to risk taking marijuana on the plane, so I promised him I'd find some west coast weed. The week before Gil arrived, I thanked Marion for hooking me up with Naveen and then asked her if she knew someone who had pot. She told me about this guy named Anthony.

"Check out this guy on the third floor. I'll walk you over, so he doesn't think you're a cop," she said.

"Good idea."

We walked up from her room on the first floor and knocked on his door. He opened after a few moments. Anthony was tall and dark skinned with black hair. He was drying his hands with a kitchen rag. His room looked a lot bigger than all the others.

"Hey, Anthony. This is Jack. We were wondering if you had any, you know…" she motioned with her hand toking to her lips.

He let out a big laugh, waved us in, and closed the door.

"Are you guys just in the mood to smoke? I have a bit."

"Nice to meet you," I said and shook his hand. "I'm actually going away for a few weeks. A friend is coming out from the east coast and I'm going to drive him back on a road trip. I was hoping to get half an ounce."

Anthony looked at Marion with a big smile.

"What do I look like a drug dealer?" He let out a big laugh.

"No, I don't want to put you in a position. I know we don't know each other or..."

"Don't be silly. I can get you some. I'll call someone I know. Give me your number. I'll call you when I have it."

"Thanks, Anthony," I said.

Marion, Anthony, and I chatted about the building for a few and then we all said goodbye.

A few hours later, Anthony called and told me to come down to his room. He let me in. I noticed his window looking out to the courtyard was open. The sun was out.

"You have a bigger room," I said.

"Well, I'm a little older than the rest of the population. I need a little more space now," he said.

"Oh yeah, me too. Nontraditional. Work, travel, and some time off. I'm twenty-three," I said.

"Damn, so am I. That's funny. Imagine all those people who are around our age who are already in a full-time job working every day? The rest of their life is planned for them!"

"That sounds like a terrible existence," I said.

"We're a little slow, but we're the lucky ones," he said with another big laugh.

Anthony handed me the big bag of pot.

"Well, there it is," he said.

"Thanks. Want to smoke?" I asked handing him the cash.

"Sure. Let me roll one."

He took out rolling papers from a notebook, and I pushed a chunk his way. He broke up the weed and then rolled us up a joint.

"I like your style. Papers, the natural way."

"Yeah, I have a little pipe, but those big glass ones make me feel like a..."

We both said it at the same time, "...crackhead" and then we laughed. Anthony had a big laugh that was contagious.

He lit up the joint. We smoked and listened to a few albums for the next several hours. First, he played the 1994 album *Throwing Cooper* by the band Live. We were good and stoned by the end. Then he hit it up a level with Pearl Jam's *Ten* from 1991. To bring us back down into a mellow spot, he put on Gin Blossom's 1992 *New Miserable Experience.*

"Ah, great musical taste. Chill stuff," I said.

"Yeah, early '90s is great! You said you're leaving for a few weeks? Are you coming back here to this building?" he asked.

"Yes, I didn't even look anywhere else. This is the cheapest, and it's in a great location. I'm in a small unit upstairs, but I haven't booked a return room yet. All my stuff is going in a storage locker while I'm away. I'll deal with it when I get back."

"Good idea. Give me a call or knock when you get back."

"I certainly will."

I thanked Anthony and carried on to prepare for my trip.

America, Summer, 2000

I picked up Gil at the airport. We went to a pizza place for our first dinner, and Gil found a bug in his calzone.

"They're right when they say no one else knows how to do pizza outside of New York," I said.

"The place is called New York Pizza," he laughed.

"This and probably a thousand other imposters west of Chicago," I said.

We went back to the room and had a couple of days to hang and party. We drank, smoked, and stared at our road maps. My old friend from high school had never been out of New York, and I had never been to many of our designated stops. The voyage would be monumental for the both of us.

After a couple of days, we moved everything into the storage unit and headed out. We went east from Portland, up and out of the Willamette Valley. We started out our trip with the *No. 4* album by Stone Temple Pilots as a tribute to my fourth car. Then it was on to the fun *Enema of the State* album by Blink 182.

Our first stop was Multnomah Falls out on the scenic Columbia River Highway. The 620-foot falls are a glorious sight. Gil was taken back by the sight. The falls leaks the water down one flight past the bridge that stands in its way. A smaller but still strong flow falls below the bridge. Green mountains are on each side. We went over to the side to sit on some rocks near some smaller streams. Gil sat a while just staring at the running water. This trip was going to provide some good solid reflection.

Mount Hood was our next destination. We crawled the scenic highway of the big mountain in the #4, and soon discovered that it snowed in June. The snow increased with altitude. The storm had grown worse by the time we reached the Timberline Lodge at six thousand feet. We decided to make this a quick tour through the lodge. I recited some lines from *The Shining*, since the exterior shots of the film were done there. We laughed back to the car and then took off down the mountain.

At our third stop, we were once again threatened by June snow. Crater Lake would have been the highest mountaintop in the northwest if it hadn't blown its top and imploded 7,700 years ago. Nevertheless, the altitude is still high enough for snow on the way up to the rim. Luckily, we made it to the spectacular view. We looked out at America's deepest Lake, so blue in the pictures, but now whitened with snow.

Hills of snow accumulated on the side of the icy road from the winter. I feared getting stuck in the snow or sliding off the side. There was no protective guardrail as we drove back down to dry land. Less than twenty minutes later and we were back on a sunny road heading to San Francisco. We were feeling good and positive. Back at my room, I had proposed a deal to smoke one last joint and then abstain until we got out of California. With such enlightening scenery, there didn't seem to be a need for substances.

"Why not experience this clear-headed?" I asked.

"Okay. I'm up for the challenge," Gil answered.

I wasn't comfortable with being burnt out on an entire road trip. I hadn't smoked in months before meeting Anthony, and it was probably a good thing because the first rain season had been hard on my mind. Pot wouldn't have made it better. I was getting by without it, but I knew Gil was a daily smoker. I wondered if he could go clean for just a little while.

We drove another two hours out of Oregon. Pine trees pointed high all around. A big blue sign with yellow lettering welcomed us to California at the Siskiyou County line. We stopped there and then again for a few laughs in Weed, California, to take pictures next to road signs.

It had been a long day. It was getting late, so we grabbed dinner and then hit the road for another hour before checking into a cheap motel in Redding.

The next morning was a straight shot down I-5 right to San Francisco. Within three hours of having breakfast, we were in the big city crossing over the historic Golden Gate Bridge. We cruised around the city. I couldn't believe how hilly the roads were. I laughed nervously—

"We're going to wreck our exhaust system on these roads!"

Gil directed me to Lombard Street, which was the most crooked and winding road in the world. It was madness. We weren't the only curious ones. This was a typical tourist trap, but the line of cars wasn't too bad. It was worth the laughs.

From there, we walked around. Trollies chugged along with their bells ringing. At the pier, incredibly loud seals barked into the summer air. We stopped to eat at Bubba Gump Shrimp, and then took the boat to Alcatraz to top it off before heading south.

Another six hours and we were in Hollywood. We got there just in time for the night life. We dumped our bags in a motel in Hollywood. We went out to a bar and had some drinks. It was strange to be back. It had been three years, but it felt like such a long time. After a few pleasant old-fashioned letters, Sarah and I had drifted. She knew I was in Portland, but we never followed up on visiting each other. I wondered how she was. I felt guilty not calling her, but I also felt a strange guilt that so much time had gone by, especially the past eight months.

"Are you going to call her?" Gil asked.

"I don't think so. It's been a while. It gets complicated."

"I hear you. What about your ex, Jane?"

"Man, like I said earlier, I think about doing it, but I don't think it's the right time. That's been even longer."

"I know how that feels. I think about my first girlfriend. I spent two years with her too. I always wonder where she is."

"Let's have a drink to that," I said.

We drank and partied for a few more days in LA. We surveyed the Hollywood Walk of Fame and stopped to take a photo at Tom Petty's star and a few others. We toured the wax museum and took pictures of the exhibits. ET. Luke, Leia, & Han. We walked by Hollywood High and read about which people went there. We spent some time at the coast too, and I was sure to drive Gil up to the rock star's house in the hills. I blasted "California" from Izzy's latest album *Ride On* as we pulled up to the gates, and I told Gil all about my encounter with the legend in Key West.

The new Izzy album was a road trip album. Songs like "Spazed" and "Trance Mission" became a soundtrack to our cross-country adventure. We went back to it every five or six CDs, as well as the new Red Hot Chili Peppers album.

Gil seemed content, but he proposed breaking out the weed on a few occasions in Hollywood. I pushed back about our deal.

"We're almost there! It'll be worth it."

We left Los Angeles and went to spend a day in San Diego. We enjoyed the San Diego Zoo, filled up on the best Mexican food we ever had, did some people watching, put some things like the bag of weed in a rented storage locker, and then decided to get on to our next destination in Mexico.

It took us only a little over an hour to cross into Mexico. Besides a whacky scene at the initial entry into Mexico, the country was just a continuation of California. All the wild things we'd heard were mere mythical stories. We drove around Tijuana for a while. Things were lively. Music was playing. People were laughing and dancing in the streets. We headed west to a beachfront hotel we had booked for one night. The hotel had a lovely blue swimming pool encased in tile that overlooked the ocean. For this one, we opted to have our own rooms unlike the previous motels where one would take the bed and one would take the couch. On one occasion, we slept in opposing directions with a partition of pillows between us. This stay in another country was special, so we splurged for the private rooms.

There was a bar down below out in the street where we hung out for the whole night at a table with some Mexican girls, as beautiful Mexican guitar music played. The girls spoke a little English, and Gil knew a little Spanish.

By two a.m., we were extremely drunk, the drunkest yet on this trip. We all went back to the room. One girl went with Gil into his room, as I talked with two others in the living room area. For a moment, I thought of my experience in the Keys with the two girls from New York, but I knew that wasn't going to happen this time. We were just unwinding from the loud bar when we heard a racket coming from Gil's room. The three of us all looked at each other, unsure as to what we were hearing. There was heavy groaning, almost a grunting, an occasional yell, an occasional scream, a slapping. When it started to sound like there was some crying, one of her friends called into the room to her in Spanish.

I didn't know what she said, but I assumed she was checking on her. The girl answered with something.

"You okay in there, Gil? Take it easy, man. Sounds a little rough," I warned.

"Yeahhhh," he answered in a hoarse, drawn-out voice.

We heard the television go on loud and decided to try to ignore them. The thinner, younger girl curled up with a blanket on the couch. The girl name Carmen and I went into the other bedroom. We kissed a little and then just kind of snuggled up together in the bed. She smelled like pineapple, and I lost consciousness in her smell.

When I woke up, her hair was in my eyes and my right arm was draped over her round waste, bare buxom breasts near my lips, plump hips like an ocean wave moved down below the sheets. She opened her brown eyes. Always those brown eyes that get me.

"Buenos dias, guapo."

"I take that as a good morning. What the helk happened?"

"I don't know, but let's make sure they're all alive."

We went out to the living room and the others were already awake. Gil was sipping coffee at the table with a big grin. He looked hung over. We all looked hung over. I looked at the clock and it was already eleven a.m. Thankfully, we paid for extra time and a late checkout so we could spend time on the beach.

The girls left after breakfast. Carmen and I hugged goodbye. She said something in Spanish, probably something about meeting me again in another life. She was a sweet girl I'd never forget.

Gil and I went out to lie down by the pool and in the Mexican sun for an hour or so.

"You okay?" I asked.

"Oh yeah, sorry. I got a little crazy. I thought we were going to kill each other at one point," said Gil.

"Yeah, we don't need that happening, especially in Mexico!"

"Nah, we're all good. Did you do her friend?" he asked.

"As much as I want to say yes, I have no idea. I was too drunk!"

"Ah, you're too much!"

We checked out of the Mexican resort around four and made our way back to the U.S. After driving to San Diego to get the stuff from the locker, we headed east for the first time on our trip. It was onto the Grand Canyon.

☆

"One more time, shall we?" I asked holding up a CD.

"On our way out!" Gil nodded.

For the third and last time on our trip, we played the *Californication* CD by Red Hot Chili Peppers, which had come out the previous year. The album, which ends with the song "Road Trippin'" was perfect for road trips, especially while in California.

We drove for a few hours before the sun went down. Black hills could be seen in the distance. This was real desert terrain with wild pointy cactus and yucca palm trees. Along Interstate 8, the temperature dramatically fluctuated at night. It would go from chilly to scorching hot in less than a minute and then suddenly back to cold. We roughed it with our shirts off and the windows down. It's not that I didn't have AC. I just didn't want to waste the gas and energy using it all the time. We decided to go natural, as Gil called it. Along the quirky interstate 8 and the mystic border of Mexico, we headed east into Arizona. We were so close to the border that at one point you could reach your hand out the window and it felt like it was Mexico.

Gil and I shut up for a while and just listened to the music and reflected. I put on an INXS CD to play the song "Beautiful Girl." I thought of Carmen. I thought of Mally, even Ginny. I thought of Sarah. I thought of all the beautiful girls I've ever known.

From I-8, the southernmost interstate, we turned north on Highway 85 until merging with Interstate 10 East, which brought us right into Phoenix. Around ten o'clock, we found a motel and checked in for some sleep.

Now that we were on our way back east, the weed deal was up. Gil took out a pipe he bought in Hollywood, and I dug out the bag of pot. We sparked up the pipe in the motel room. Gil took in some big hits. He was right back on it like there hadn't been any time away.

"We did good. All the way down the coast. A whole week without smoke. Is that the first time in a while for you?" I asked.

"Yeah, you know I think about quitting. I really do."

"So what stops you?"

"Honestly, I don't think I can," he said taking a hit.

"I've had my moments when I've quit. Somehow it finds me again, but I've learned to moderate it. You think you're addicted?"

"Well..." he hesitated.

"I don't mean to accuse you or put you on the spot."

"No, no, it's okay. It just takes the edge off for me," he said.

"It's all natural. There's a lot worse," I said.

"It's not like we're smoking crack!" he said and laughed.

"We'll probably grow out of it as we get older anyway," I said.

We laughed. But somehow, I felt like he was never going to grow out of this. I let him smoke a bit more on his own.

I took a walk for a few blocks around the motel. I felt the strange feeling I had had when I was in Arizona the last time. I looked around. The night sky. The air. The odd landscape. It was like another planet to me.

The next morning, we grabbed a gas station breakfast and jumped back on Interstate 17 North to the Grand Canyon. We arrived a few hours later and ate at a Wendy's restaurant just out front to the entrance of the national park.

At the canyon, we walked around to different spots to try to see it from different angles. This giant hole in the Earth was magnificent and stretched on for miles. The layers of rock were shades of orange, brown, and a red seen nowhere else. I stared out at this overwhelming open pit.

It was burning hot, so we took off our shirts. I walked out on a cliff overlooking the canyon.

"Let me get a picture of that," Gil said.

I put my arms up in victory with a giant smile on my face. This was a moment in time. We knew how fortunate we were to be out there on the road seeing the wonders of America. Some would never make it out of their own backyards. Too poor. Too sick. Too immersed in work. Too sheltered by a bubble of small-town ignorance or big city pride. But here we were out in the world.

"Let me get you, Gil. Just watch your step," I said.

"Yeah, one step back and I'm a goner!" he said.

Gil went out on the ledge and did his victory wave.

When we were done with the photos, Gil and I sat for a long drink of water, which was important out there in the crazy heat.

"Are you ever going to talk about her?" Gil asked.

"Who? Jane? I told you..."

"No, you know, the one after her..." he said.

"No. I don't think so. Not yet. It was a tough break."

"Hey, that's cool. I don't mean to pressure you."

"I know it's good to talk about things. How about you, and what happened at college upstate?" I asked.

Gil tensed up, and I immediately regrated asking.

"Sorry, I didn't mean to throw a tough one back at you."

"No, it's fair game," he said.

"No, that's not fair. I'm sorry," I said.

"I was going to say something, but then I saw how easygoing things were at your college. I felt stupid," he said.

"No, man. Don't. You know I'm in that old building with slightly older kids. I'm sure there's partying at my university in other buildings."

"Honestly, I don't think I ever want to talk about it again. It was just abusive frat boy shit. Don't worry, I'm all right. I'm a big boy," Gil said.

"Well, if you ever need to talk, I'm here."

We sat for a while in a quiet spot looking out at the canyon.

After about fifteen minutes, some Asian men with big cameras came along. We heard their giant laughs before we saw them. They were a jolly group of tourists. Gil and I looked at each other and laughed. It was awesome to see people so happy just to tour our country, the great place we were born.

☆

After Arizona, we moved toward the middle of the country. We were tired, running out of money, and very restless at this point. Gil freaked out the next morning in New Mexico when a man crawled out of the dumpster he was pissing on. The man demanded a cigarette. I don't know why, but Gil was freaked out.

"Get me the hell out of this state," he said.

I laughed and drove on, only to have my own breakdown in Texas. At a rest stop, I got out and walked around, suddenly panicked at the prospect of going back to New York. I was delirious and unsure of returning to New York, even for a visit.

"You mind jumping on a train for the rest of the trip back? I'm not sure I can do this," I said.

"Oh man, but our plans. Come on, you have to finish this."

"I don't know, man. I don't know."

"If you really need to," said Gil.

After some time out of the car with a bottle of water, I decided to continue and suggested he drive for a while.

Gil took over the wheel for the whole middle of the country. It was like we were in the middle of nowhere, lost, going around in circles in one giant loop. The land went on and on. The highways out there were nameless. We were full of fright.

We flew through Oklahoma on I-40, and then we stopped to see some weird sights in Arkansas. We spent the night there in a motel outside of the national forest and then went for a little hike in the morning to get some exercise. From there, it was five hours to Memphis.

The last great site we saw on our trip was Graceland in Tennessee. The property stretched far and wide. The house was pure royalty, not so much in size, but in grace and style. The inside of the house was exactly as Elvis had left it when he passed in 1977. Shag carpets going upstairs, three TVs in the den, a wall full of awards. Outside was a small swimming pool, smaller than Hemingway's. Around a small pond sat the family gravestones.

We listened to an Elvis greatest hits disc on the way to Nashville. We spent some time walking around Nashville and really enjoyed the city. I wanted to spend the night, but we were low on cash. From Nashville, we headed north on I-65 and connected with I-64 in Lexington, Kentucky. Green hills but bad air. Gil continued the drive as I relaxed and blew my smoke out the window in thought. A large crucifix stood on the side of the road. Gil played a new CD by Matchbox Twenty, and a brilliant song titled "Rest Stop" came on just when we needed the inspiration.

Lightning strikes in the blue day sky entertained me and bugged Gil out as he took us into West Virginia. It was on through the night into Pennsylvania. All the roads we had been on merged into I-78, which would take us right home into New York. I took over in the middle of the night for the final leg of the tour.

Gil had fallen asleep, exhausted from the long haul he'd accomplished. The sun emerged while we were in the Holland Tunnel. On the other side, it seemed like a whole new world. The pulse of New York City gripped me. Gill awoke. We could feel the city's energy, even at this time of the day. Lower Manhattan only took minutes to get through this early in the morning. On the Williamsburg Bridge, the sun popped higher in the morning sky. I played "New York State of Mind" by Billy Joel, and Gil smiled, proud to be home. We cruised through Brooklyn and jumped on the Belt Parkway heading out to Suffolk County as the rush hour traffic started to clog up the highway in the opposite direction. We were on the right side of things. If only we could've kept it that way.

Hometown

I dropped Gil off. We needed some solitude and rest after such a voyage. We made plans to see each other one more time before I got back out on the road. We'd have some beers, light up the bong, and go through all the photos. We'd laugh and cry over the memories of our 2000 road trip. And then we'd sever ourselves from the awkwardness of a strange summer adventure with underlying pain, and highs and lows too difficult to face again. Gil would fall right back into his everyday New York life, and I would soon return to my new, indeterminable life.

I drove around the old town thinking of all the people I had once known there. It seemed like no one was left. Andy and Jeff had just lost their mother and moved out to Los Angeles while Gil and I were travelling back. We had missed each other like ships passing in the night. I drove through Main Street and felt like a stranger in a strange town. No one would recognize me here. The old town wasn't my hometown, maybe never was, but Long Island was. All of Long Island would always feel like one big home.

I spent one week at my grandmother Rosa's house. She was also getting ready to leave New York. She and Andre had sold the house and had just weeks left. They were spending a lot more time in Florida, and now they were selling the New York house to dedicate more time to living on a farm in Virginia.

I enjoyed the week at their house sleeping in the guest room upstairs overlooking the bay. All the family memories flooded back. This would be it. They were selling the family headquarters, and there wouldn't be anyone left in New York.

That night, I fell asleep to the sound of the bay waves. In my dream, I was walking up to the house. The front lawn is frosty. In the front yard out past the bent tree sits a pond of goldfish sheltered by a sheet of thin ice. I walk inside to a tree of decorations and lights with bows and gifts below where we children kneel opening the suspense of weeks, while bleached-blond Aunt Judy drinks wine thinking of her next painting, and Granny is in the kitchen checking the lamb, thinking of her next poem or story, as Great Grandpa is slicing an apple using a knife as a fork as he laughs at our president and his "flag waving idiots", and Uncle Joel is cross-legged in a chair talking stocks with Andre over a scotch, and Aunt Gloria sits to share her pictures of Africa with us kids, and Aunt Annie sings "Silent Night" at the piano, and I laugh because it's never silent here. The aroma of lamb permeates through the house, Grandma Rosa rings the dinner bell, and the kids take their place at the table in the next room, but I stay and stare at the stone fireplace with wooden mantle, fire entrancing me until someone taps me on the shoulder telling me it's time to go.

Against the Wind

Out on the highway in the middle of the country, there were two roads that went off below a bridge heading in different directions. A divide of grass sat between them. Each side had ample space. The roads seemed to go on forever, but from the bridge there was a great glare of a circle around this scene, like a photograph with a flash ring around it.

I didn't know what was in the distance. I wanted to know. The curiosity of the unknown and the desire to be free from all I'd ever known were the reasons why I was back out there. And I loved a lot about Oregon.

The way back was almost all on Interstate 80. From New York straight through the Midwest of Iowa and Nebraska. I took the same familiar route through southern Wyoming, but instead of heading northwest through Utah, this time I decided to continue straight on 80 right into Nevada. I thought of a Billy Joel song "Stop in Nevada" and dug out the CD to play. I spent a night in Reno and then went to see Lake Tahoe the next morning.

The beauty of the blue lake prompted me to venture down to Yosemite National Park. It was only two and half hours away, so I couldn't resist. I didn't have a camping reservation or a tent, but at least I could see some of the park. I started near Mt. Dana and wrapped around the park for an entire day stopping at lakes, vista points, and trailheads. I didn't want to leave the car alone for too long, so my hikes were short but refreshing. I spent the night alone in the car in a campground parking lot. I watched black bears cross right in front of my car as they roamed around looking for food.

In the morning, I left the majestic Yosemite and made my way west to I-5 to begin the journey north to Portland. But I ventured hours off course to see Crater Lake again. I spent just an hour staring out at the beautiful blue lake, this time without any snow to worry about. It was a worthy detour to touch my soul.

When I got back to I-5 to head north again, I popped in a mixed CD. Bob Seger's "Against the Wind" came on and the lyrics obviously reminded me of Jane. I'd been closer to her than I'd been in years, right there in her new home state. Yet I still couldn't go to her, even when I was minutes away driving through her city. I couldn't go back there. She seemed like so long ago. There I was still running, and yet she surely had moved on. I wondered if I had really lost my way like the poor guy in the song. I wondered if she even thought of me and wondered.

"What a sad song," I said out loud to myself. "What a sad fucking song."

Tears followed.

"Shit," I said again acknowledging the years that had gone by. I hit the gas and zoomed up the highway trying to leave the pain behind in the dust.

A song titled "The Comfort of Strangers" came on next by a guy named Jamie Walters. For a moment, I thought I was going to have to pull over to the side of the road to sob like a basket-case, but then something in the song pulled me up and made me feel better about everything. The music was something I never lost. It was always there. It was part of me. It made me alive.

"It's alright" by Candlebox came on next. Their old songs got me through my worst times out in my car as I was homeless and out of school for eighty-nine days. Now it was six years later, and a new song was there to bring me into the light of the night on my travels. It would be alright. I had lost love, but it would be alright. I kept telling myself. It would be alright.

Portland, Summer, 2000

I was back in Portland for round two. I checked in at the building and my new floor manager, a guy named Sidi from Nigeria, met me in the office. I paid him the pro-rated rent until the 31st, along with the full $290 for the following month. Then he brought me up to my new room. He said they had a good room for me on the third floor this time. We arrived at room 308. I looked at the door across from mine. This was going to be a whole new experience this time with Anthony right across the hall.

After settling in, I knocked on his door and backed up into my doorway to show him where I'd landed.

He opened up. "What the ...!" he yelled and let out that big laugh of his. He was surprised but genuinely happy to see me.

Anthony welcomed me in and took out a sandwich bag of marijuana. We sat down in his dim lit room with dirty dishes all over the place, a bit more disheveled than the neater guy I had met last time.

"Man, sorry for the mess in here. I've been working a lot. I have to catch up on things," he said.

Still, the place had a maturity to it that I could appreciate. Two healthy plants on the windowsill made all the difference. After rolling a fat joint, we smoked it and sat there a while talking and listening to an old Santana album. The room was fogged out, and we were seriously stoned.

"So how was the trip east? You from New York?"

"What an adventure! Yes, I'm from Long Island."

"You drove all the way back? Hard core!"

"I guess so. It's draining and energizing at the same time. Are you originally from Oregon?" I asked.

"Have you ever heard of the Nez Perce?" Anthony asked.

"No, what's that?" I asked.

"It's my tribe back where I grew up in Idaho. I moved to Oregon as a teen, but I have family back there still."

"Man, you're Native American? That's cool."

"Thanks."

"You'll have to tell me all about the culture someday soon."

"Absolutely," he replied.

Then Anthony told me about his ex-girlfriend.

"You can't live with 'em, you can't live without 'em. She was crazy anyway. She partied like a teenager," he said laughing.

"Yes, I think I know how you feel," I said.

I looked over and spotted something disturbing out his window. Anthony's window overlooked the courtyard and faced the other side of the U-shaped building. On the other side was the men's bathroom with a sink right in front of the window. In that open window, stood a chubby naked guy bent over the sink. It looked like he was brushing his teeth.

"Ah, what is that?" I said laughing.

"That's the coach! He's some kind of jock guy. You'll walk in on him doing it sometimes. No care at all. You'll see."

He picked up a camera from his dresser and went to the window and snapped a picture.

"You're too funny," I laughed.

We went back to smoking and listening to the Temple of the Dog CD. I had found a friend.

☆

I was sitting in my room with the door open a week after moving in, when a woman stormed in with a beer bottle in her hand. It was eleven o'clock in the morning.

She was tall and dressed in tattered blue jeans, a black t-shirt, and black boots. She had black rimmed glasses and her dark hair was a mess.

"Hey neighbor, I just moved in next door," she said.

"Hi there, come on in." But she was already there. She sat down on my windowsill and lit a cigarette.

"I'm Alana. Nice to meet you," she said and then clinked her beer bottle on my coffee mug.

"Where are you from?" she asked.

"I'm Jack. New York. How about you?"

"No way! Cool. I'm from Illinois, right outside of Chicago."

"Pizza competitors," I said.

"Don't worry, New York is better. How long you been here?"

"I just got back from New York. I was on a cross country adventure for a few weeks. I lived here last year. Moved here in '99."

"This fucking room is so small. I'm so out of here soon."

"It takes getting used to."

"Not something I'm going to do, but we'll make it as fun as we can."

Then she told me all about her breakup with a guy named Mick who she was living with back in Illinois. They had a blow-out in the street in front of the apartment they shared.

"I cursed him out in the street and slapped him around like a bitch, and left him with a whole month's rent to pay by himself. That's what he gets for screwing me over, that man pig."

I was taken back by her brashness, but I knew I would be safe as long as I was a neutral, platonic friend.

☆

Alana and Anthony met, and they were like night and day from day one. She studied art; he studied business. But they had one definite thing in common— the ability to drink a shit load of alcohol in one night. The whole month of August was a drunken blur. I would pass out at one a.m., emerge from my room at three a.m. to go to the bathroom, and they'd still be there drinking away. That was on the weekdays. On the weekends, we would hit the local bars and stay out until the sun came up. Then we'd head to breakfast at the same sleazy all-night joint. I barely touched anything. The place gave me the creeps. I couldn't even drink the coffee because I couldn't bear to pour the milk in my cup from a baby bottle with a nipple.

One late night during the week, there was a knock at my door. I could hear it was Alana and Anthony coming back from being out somewhere. I was in bed already with the lights out with a classical piano CD playing gently in the background. I wasn't going to get up for them at this point, so I ignored it. I could hear them through the door laughing.

"Just leave it for him," he said.

"Brought you a gift, Jack," she said.

I heard something placed down against my door. I could only imagine a bottle of liquor they drank and left at my door.

In the morning, I woke up and had forgotten all about the knock until I went to leave for class. Outside my door was a flowerpot in the shape of a woman's head with sprouting green leaves that exploded with bursts of red from their centers. The plant appeared healthy. The crafted head was a beautiful, brown-haired woman from the shoulder up. The woman's hand draped about her shoulder delicately positioning a bright red rose just under her nose. Her elegant shoulder held the top seam of a green dress around the lower top of her back. In her chocolate hair were scattered heads of roses that appeared to be blossoming from her hair. Out of the top of her grew the healthy plant as if it were her thoughts branching out into the infinite possibilities of the world.

The cement pot was heavy. I took her in and placed her above my work desk where she would be in my presence.

Later that day, I thanked Alana.

"She's perfect for you," she replied.

"Not sure if that's a compliment or insult. But where in the world did you get her?"

"Gosh, we were drunk. I don't remember," said Alana.

"So you stole it? Just great!"

"Just borrowed. Don't worry."

"She is fine looking. I think I'll write a poem about her and call it Hard Love!"

She let out a big laugh.

"What were you two doing out there last night?"

"Just drinking beers."

"You two drink alcohol like it's root beer," I said.

"Here, I gave one to Anthony too. We'll make a statement," she said handing me a yellow sticker that read in bright red letters: *Warning: Radioactive.* I looked at Anthony's door and there it was.

"Thanks. Nice way to bond," I said.

The three of us stuck the stickers on the right-hand corners of our doors. We were now an official club. Dangerous. Ready to self-destruct.

A foreign exchange student from Spain named Santiago moved into the room on the other side of me. Alana, Anthony, and I befriended Santiago and took him out for a Friday night in the city. He was a small guy, smaller than me, at five foot three, with beady intelligent eyes. His English wasn't the best, but he had the best smile and laugh. We all got a kick out of him. We had one hell of a time that night. Anthony and Alana got destroyed on liquor. Santiago and I drank slower and kept a healthier pace.

"It's nice to meet someone who doesn't drink like a fish."

"They're a little loco, eh?" he said.

On the way home, we passed some panhandling kids on the sidewalk. Alana turned to them.

"Get a job." she said.

I looked at her in shock as we continued down the street.

"They're perfectly capable. Some of these runaways are spoiled rich kids. I read about it and even talked to some of them. They come here, but they have a safety net somewhere out there waiting for them to come to their senses. They need tough love."

"It's not like we have money to give them anyway," I said.

"In many cases you're just feeding a drug addiction if you give them cash," Anthony said.

"Some are junkies, but some are just brats acting out. I'm all about teaching them self-reliance," Alana said.

I thought of Professor Kohl and Ralph Waldo Emerson.

"Santiago, do you have beggars in Spain?" asked Anthony.

"A few," he replied. "Mostly immigrants."

"I just usually ignore them. New York had a few cases of crazy rich guys going out on the street just for kicks. They'd rub dirt all over their faces, wrap themselves in sheets, throw themselves on the sidewalk, and then at the end of the day they'd laugh their way back up to their ritzy penthouse apartment," I said.

"See. I wouldn't be sweet and nice with them either," she said. "Takers. Fuck takers."

Santiago, Anthony, and I looked at each other and laughed at Alana's toughness. She was one of a kind.

☆

On a Saturday in August, Anthony had three tickets to a Portland minor league baseball game. I didn't care much for the game, but I had never been to a game in a stadium, so it would be a new experience. I knew Santiago would get a kick of it too. The three of us had a blast. There's a picture of us screaming with excitement over a game we really cared nothing about.

We drank bad beer, ate popcorn, and yelled our heads off for the Portland team to win the game. Anthony bought the three of us souvenir balls on our way out of the stadium.

I appreciated these kinds of breaks that got us off campus. My summer science class had ended and left me open to strolling the park and drinking pina coladas in my room. If Anthony hadn't had a job a few days a week in an office, we would've been in big trouble because we partied like rock stars when the bunch of us were together.

Sleepwalker

In late August, new folks moved in to get ready for the fall quarter in September. All of them were younger than Anthony, Alana, and I, but we knew that going into this. We were a little slower, but a little more experienced at life. I'd like to think that was a good thing.

Robin moved to Oregon from Michigan where he had been raised by his father. His mother and stepfather lived on the outskirts of Portland, so it was a secure move. Far away from home, yet close to family. Robin was a twenty-one-year-old guy who wore hats all the time. I knew I liked him right off the bat. He was soft-spoken, but he'd let out these crazy hyena laughs. He had a serious look on his face. You could tell this guy was thinking about things.

Michael was a scruffy looking twenty-one-year-old with the best flannel shirts. He moved from Vermont. His journey to the northwest was farther than mine. I figured we'd click, but I found that we had the least to talk about for some reason. Maybe he thought I was a crazy man. But he could drink well with Anthony and Alana, so they took to him right away.

Scott was from Sacramento, California. He was an eighteen-year-old, long-haired, theater major. He wasn't much of a drinker, but he was funny and eccentric. With wild eyes and all, he'd drop in and say hello. Just as a conversation took off, he'd slip out quietly and mysteriously. Some days he was dressed normal, but some days he wore outrageous costumes of tights and fringe shirts with black mascara on his face. He was a born entertainer.

We all got an invitation from Marion to go down to her room on the final Friday night of August. She was able to throw small parties because she had one of the bigger rooms like Anthony. We met some of her new friends and all got to know each other.

Bonnie was one of Marion's friends and also lived on the first floor. She was nineteen and from Seattle. Bonnie and Marion were opposites, but they were inseparable. Bonnie was short and dark haired. Marion was tall and blonde. They were both younger than Anthony, Alana, and me, yet their maturity and smarts were impressive, and far more advanced than ours.

When the younger crowd tired out, Alana was eager to break away and get into the serious partying. We went upstairs to Anthony's room to smoke and drink a while. To her delight, we all stood back in horror as she revealed her latest art project— a squirrel head coming out of a human torso.

"What's it called? Hard Death?" I asked.

"Very funny," she said.

"My 'Hard Love' is prettier," I said.

"I won't disagree," she said and laughed.

We all talked for a while before Santiago retired for the night. I checked out an hour later and went to bed.

When I woke up the next morning and went to open my door, there they were with the door wide open, still drinking and smoking.

"Are you two kidding me?"

"Ah, shut up. We're vampires, didn't you know it?" she said.

Anthony showed his teeth and laughed.

Eyes Wide Open

On the first of September, a bunch of us took a drive. Anthony took Marion and Bonnie in his car, and I took Robin and Santiago in mine. No one else was interested in climbing a mountain. We didn't know how far we'd even get up the mountain, but we were going to take a chance. Mt. Hood is Oregon's largest mountain at 11,249 feet tall. It is a potentially active stratovolcano, which means it could very well blow its top just like Mt. St. Helens did in 1980.

It was a beautifully sunny day with clear skies. We parked the cars and set out on our long up-hill walk. Some of the steep inclines were challenging, and some of us needed a hand along the way. Marion and Bonnie were troopers all the way up. Robin and I had the toughest time, but we pushed on.

"It's the cigarettes. The tobacco giants. These million-dollar companies are killing us and getting richer and richer," I said.

"Bastards," Robin said.

We did well, considering we weren't in tip-top shape. The climb took several hours. When we reached the top, Santiago let out a big yell of excitement. Bonnie dipped her hand in the snow at the top and gasped. We were all charged with emotion. There we were walking in snow and sliding on ice at the top of a mountain. Not another soul could be seen or heard. We were even above the clouds and the birds. We looked out at the magnificent sky. This topped anything I'd ever seen in all my travels.

"This is deeply spiritual. Do you all realize what we've done?" Bonnie asked.

"This is one of those moments in life," I said.

"We're probably never going to get to do something like this again," Robin added.

"Thank you all for bringing me," said Santiago.

"Guys, who has a camera?" asked Marion.

It was then we realized none of us had brought a camera to document the climb up Mt. Hood. The memory would remain in all our hearts.

"How could we?" I asked.

"It's all going to be in our hearts," said Anthony. "Let's all never forget this. It's a special moment. Let's give each other a hug."

We all did a big group hug and then looked out at the world. We were coming for you, world. We were going to make things happen in this life.

It was cold and difficult to breathe up there, and with the day starting to wind down, we agreed to head back down the mountain. We all looked at each other before we left the top, knowing we had shared something special.

☆

A few days later, it was sadly time for Santiago to return to Madrid. He was in Portland for a once in a lifetime summer experience, and we were all honored to have shared it with him. We had a going away dinner for him and wished him well. I promised to write and visit him someday.

Into the Night

One night a few days into September, Alana knocked on my door with a visitor by her side.

"Hi, Jack. This is Lucy. We're going to a party tonight."

"Hi, Lucy. Nice to meet you. I'm not sure if I was..."

Lucy grabbed me by the hand and looked at Alana.

"Oh, he's cute," she said to our friend.

"So where are we going?" I asked.

"We're going to a house party. Lucy is friends with my friend Gail, down on the second floor. Have you met her?" asked Alana.

"Yes, I think I ran into you two a few weeks ago."

"First, we need to go get wine at the store. Me and you," said Lucy. She took me by the hand and I closed my door behind me. She led me downstairs, out the door, and across the street to the Plaid Pantry to buy a bottle of wine. The clerk I usually saw there gave me a wink. Lucy and I walked back to my room with the wine, arm in arm, like two high school lovers.

Alana was waiting for us. Lucy had a car, but I volunteered to drive. I ran out to the parking garage and then picked them up out front. Lucy got into the front seat. Alana climbed into the back.

We crossed the bridge into southeast and drove through a residential neighborhood until we found a small green house.

Lucy turned to me when Alana found the house.

"We'll just go in for a little while, okay," she said.

"Sounds like a plan," I said.

The three of us went into the house. It was an alright crowd. Alana was getting into it right away with these people. I guess it was her kind of folks. I'd never seen her so social. I opened the wine bottle we brought and poured Alana a full cup. Lucy and I walked off and found a spot to talk. I poured her a cup and took a few sips. She drank some of it while we told each other about ourselves. She was twenty-nine years old, almost thirty, and worked for a furniture sales company. She finished community college but never went on after that. She was also a former dancer at a place in central Oregon.

"So what does that mean? How much did you…"

"Use your imagination," she laughed. "But I didn't do anything with any of the guys."

I looked at her and imagined drooling middle-aged men with suspenders on over their bellies, drinking their smelly beers, eating chicken wings, hollering at her to do things to herself. Or men in suits holding cash in their hands ushering her to come sit on their laps so they could stick their fingers in her. Barbarians and the beauty.

"It paid well, but then it was time to grow up. I only did it for a year. Don't worry, I never did anything else like that for cash."

"That's all interesting but I think you're above all that."

"Well, thank you. I think you're pretty special too. Alana told me all about you."

"Really?" I asked.

"Really."

Lucy got up and put a leg over me and sat on my lap with her red plastic drink cup in hand.

"You want to go have our own party?" she asked.

I could smell strawberries in her blond hair.

"Let's go," I said.

We got right up and went to give Alana the rest of the bottle. She took it and told us not to worry, that she'd catch a ride.

I drove us back toward the bridge. Just as I approached, Lucy leaned over and started to kiss me all over as I drove. I gripped the steering wheel as we crossed over the bridge.

"We're going to die!" I yelled.

"We'll finish this inside," she said with a laugh.

We walked back from the parking garage and went up to my floor. The building was pretty empty on this Friday night. We stopped at the ladies' room so she could go, and then we went back to my room. I popped open a bottle of white wine I had stored in my fridge. We enjoyed a quick cold glass, and then I told her I'd be right back. I went around the corner to the men's room.

When I returned to my room, she was sitting on my bed in white lingerie. Had she brought this in her bag? Did she normally carry this around? I didn't know what to make of it.

Lucy had lit my beachy-summer-scented candle, turned off the lights, and turned on the local jazz radio station.

With six years on me, this woman said things and made sounds I'd never heard before. She made me feel things I'd never felt. She flipped us over and got on top in control, but it wasn't forced. This instinctual passion was happening to both of us. Her blonde hair draped over the front of her face. The candlelight made her skin glow, and her blue eyes peered down into mine once in a while in between closing them with pleasure. Our summer sweat mixed. We moved with the music, like the ocean, like birds in flight. It felt like we were floating off the ground. "Into the Night" by Benny Mardones came on the radio.

Now we were escaping the world, flying off into the night, drifting, coming together in the sky. Lucy and I were all alone, united in the darkness with stars all around us.

This moment in the night sky, this was love.

Knock Down Walls

The final batch of people moved in. Jill from Utah moved in next door to me to the right in Santiago's old room. Next to her, Leslie from central Oregon moved in. They were both friendly. We all introduced ourselves on Saturday. Robin, Michael, and Scott came over from the other wing. Marion and Bonnie came upstairs. Alana, Anthony, and I opened our doors. We gave out drinks and had a hall party. We warned everyone that if Sidi the hall manager came by, which he hardly did, that we all needed to hide our alcohol. Alana, Robin, Marion, and I were the real smokers, so we fogged the place out with our cigarettes, but others joined in. Anthony was a more casual smoker. He could smoke at night but go all day without needing one. I had no idea how he did it.

Anthony and I went back and forth playing tunes. First, he played *Blood Sugar Sex Magik* by Red Hot Chili Peppers. Then I played an album titled *Sugar* by a band called Tonic. We laughed our heads off for a few hours into the night. Around one a.m., we calmed it down and broke into smaller groups inside our rooms for a while more. It was nice to meet everyone before classes started the following Monday.

☆

I continued my work at the computer lab from the previous year. The lab was in the campus library, a beautiful but modern building. The lab was to the right when entering the building, and it was open twenty-four hours a day. I worked two night shifts from seven to eleven and one overnight shift. I spent hours surfing the young and evolving web, looking up both important and useless facts and opinions. I got into looking up criminal records on people I once went to school with, especially the ones who had moved to Florida where they posted mugshots online.

It was always two of us on duty, and I worked with mostly computer science majors, mostly from other countries. Being an English major, I was the odd guy out, but they all liked me for some reason. My favorite shifts were with Chang Soo from Korea and his friend Ryosuke from Japan. We realized we all lived in the same building. They were on the second floor. We had a few good long talks about their countries, about the United States, and the future of computers. I learned a lot every time I talked to them. They were a break from the normal American conversations, and a break away from what was becoming a messy life outside of work.

☆

One night, Lucy, Alana, and I went out to see a movie at the Baghdad Theater, which served beers. Alana was able to drink a good number of them during the show. Since Lucy was driving, I drank a few hefeweizens, the only beer really tolerable at this point. After the movie, we hung out at the bar. When Lucy stepped away to the bathroom, Alana asked about her.

"Hey, I like her. She's spunky. You digging her?" she asked.

"Yes, very much. Thank you."

"Gail and I ran into her in the street. She knew her from a long time ago. I thought of you right away. Have fun."

Lucy

Lucy started to come over every couple of days. We'd go out for drinks and dinner. We'd exercise at the campus gym or play racquetball, and then go back to my room for a different kind of workout. I was having a good time.

In mid-September, we attended Lucy's mother's fiftieth birthday barbecue. She invited Alana and told me to bring another friend if I wanted, so Anthony came along. We ate the delicious food and soaked our throats with the spiked punch. Her mother and half the family got sloshed on tequila. After the dinner festivities and a birthday cake, we gathered around the fire pit and listened to Lucy's uncle tell stories of Vietnam, and the 60's, and then jail. As entertained as we all were, there was a brewing conflict within me. While I was having fun with this exciting lady, I wondered where this was all going.

One night, we got together with her friend Gail. I finally got to really meet her. She was dreary and dull. She talked slow, like a permanent drunk. I made the mistake of suggesting we party.

"Oh, you guys want to party tonight, eh? I know someone who we can get coke from. You want to go in on a bag?"

Lucy looked at me.

"That's been a long time for me," she said.

"Same here for me," I said.

"Oh, I'm just throwing it out there," Gail said.

"I don't know, Gail, why don't we..."

Gail cut off Lucy mid-sentence.

"We could just do a little for old time's sake." Gail said.

"Whatever you two want to do," I told them.

I stayed behind while Lucy and Gail went to go purchase the cocaine. There was no way I was stepping foot in some drug dealer's living room, hell not even a front lawn.

While I waited for them, I hung back with this bony guy from down the hall named Harry. Gail knew him and had bumped into him in the hallway and told him of our plans. He wanted in on the action. We talked about the music scene while we waited.

Harry had neon blue hair and piercings here and there, but besides his punk image, he still worshiped his favorite childhood band Nirvana. I pictured Kurt somewhere in this guy's shadows screaming, "let go, let go already."

The women finally came back with the bag. I had imagined the worst possible scenarios, but they appeared unscathed.

"How much did it cost?" I asked.

"One hundred," said Lucy.

"Damn, it *is* a rich man's drug," I said.

"I thought you said you did it before," said Gail.

"Yes, but I never bought it. Never will."

"Well, you just did," she said holding out her hand.

I placed a twenty and a five in her hand. This seemed like the beginning of all the after-school specials I'd ever seen on some kid who gets hooked on coke. Always an accident.

The four of us snorted up around two or three lines each, while also sipping on strawberry daiquiris. We were blasted into next week. Harry slipped out the door at one point, either sick from partying or disgusted by our senseless conversation, but probably just craving Nirvana.

After some time, the three of us took a stroll through the city. We ended up at the waterfront and took a seat on the rocks by the serene shore of the Willamette River. For two hours, we sat listening to Gail's life story; how she had done too much mescaline; how she had beaten up her ex-boyfriend, the only one who had ever truly loved her; and how they had found him dead in bed one night from a bad mix; how she once sucked dick for coke; how she fucked too many strange old men for great sums of money; how she still appreciated the doctor's precision on her new breasts....

My high had been shot to a dangerous low in these two hours of Gail's life confessions.

"How do you know each other again?" I asked after a while.

"Oh, way back from school a long time ago," said Lucy. She downplayed their connection, which made me feel a little better.

"You two want to do another line?" Gail asked.

After hearing all that, yeah. So we snorted a final set on the waterfront. The same waterfront I had jogged at with Mally a few times. I wondered where she was these days. The kind of mixed-up feelings I had with her paled in comparison to this.

We roamed the night. I insisted on walking to keep things flowing, so to not fall back into some depressing narrative from Gail's tragic life. The blazing city seemed to hover over us as we walked along. We walked back towards the university. It was quite a hike, but we had a burst of energy to push us there. We passed a disco-blasting meat-market club. It reminded me how much I disliked those clubs. I hated dancing, but I did a little dance out on the sidewalk as we walked past. Lucy and Gail laughed.

Gail retreated to her room when we got back to the building. Lucy and I went to my room, and made a mess of the place. Against the wall. On the desk with papers and books flying around. On the sink with running water, splashing it on each other. On the chair. On the floor. On the bed in the window frame with her head peeking out the third-floor window facing the building across as I held her in by the hips. This time it was the rock station playing. Ramble On. Break on Through. Rocket Queen.

When we were finally finished, we held each other and cried awhile for some reason. We sat there a long while in the dark. We started to crash. She fell asleep first. I sat at the edge of the bed at 3 a.m. staring at her wondering if I was gaining her or losing her. How would she destroy my heart like the others? When would the bad creep in like it often did to steal the best things in life?

Change (In the House of Flies)

Lucy and I started enjoying more time out. My room was surrounded by neighbors now that the semester was fully underway. They were young. She was older. It didn't seem right to bring a lady around college stuff, even if she was fun and young at heart.

We went to her place, just so she could show me why we couldn't spend too much time there. It was an upstairs third floor apartment, above her grandmother's house. The room was nice, and she had a gorgeous white cat who walked all over my back as I stretched out on her bed. But her grandmother never left, and it felt awkward to have her down there.

If we weren't at each other's places, we were out drinking or walking around. We didn't talk about that night with Gail for a few days, but then it came up and we finally agreed we didn't want to do cocaine again or see Gail again.

"Honestly, when I think about it. I've had alcohol every single day for the past two months. My body is feeling it."

As we realized our crux of not being able to go somewhere quiet and sober together, she proposed something.

"Why don't we get a place together?"

"Like move in?"

"Yeah, you said you knew of that good apartment complex you lived in. We could get a two bedroom," she said.

"That would be great, but I'm not sure I make enough."

"I'll pay more since I work full-time. We can do the math later. Think about it."

☆

A few nights later, Lucy and I quietly snuck up to her bedroom. Lying there after quiet sex, she told me some strange thing about another guy and something about him wanting to have a different kind of sex with her, and something about what I thought she should say to him. I told her I didn't understand.

"How many guys are you seeing?" I asked.

"No, no, no, it's not like that. What do you think I am? He's a friend from work, and he mentioned it. I just wanted to see what you thought about that."

"What do you think I think about that?" I asked.

"About the guy or the other kind of sex?"

"I'm really not sure. Both, I guess," I said.

"I'm seeing only you now," she said.

"I guess you should say what you think is right. Do friends say that kind of thing to friends or do men who harass women at work say those things? Tell him you already have a guy to do that."

"I will. And we can do whatever you want to," she said.

I was weirded out and the conversation refreshed my internal feelings that something just wasn't right with this. How was I supposed to move in with a person I was so unsure about?

Prior to my birthday in October, Lucy had proposed we spend the weekend on the coast in a motel, maybe even the same one Mally and I had used. Lucy left three messages on my machine, and then she quit. The second message was when she realized I had checked out and she'd lost me. The third was a lecture to make me feel guilty, something about being more mature and talking things out.

I had taken a drive by myself in the opposite direction. I don't know why I ended it like that. It was a familiar urge. Another doomed relationship. Something had gone wrong. I'll be what I am.

You May Be Right

The highlight of my fall classes was Contemporary Literature with Professor Mariels, who would just sit and tell stories to address the assigned literature. Analogies and metaphors were a great way to get us thinking about the poems, stories, and novels. The professor explained how Sam in Richard Russo's *The Risk Pool* was representative of Uncle Sam. The character was really part of a bigger allegory for our nation. Sam was young and went through problems with his mother and father. Eventually, he worked things out and grew up, just like our country did. It was a fascinating way to look at literature, and I felt enlightened every day in his class.

But even as the course work started to increase, so did the partying. Robin would show up already sloshed. He sometimes brought his acoustic guitar, which always cheered everyone up. Just sitting there drinking was depressing to me. We had to be listening to or making music or at least talking about something deep, or the party just wasn't a party. I held a few parties in my tiny room. It was all about the music. I'd play Billy Joel's "You May Be Right" and lead a sing along of the track, flipping the lights off when he got to the part about turning out the lights. Everyone would cheer and go crazy.

On other days, Robin, Anthony, and I would sit for hours smoking pot and listening to the weirdest music we could find. They introduced me to some new stuff. Robin liked all kinds of mellow stuff. He put in some newer Johnny Cash. I'd never heard such music. The songs were brilliant covers of popular songs by Neil Diamond, U2, Tom Petty, and others. Deep and sad songs, yet they made us feel better about our own lives. We actually laughed our heads off. It was cathartic.

Both Robin and Anthony had acoustic guitars and so we spent hours playing and singing. Anthony brought over a bunch of old Native American drums and beat away on them. We were like a band in progress. We even named ourselves Psybor.

When the whole gang was back together for parties, we'd have wild sing-alongs. I plugged my microphone into my stereo speakers and blasted it at full volume to our own garage rendition of "Knockin' on Heaven's Door." I don't think anyone will ever beat our record— highest decibels reached in the building. We were told later that day that our performance was heard down in the lobby of the building. All the way from the third floor!

Jill was my happy and witty neighbor. She was mysterious and didn't feel the need to party. She'd have a sip of a drink here and there, but nothing major. Being from Utah, this scene must have looked wild to her. Still, she was non-judgmental. In a way, she kind of looked out for all of us. One night Leslie had had too much to drink, and Jill was sure to walk her back to her room and get her safely set in bed. Not that anyone had to worry about any of us. We were an eclectic group of odd people, but we were decent.

Sea Above, Sky Below

Alana seemed a little put off by the younger group and the changing vibe. She grew distant. Anthony and I saw less of her.

When I asked her one day what was up, she said she was turned off by the group dynamic. She wanted to do her own thing.

"Hey, I totally get it. I'm also having trouble focusing on what I want to do. What I'm here to do. It's the story of my life."

"Yeah, I'm looking for apartments," she said.

"Really, already? It feels like you just got here."

"I'm just looking. But when I find the right situation, maybe some roommates, I'm going to jump ship. I'll still visit you though."

"Good to hear this!"

She asked me to go to a concert and I agreed to go. I was open to explore Alana's artsy indie music. She knew I liked rock, the commercial stuff as she called it. She didn't like anything "commercial" which meant they couldn't be too successful. I argued they're still commercial if they're selling tickets, but then she changed it to "corporate mainstream."

In late October, we went to the Crystal Ballroom in Portland to see a three-piece band called The Dirty Three from Australia. The music was all instrumental with a violinist, guitar player, and drummer. They hypnotized me, and I came out of there feeling like I travelled the world.

"That was nice. Really different. Thank you, Alana."

"I wouldn't steer you wrong. But what happened with Lucy? I liked her."

"Yeah, things got weird. I don't know," I said.

"Well, at least you had some fun."

☆

For Halloween, we all had different events to go to, but Leslie and I didn't have plans, so we ended up hanging together. Leslie was the cheerful social one. She talked to everyone. She had piercing blue eyes, dark black hair, and a wide-stretching smile that lit up the room. She was also a fellow English major, the only other one out of the group. She had a knack for writing. We exchanged bits we wrote and talked about literature. We agreed to take British Romantic Poetry Part I in the winter term together.

We grabbed our pumpkins and sat down in her room with a knife and newspapers to put underneath. We cut the tops off.

"So what you want to do is close your eyes. Reach into the pumpkin and pull everything out that way," she said.

"Blind?"

"Yes, feel it."

I reached in to pull out the slimy insides of the pumpkin.

"Ooh, that feels weird. Oddly nice," I said.

"Sensual, eh?"

I opened my eyes, and we laughed. After carving them, we put candles in the pumpkins and lit them. We placed them together on her windowsill and took a picture.

"You can keep mine here. My gift to you," I said.

"Ah, thanks. They do look inseparable."

☆

In early November, Anthony, Robin, and I went to see a former teen actor who now had a rock band. He was one of those heartthrobs who starred in mostly low budget flicks. Now, years after being on the "Where are they now" list and surviving a drug addiction, he had his own band and traveled around in a van from city to city to play in bars and small clubs. I reached my hand up onto the stage and he gladly shook it. I enjoyed a few of his movies as a kid, and his music wasn't bad, but he had come out in a clown suit and changed his outfit a few times throughout the show. On one song he sang through a four-foot-long cone. Absurdity.

The club was filled with women my age who never let go of their childhood crush. They were way into the guy on stage to even notice us. There was this one girl who clutched a sweater to her chest the whole show, just staring up at the guy. I couldn't believe it. I could've loved this girl. Anyone in this club could've loved her, but all she wanted was this actor, a broken man living off his past fame who probably would've used her anyway. I was a nothing man to someone like her.

On the walk home, I got upset. I felt like no one else in our group was taking music as serious as they should.

"If that goofy guy could go out and get gigs and play music, so could we. We have talent. We have to get out there in the real world and share our message," I screamed in a drunken rage.

"What message?" asked Robin.

The guys just laughed at me. They thought I was joking.

☆

Just two days after we saw the clown, Bonnie and Marion came over to ask if Anthony and I wanted to go to Pearl Jam with them.

"Absolutely! How much?" I asked.

"Don't worry about it," Bonnie said.

"No, come on. We'll give you something," I offered.

"Just buy the drinks," she said.

"You got it," snapped Anthony.

"Let's do this," said Marion.

The show was legendary. Nearly three hours. Nearly thirty songs. Mike McCready and his crazy long guitar solos. There we were in the middle towards the front all mixed into the crowd cheering and singing along. It was the time of our lives.

The show closed with a cover of the Neil Young song "Fuckin' Up" which reminded me of my recent mistakes. It made me feel better. Right from the first line about a traveler on the road, I knew this was totally my song!

I loved these people. Anthony was like a long-lost best friend. I always called Marion the Scandinavian princess because she looked like she was from somewhere up there. Her height was no match for little me, so I never looked at her any other way, but she was stunning. Bonnie was equally amazing, but she looked southern European, Spanish or Italian. While she was a compatible size, I felt all of us had been up the mountain together. That was something that shouldn't be ruined with other emotions. Anthony and I never talked about it, but I sensed he felt the same way about these two brilliant ladies. It was a relief to be friends without complications or expectations. Maybe they felt the same.

And despite my love for these people, I was always a step away from throwing it all away.

Grey

The whole group of us went out to dinner together before the holiday break. Only Alana was absent. She had already left to visit her father in Colorado, and she wouldn't have been up for such a crowd anyway. We went to a fine restaurant and treated ourselves. With the meal, we ordered some bottles of red and white wine. We kept it classy. The waiter took a picture of us at the table. We never looked better.

Then everyone went their own way.

Even though there wasn't much family left in New York, I decided to go back just for three nights. I found a cheap flight and wanted to see how it would feel to spend time in the city.

My aunt and I never really sparked up a relationship, so I wasn't going out to Long Island to visit her. She was distant, into her own thing. My uncle, on the other hand, had kept in touch with me with occasional letters, but then he turned on me.

In his previous letter, he got political and bashed on Al Gore who had just been through a controversial election that resulted in a recount in the state where his opponent's brother was governor. There had been shady activities in the state's electoral process and a recount was ordered by the courts, but the Bush team convinced the Supreme Court to stop the recount, which awarded Bush the White House. It was a devastating blow to democracy. I didn't share any of my feelings with my uncle. He chose to open this up.

My uncle Al hated the other Al, and he let me know loudly. I couldn't understand. The Al I was related to and the Al I was voting for had more in common. They were kind and helpful. They were respectful. They both seemed calm and gentle. But then I remembered his blow up on my grandmother before she passed. I remembered the unbelievable stories my father told me about his brother jumping out to fight kids in their town. I remembered callous stories Al himself told me over breakfast about people he'd pull over. I missed another side to him, but there it was staring at me now on the pages of a letter. An onslaught of aggression.

When he wrote to me with the attacks on my candidate, I wrote him back nicely telling him that I didn't want to get into this kind of thing with him. Al answered back with a series of personal attacks: "Don't you realize anything? Aren't you in college? Do you think you're too smart now? Do you hear yourself? Do you remember what I did for you?" He somehow expected me to pledge eternal allegiance to him now. This was heartbreaking, and so I wasn't going to Long Island this time. There didn't seem like anything left there for me.

I arrived at JFK and took a train to Manhattan. I took the elevator up to my upper floor room with an overwhelming view of the city. I waved at the Empire State Building. I ate my take-out dinner from the windowsill looking out at all the life down below.

On my second day, I went to the Museum of Natural History. It was as I remembered it when my Aunt Gloria took us in the '80s. The giant whale fossil hovered over my head. The dinosaur fossils were the most spectacular. The past preserved forever.

On my third day, I walked all the way downtown to the World Trade Center. I don't know why I was drawn to the buildings, but I was. I just wanted to look at them. I had been in them when I was young. Don took us, and we went all the way to the roof. It was the best view of the city. I stopped at the buildings and looked up barely able to see the top from the sidewalk. The Twin Towers stared down at me with their beautiful steel and glass architecture. I spent a minute or two, and then walked off to a bakery I knew of, so I could enjoy some Italian pastries and a coffee. Then I walked back up to midtown where my hotel was.

My fourth and final day was Christmas day. It was another quiet and lonely Christmas. I ate breakfast and lunch at the hotel. Then it was time to head to the airport for a Christmas flight home. I got a deal because hardly anyone flew on the actual holiday. Most people waited until the next day to leave.

There didn't seem to be much of a point to go home to New York for the holidays this year, but it was better than staying at the building on campus all alone again. Going back to New York made me feel like I had somewhere to go. Some kind of hometown. Some kind of satisfaction settled in me to be back there in the place, both a tribute and goodbye. Now I was eager to get home to my new life under grey skies.

Black Eyed Dog

The winter quarter started. In British Romantic Literature Part I, Professor Mariels used his same manner of storytelling to help us appreciate and understand the literature of Wordsworth, Coleridge, and his favorite William Blake. Leslie took the class with me this time. We'd get together to study and read poetry out loud. She raved about Wordsworth, and I obsessed over Blake. We ended up jointly reading out loud the entire "Rime of the Ancient Mariner" poem by Coleridge at least three times.

My other English class was Literary Criticism. At first, I liked the professor. He dressed in black jeans and a leather jacket and had gone to school on the east coast. I tried to spark up conversation with him about New York, but he was difficult to talk to. Instead of sharing wisdom like Professor Kohl or Donovan or telling great allegories like Dr. Mariels, this new professor would ask bizarre questions and stand there staring out into silence. The one or two kids he'd spark up conversation with would eventually chime in, and suddenly we were all invisible witnesses. The selected article readings were nothing but scholars making assumptions about authors and concocting wild theories about the stories and poems of others. One day, the professor clumsily stepped his foot backwards right into the trash can.

I was reminded of a poem about education from Donovan's class by the great Walt Whitman—

…Till rising and gliding out I wander'd off by myself,
In the mystical moist night-air, and from time to time,
Look'd up in perfect silence at the stars.

On the weekends, things got blurry. When I'd hang with Robin, we'd smoke his pipe until we were ripped. He always played mellow music. One day, he put on something I'd never heard.

"Who is this?"

"This guy only made three albums. He died young. Poor guy swallowed a bottle of pills."

I looked at the CD he handed me. It read Nick Drake.

"Listen, you have to hear this next one."

"Black eyed dog" came on and I was entranced. The poetic lyrics made us both giggle with delight. I couldn't believe how good it was. Robin gently sang the first verse along with Nick and then broke out with a big laugh. It was greatness. It was one of those ah-ha moments I wish I could repeat over and over.

☆

Alana and Anthony were still drinking more than I could handle. With pot, I felt like I could moderate how much I did, but with the kind of drinking they did, I felt silly. I was out of my league. I couldn't handle their consumption, yet I was still drinking more than I wanted to.

One afternoon, I tried to get out with Anthony and just take a walk. He was excited about the idea of exploring the West Hills, which looked down on our building from the other side, where my old room was. We took a walk up into the hills and came out into a neighborhood of upper-class homes. It was hard to see all this from where we were at the bottom of the valley. This was another world. These people had paid their dues. They were successful. They were ahead of us and above us. How would we ever catch up?

When Anthony and I got back, he cracked open a beer and offered me one. I gave in and took one. He didn't know the confusion and unhappiness growing in my mind. He just wanted to be a good, welcoming friend.

"Have a seat. I've been wanting to show you this," he said.

He pointed to a big brown trunk, and we each took a seat.

He opened the old trunk and pulled out a Nez Perce headdress with feathers and all. He put it on and smiled.

"What the… This is amazing."

"Thanks, brother," he said.

"This is a box of history, right here in your room."

He pulled out more clothing all made from animal skins that had intricate beading attached. He pulled something else out of the box and plucked a long black feather out of a little horn and handed it to me.

"Keep this. It's good luck," he said

"Man, I'm honored. I'll never let it go."

We shook hands. A while later, I went and put the feather in a safe place hidden away in my room. I would need it.

Something Vague

On a Tuesday in the last week of February, Alana and I got together to go see a show that evening in Seattle. We went to our morning classes, and then we got in the car and drove up in my Toyota.

"Thanks for coming to the show. I think you'll like them."

"Hey, it's just good to see you. I don't see you so much these days," I said.

"I know. If I'm not getting shitfaced, I'm off exploring."

"Understood. I've been wanting to scale back. Turn inward."

"Hey, if I find a house rental and there's an extra room, would you consider it?" she asked.

"Maybe," I replied.

"I'll let you know. Staying in that place is tough on the soul."

We laughed and then set out for the venue. It was a dark, small intimate place that reminded me of a school gym.

It was a small indie band. She said the lead singer was prophetic, but I didn't see it. I wasn't impressed, but then he played one brilliant song where he mentioned a coffin as an apartment. The song had poetic lyrics and an explosive end that tapped my soul and captured what I was feeling. All you need is one song to make it onto the soundtrack of life. I was ultimately glad we went.

☆

The next morning, I was back in my room waiting to go to my other favorite class, History of Rock 'N Roll. I was sitting at my desk when the coffee cup in front of me started to rattle. The whole room was shaking. I stood and made my way to the door. It felt like I was in a shoe box and someone was shaking it. A few books on my shelf fell off to the floor. The slap of the landing books made me jump. Just as I got to the doorframe, the shaking stopped.

Alana popped out of her room. "Did you feel that?"

Jill came out of her room. "What in the world?"

A guy all the way down the hall peaked his head out his door and waved. Then Scott came walking down the hall with an exaggerated bounce in his step.

"I almost bounced off the wall for real just now," he said.

"Whoa. A real one. That was a first for me," I said.

"Same here," Alana said.

"I've felt some and that was a decent one," Scott said.

"I think we better get out of this old building in case there's an aftershock," Jill said.

"Good idea," I said.

I quickly gathered up some things and just as I was heading out, Sidi came around announcing an evacuation.

"We need to leave for a while. They need to inspect the building," he shouted.

"I hope so. The building's like a hundred years old," Alana said as she walked out with an unlit cigarette in her hand.

We all hung around out front for a while. Thankfully, it was a rare clear day and not so cold. I walked around for a while and skipped class. I was too shook up to sit in class.

In the days that followed, I had this sudden anxiety that the building was going to have some kind of structural failure. I envisioned it collapsing with us inside, crushed under the weight of one hundred years.

Spies

After a week, I felt a little better about the building, but something was different with all of us after the earthquake. Anxiety started to bubble from within me. One night, I felt a small lump in my throat. It felt like something was going to choke me out. I decided it would be best to close my eyes and sleep it off.

But then my sleep started to suffer. I started hearing things from the room upstairs late into the night. I'd put my ear to the walls on each side to prove it wasn't Alana or Jill. As embarrassing as it was, I asked them if they were hearing anything. They both thought I was fooling around with them.

Like clockwork, I would hear the noises— a shaking, the pounding of desk metal, slapping of skin, bouncing mattress coils, moaning and crying. A girl lived up there, but I didn't know her. It surely just had to be her and a lover. Simple explanation.

But when I went up to confirm the all-night-fest, all was quiet when I listened outside her door. When I went back down to my room, the noises would start up again. When I finally knocked on her door in the morning, she opened the door, but there wasn't anyone else in her room. She looked at me like I was crazy when I told her I was hearing a lot of noises coming from her room.

Night after night, I was kept up by the sounds. I couldn't fall asleep. I was forced to drink coffee and smoke and play my music. I found a couple of UK artists, Travis and Coldplay, and I played their CDs nonstop. But even the music couldn't block out these wild noises. I became nocturnal. I'd stay up all night, go to class in the morning, and then sleep the rest of the day while everyone was out and about. I started up another two overnight shifts at the lab. On my nights off, I'd leave my door wide open with the hopes that someone would come by and hear it, and save me from the madness, but no one was around. They were all sleeping. And Anthony was laying low for a while with a girl off campus, otherwise he surely would've seen me in there suffering from across the hall. When I couldn't stand the night tremors, I'd go for walks in the city. I'd grab coffee at 7-Eleven and stroll around like a wanderer.

One night, I'd had it. I didn't want to run from the noise anymore. I bought a bottle of White Zinfandel at Plaid Pantry and went up to my room to face the demons. I would flush them out. I downed the bottle. The song "God of Wine" came on by Third Eye Blind. I lit a cigarette and challenged the sounds to come get me. When the song echoed to a conclusion, I snuffed out my smoke and slid into bed to stare at the ceiling in the dark. I fell asleep before the sounds could get me. I knew I couldn't possibly drink a bottle of wine every night to keep them away.

As the winter quarter came to a close at the end of March, the sounds stopped. The first night it didn't happen without any wine shocked me. I was used to this madness now. Where had it gone? I put my head out the window and looked up to find a bunch of pigeons making noises on the ledge above. They spotted me and flew away. I felt like I was cracking up or being haunted by some karmic ghost for something I'd done. I needed that good luck feather to start working.

Little Room

Alana had another set of tickets to a concert. We once again made the drive up to Seattle, but we left earlier this time. We had the week off, so we spent time exploring the city. It was a typical rainy day in Seattle. This city had that similar Pacific Northwest feel that Portland had, but Seattle was much bigger and busier. It had grungy spots. It had classy big money spots. It had touristy spots. It had trendy and artsy spots. We worked our way around.

We were surprised to see buildings with damage. At 6.8, it had been a decent quake. Some buildings had cracks. Some had warning signs. Some elevators were still out of order.

We wandered the market, toured the museum of art, browsed a private bookstore, and then went to a café for dinner.

"They freak me out," she said motioning to a dwarf.

"Why?"

"Little people. I don't know why."

"At least you're being honest about your fears," I said.

She laughed big. Then I told her about my hearing of noises.

"At least you're not losing your mind with pigeons," I said

"I told you we need to get out of that building!" she said.

We finished up our dinner and then headed over to the show at the famous Paramount Theater. The performer was Nick Cave. He was normally with a band, but he was doing a rare solo show. He sat at a piano and played his hits. He had black hair and a wildly deep voice. "The Mercy Seat" really grabbed me.

"Wow," I turned and said to Alana after the song, "Damn."

"Look at all these sad bastards here tonight," said Alana.

I looked around at the pink-haired kids and artsy adults.

"And we're two of them now," she said.

"Thanks, Alana. No, really. I really needed to get out of the demon den for a while. This was well needed."

When we returned to Portland, Alana lent me a few Nick Cave CDs. I was eager to listen to them, but when I did, I didn't get the same feeling. The songs with the full band didn't do it for me the way him sitting at a piano had. I gave the CDs back to Alana.

"What else do you have? Anything new?"

"Hold on." She went back and returned with a CD.

"This album isn't even out yet, but I have an advanced copy. 'Little Room' will remind you of our room problems."

The side of the disc read The White Stripes.

"Is it only the two of them in the band?"

"Wait until you hear them though!"

☆

A girl came by looking for someone one night while a bunch of us were drinking in the hall, and she approached me.

"Have you seen Regina?"

"No, sorry, who's that?"

"The first door on the right," she said.

"Oh, the..."

"Yes, the lesbian. That's my girlfriend."

"Yeah, sorry. I haven't. Anyone else?"

Everyone said no and continued with what they were doing.

"Damn, maybe she's still at work. I think I'm actually a couple of hours early. I mixed up my days," the girl said.

"You can hang here if you want," I said.

"Do you want a beer?" asked Anthony.

"Okay. I'm Mindy," she waved and then sat down.

I fetched Mindy a drink from the cooler. Her and I got into talking for a while. She stopped drinking after two bottles and then asked if I could show her the bathroom. I walked her down the hall.

"Have you ever seen the women's room?" she asked.

"No, why would I?" I asked.

"Just wondering how much nicer it is."

Mindy had a point. She opened the door, and I looked inside.

"Damn, a bathtub. I want to take a bath," I said.

"I'll take one," she said as I walked in to inspect it.

"Oh, really," I said awkwardly and realized I was in the girl's bathroom with my neighbor's lesbian partner talking about taking a bath. I instantly thought of Ginny and her psycho bath rituals.

"No, I'm kidding, but there's a towel. Feel free," I said.

"I'm going to. Stay and talk a bit."

Mindy turned the faucet and started to fill the tub. There was bubble bath on the stand, and she added it to the water. I stood there awkwardly waiting to figure out where this was going.

Mindy started undressing. She had a thick figure. Out came her giant breasts. Each nipple had an earring through it. Then she slipped off her pants. Another ring was down below. She was sure to point it out to me. She flashed another earring through her tongue. She had pale skin with some red blotches from the warm water. No tattoos though. She had short blonde-red hair with a hint of pink dye. She got into the tub and covered herself with bubbles.

"Why don't you get in now?"

"Oh, I don't know. What about Regina?"

"She doesn't care."

"But I thought you were…"

"I like men too. It's been a while though. Come on."

An hour later, Mindy was dressing back at my room. The music was still playing loud on my stereo, but it hadn't mattered because the crowd had moved on to another floor. She said goodbye and went three doors down to see if Regina was back yet.

With my door cracked, I could hear them.

"Why is your hair wet?"

I couldn't hear Mindy's answer.

"You what?" cried Regina.

I closed my door and locked it. Some yelling went on for a little while and then fell from range. They must have made up.

Spring, 2001

One of my four spring semester classes stood out. In British Romantic Literature Part II with Professor Mariels, we studied the quests and rebellion of the next generation of poets— Lord Byron, Percy Shelley, and John Keats. The professor's excitement for these authors was contagious. Shelley wanted to change the world. Byron wanted to have fun. Keats wanted to experience beauty. Everything us young people wanted. Leslie and I sat there in class floored by Professor Mariels' analogies of wisdom—

"Magic is in the moment— that moment is like a hot fudge sundae that inevitably melts into slush on the sidewalk."

The room was silent as we pondered such a simple reality.

These poets lived fast and died young. They wrote of darkness, truth, and beauty. There was sorrow in their work, yet there was hope. We could learn from their tragic existence. We could be better and happier. We could try.

☆

One night, Jill told me to fill her cup. This wasn't like her. She ended up getting sick in front of everybody, right in my sink of dirty dishes. She stood, ran to the sink, and vomited chunks, while I stood over her blocking her from of our neighbors. A few days later, she got very drunk again and could barely walk. I carried her to her to bed next door and tucked her in. Leslie checked on her a few hours later.

Leslie also seemed troubled. Robin was ripped. Scott was hiding out. Michael was getting destroyed on hard liquor and passing out on people's floors. Then Anthony's off campus girlfriend dumped him. Even though I was no longer hearing noises, I was still tense. I suspected we were all going through something and wondered if the earthquake had triggered some kind of avalanche of bad luck for the rest of the year.

☆

In mid-April, Alana suggested we take a ride and get breakfast out somewhere in the countryside. We took a pleasant one-hour ride from the city. Over breakfast, Alana confided in me.

"Jake is a man-pig."

"You mean a snake? Jake the snake. The guy on the second floor from Nebraska? What do you mean?"

"He's a man-pig. He hit on me."

"You know he is a man. That's what a lot of them do."

"Yes, but most of them don't do it butt-naked."

"No way, what happened? I mean, are you alright?"

I spotted a dwarf across the room. He was hopping off a stool at the counter. I didn't mention it to Alana.

"We were down in the television lounge, you know, the one in the basement. We had a few beers. This was four nights ago. He took off all his clothes and sat down next to me. He asked me to..."

"What? He got naked and asked you to..."

I shut my mouth upon realizing how loud I was and how half the restaurant seemed to be staring over at our table.

"Totally naked?" I whispered.

"Yes, absolutely naked."

"What did you do?"

"I laughed."

"You laughed?"

"I laughed and I laughed right in his redneck face," she said.

I laughed at this.

"And then what?" I asked.

"He begged for a blow job."

"What? Are you joking?"

"No, I'm dead serious. He begged."

"So what did you do?"

"I laughed in his face again, but he grabbed my arm. Then I whacked him with my elbow right in the jaw. He held on. He's a strong son of a bitch. Then I planted a boot right in his chest. He grabbed my leg, and thankfully Michael walked in on it. Jake let go right away, and I walked out on him. Michael followed me and wanted to know. I told him not to tell anyone."

"God, I don't know what to say. This could've been worse."

"You know what this means now, don't you? I have to move out of here like tomorrow."

"I know you've been looking, but how are you going to do it this quickly?" I asked.

"I'm not happy with the shitty room anyway. I need more space. Now it's a matter of safety," she said.

"Why don't you report this?"

"I probably will. They should know a predator is in the building with all those young girls."

"Yes, I think so. But again, where are you going to go?"

"I found something already. Remember Gail?" she asked.

"Oh god, Alana, are you sure you want to do that?"

"I know. I know, but she won't be around too much. We found a good two bedroom at that place you used to live."

Alana and I watched the dwarf pass by our table, and we looked at each other and smiled.

"You're making progress. Need some help moving?"

"Thanks, I'd love the help," she said.

Two days later, I was helping Alana move out. We packed my car twice and the job was done. I helped her get set up, but then wanted to get going in case Gail came by. I told Alana to be careful and call me if she needed anything.

Late that night, I heard a ruckus outside my door. I crept up to the peephole and saw Anthony with one leg raised in the air humping his door. I opened my door, and he laughed wildly at me.

"Jack, Long Island man. What's up? You wanna party?"

He was laughing loudly. This was the drunkest I'd ever seen him. He had reached his limit.

"No man, it's late for me. I was just getting ready to..."

"Oh, come on," he said laughing. "Look at these babes," he said pointing to pinups of swimsuit models on his door, to which he was thrusting against.

I had no idea why the posters were hanging on his door.

"Yes, they look good, but..."

"Come on, man. Have a beer with me."

"I don't know. I was getting into bed. I have some studies."

Jill stepped out of her room in her pajamas.

"What's going on, guys?" she asked.

"Sorry, Jill. I know it's late. Anthony was getting home."

"Are you alright?" she asked him.

"Yeah, hey Jill, you wanna party too?"

"No, I was in bed, Anthony."

"Even better!" he said laughing.

She just looked at him and he stopped.

"Sorry. That was stupid. I didn't mean to wake you all up."

"It looks like you're already all partied out tonight anyway. Where were you?" she asked.

"A family reunion," he replied laughing again.

"Are you upset over the breakup?" she asked.

"No, no, I'll get over it."

"Plenty of fish in the sea, right?" she said.

"Yeah, that's her loss, Anthony," I said.

"All right, go get some sleep," she said.

"All right, both of you too. Sleep well," he said.

Jill and I smiled at each other, and we closed our doors. I watched Anthony through my peephole as he fumbled with his keys, turned on the light, and closed his door for the night.

☆

Two weeks later, Alana called me late one night.

"I need to get out of here."

"Why, what's going on?"

"This girl is nuts."

"I tried to tell you."

"Yeah, but she's a graduate student," said Alana.

"Doesn't matter at all," I said.

"I guess not. She's just disgusting."

"Why? What's she doing?"

"She's a slob, and she occasionally binges and gets sloshed, but the thing that pushed me over the edge were the hairs in the bathtub. She left a mess of pubic hair in there."

"How do you know it was..."

"Come on, it was absolutely the hair from her coochie."

"Nothing wrong with a little landscaping," I said.

Alana laughed hard.

"But not in the bathtub that I have to shower in!"

"So what's the plan?"

"I found a house rental with some folks in southeast. I'm going over to meet them tomorrow."

"All right. Let me know what happens."

The following evening, Alana called to tell me it was a go. I went by the next day while Gail was out. We cleaned out Alana's belongings in two trips again. I helped move her in and briefly met her new roommates.

"By the way, here's the White Stripes CD back. I really love this album. But you're going to hate them in like a year when they're huge."

She laughed.

I wished her well in her new room in the house.

☆

A week later, Alana came by to visit. Her head was shaved.

"What the..." I said.

"I'm ready for anything now."

Now she really looked like someone I wouldn't mess with.

Alana had filed a report on Jake, and while I had recently seen him around and worried of his retaliation toward her, she felt safe with me and Anthony. And with her new look, she felt empowered. I didn't think he'd be around for much longer anyway.

The three of us ran into Regina down the hall. She invited us over for a drink. She had a whole cooler of wine coolers on her bed. Although they would have preferred beer, wine, or hard liquor, they took the invitation to alcohol without hesitation. We went into the room and realized she had one of the bigger rooms, like Marion and Anthony. I didn't mention Mindy, but I wondered if they were still together. Alana read my mind.

"You still with the girl with the pink in her hair?" she asked.

"No, Mindy got knocked up."

I coughed on my wine cooler.

"Oh, sorry," said Alana with a big smile.

As the anxiety grew in me, Alana and Anthony got into the drinks.

"Remember, guys, we have that thing at eight," I said.

"What..." Anthony started to ask.

"Yeah, the movie. We'll have plenty of time," Alana piped in.

I got up to look at Regina's music collection.

"Oh, David Bowie's great," I said.

"He's a legend. A bi-sexual too," Regina said with a wink.

I continued looking through the collection as Alana and Anthony sat and drank half the damned cooler. Everything was good times until they started to bicker. This was no ordinary argument. A bicker turned into a fierce shouting match, which quickly escalated into a shoving match. Alana was a big girl with a big mouth. She stepped right up to Anthony and shoved him. He shouted back. They wrestled about as empty bottles smashed and rolled across the small apartment. It was a bar room brawl, and I wasn't going to get into the middle. It happened too quickly. Before we knew it, Alana had lost her balance and fell straight back into Regina's frog tank. The glass tank crashed to the floor and broke into pieces. Regina started to scream at my two unrecognizable warrior friends.

"Stop guys! My Betsy! Where is she? Do you see her, Jack?"

"Who?"

"Betsy, my frog."

I got down on my hands and knees to look for her pet frog. Alana was now on her feet and Anthony withdrew to the doorway. They both started to laugh at the scene. They wailed and wailed.

"I found her. She's safe," I said.

Betsy was safely inside a little porcelain house. Regina cried with joy. Anthony and Alana apologized and walked out of the room. They tried to hold back the loud heckles of laughter.

"My friends will pay for a new tank. I'll make sure."

"Okay, thanks. And Jack, don't worry, no one's pregnant."

She knew the whole time.

☆

On the Sunday before final exams, a bunch of us went on a fieldtrip. Leslie, Jill, and Scott jumped into my car. Robin, Bonnie, and Marion jumped in with Anthony. We drove up and over to the zoo, which was only five minutes from where we lived. When we got there, a cloud of smoke poured out of Anthony's car.

"Ah, come on, guys. You can't even go to the zoo without getting baked?" I asked.

"It's like right out of *Dazed and Confused!*" said Scott.

We all laughed at the movie reference and then walked in for an afternoon with the animals.

"You should see the Bronx Zoo. It's a fantastic zoo. But damn, this is just as nice. Look at those pandas!" I pointed.

Later, in front of the zebra habitat, Leslie leaned in and told Scott and I the news. She was dropping out of school for a while and moving back home to the countryside of her hometown in

Bend, Oregon. Two zebras faced away from each other with their asses pointing at each other. A tree stood in the middle.

"The city life just isn't for me. I'm going to miss you guys, especially you two, but I just need to go home."

"You know, I've been there. It's a beautiful place," I said.

"I'll be back to visit all you beautiful people."

"You better," said Scott.

"We're losing the little bit of sunshine we have," I told her.

We all hugged. We knew things were changing. Sometimes we just can't leave ourselves behind, and when we try to, we end up going back.

☆

On the day of my last final, I ran into Robin in the hall.

"Hey, I'm heading out for a couple of weeks," I said.

"Where you headed?"

"I'm going to LA for a couple of weeks. I have a couple of buddies from New York I haven't seen in a while."

"That's cool. I'm hanging here for the whole summer. Maybe a trip up to Seattle next month. Let me know when you're back."

"Nice. Will do, Robin. I'll see you in a couple of weeks."

"Safe travels," he said.

It had been a while since I'd been on the big highway, but the time was finally right.

My Song

Upon taking the last of my final exams, I relaxed for a few hours and decided to leave on my trip in the late afternoon. I jumped on Interstate 5. The buzz of the road was a shock at first after months of more relaxed city driving. But I found my groove, turned on some tunes, and headed south through the vivid Oregon landscape. By the time I reached Salem an hour and a half later, the early June sun had begun to descend. According to the radio, the forecast ahead was clear.

Three more hours rolled by, and the sun was gone. The fluorescent yellow lines in the middle of the road began to blur my eyes, and I needed a rest. I was hungry, but it was far too early in the voyage to be rewarding myself with a sit-down Denny's stop. I exited and pulled into the nearest gas station. I thought of a packaged dinner from the station food mart, maybe a donut or something, but then I spotted a burger joint next door. I pumped $12.75 and maxed out the tank. Then I drove next door to the drive-thru and ordered a value meal. The counter girl was the friendliest fast-food worker alive. I couldn't understand it.

Within fifteen minutes, I had munched down the food and jumped back onto the road. I popped in a Ray Charles Greatest Hits CD, and I felt something odd during the song "Lonely Avenue." The next song never came on because I jammed it off after feeling a giant lump in my throat. I gulped my Mountain Dew until it was Mountain done, and I smoked cigarette after cigarette hoping to smoke away the fear. I even considered turning around for home but knew it was too late.

I started to gag. Panic overcame me as I began to search for an emergency exit. I pulled off into a rest area and proceeded to vomit into my hands. All that came up was the liquid of the Mountain Dew. It was as if all the food I had just eaten was lodged in my throat. The lump persisted, and my fear grew. I looked around. The rest area was dark, and this frightened me. What if I was attacked by some beastly man that had had enough of trucking the interstate and decided to give up his life of delivering goods for a life of roadside murders? What if I died in my car, all alone in the dark, hundreds of miles from home? The sheriffs wouldn't notice me until morning if I was lucky, but by then I would have already turned grey. The temperature seemed to drastically drop. Now shaking from the cold, I fought the wrenching gag in my throat. I was uncertain of what would happen to me in the wild loneliness of the interstate highway.

Pulling out of the exit, I zoomed back onto the freeway, once more hoping the devious obstruction would melt from my throat or that I would at least find a place of safety. Speeding along in the right lane, I noticed the green road signs said there would be a gas station at the next exit. I roared off the ramp and quickly found the station. I pulled into the lot, abandoned my car, and ran into the food mart. A scruffy kid waited behind the counter.

"Can I help ya?" he asked with an odd accent.

"Yes," grasping my throat.

"I think I'm choking on something. Do you think I could grab a cup of water?"

"Sure, right over there by the coffee machines."

I poured myself a cup of cold water and gulped it down. Nothing. I poured another cup and drank it down. Still nothing. Then I poured a cup of hot coffee, figuring that if the cold drink wouldn't help, perhaps the hot one would. I handed the clerk a dollar for the coffee.

"Are ya alright?" he asked reading my desperation.

"Yeah, I think so. I think it's a piece of food from a sandwich I ate. Do you know how to get to the hospital?"

"I don't know where it is. Do ya want me to call 911?"

"No, that won't do anything. Thanks anyway."

I departed the mart and sat back down in my car, slowly sipping the hot coffee. Suddenly the gag began to tug hard at my throat. Spilling some of the coffee, I placed it on the dashboard and got out of the car. Finding the restroom on the side of the mart building, I went in, closed the door, and looked down at a very unsanitary toilet bowl. I found myself at the base of this filth, with my finger in my mouth, and bile all over my shirt.

Up came the little bit of coffee I had drank, then the two cups of water, and then the rest of the Mountain Dew. Liquid seemed to shoot out from my face. I sat there for a while praying in panic. In horror, I thought of the shaggy-haired gas station clerk finding me hours later, dead on the floor of his unsanitary urinating grounds. What a sad death this would be. I chose to fight on, at least enough to stand and head out to find a hospital.

Exiting the restroom, I noticed a car parked at the gas pumps with sirens atop it. I walked over and discovered a female security officer sitting in the driver's seat. I waved for her attention, and she rolled down her window.

"What can I do for you?"

"Do you know how to get to the local hospital?"

"Sure, it's actually the next exit. Go right, heading east. Go down that long road for about two miles and it's on the left-hand side. You won't miss it, there are signs all along the way."

"Thank you, officer."

Back in the car, I realized she hadn't even asked if I was alright. Surely, I looked like a panicked and sickly man, at the least some kind of traveling junkie going through withdrawal. Maybe she didn't want to get caught up in that kind of thing. It didn't matter. She had given me direction. Speeding back out onto I-5, I traveled to the next exit, numbers and names totally escaping me.

The gagging was now to a controlled minimum. Turning right, I headed east down a long winding road for about two miles until I came to the hospital sign. Missing the first entrance, I entered through the second driveway, which brought me around to what appeared to be the back of the hospital. The sign stated that it was the emergency room entrance. My arrival seemed perfect.

Barging up to the doors, I discovered they were locked. All was quiet at this ER. I looked around. There were no cars in the parking lot, and the hospital was dark, unlike the busy ones in big cities. I ran back to my car, and I wondered how hospital doors could be closed to the public. Had this town been taken over by aliens?

Driving back around to the front entrance, I saw there were several cars parked in the lot. I felt a new hope. I reached the front doors and once again they were locked. How could this be?

"Hello!" a female voice echoed through an intercom. "What can I do for you?"

Peering through the front windows, I located the source of the voice. In a setback office, she sat at a counter.

"Hi, this is going to sound really stupid, but I'm traveling on the road, and I got this lump in my throat."

The doors automatically opened to the sides. I stared straight ahead at the female.

"Come on in," she welcomed.

As I approached her, I began to fill with uncanny emotion. She looked familiar, yet intriguingly different. She seemed like a compilation of all the women I ever loved. One by one, all my past loves began to emerge within this mysterious front desk clerk. Women from my family even showed up in the mix. From this mosaic of features, she became her own entity. Moving closer to her, I noticed her sandy blonde hair, which was much like that of the very first girl I had had a crush on in second grade. She had on a tight baby blue shirt, the color of the sky in a memory from childhood. I had entered the hospital, a home of death and of repair, and yet I was still unsure whether I had either. Here I was in a state of insanity.

"Hello. Tell me what's happening," she said.

"This is going to sound ridiculous, but I stopped for something to eat, and after getting back on the road I felt a lump in my throat and started to gag. I think there's a piece of lettuce or something stuck in there. Or maybe an allergy."

"You feel something in your throat, but you can breathe?"

"Yes, I think..." I stopped to check my breathing. "Yes, it's in the other pipe, and just really uncomfortable."

"Would you like to see a doctor?"

"I think I'd better."

"Hold on one sec and I'll page her."

"Thanks. I thought for a minute that you were closed. It's pretty dark out there."

"I know. It's slow on the nightshift. But occasionally we get someone in from the road choking on lettuce," she said with a grin.

My level of panic dropped.

"You must get tired here all night. How do you stay up all night?" I asked.

"Oh, you get used to it."

She paged the doctor, and then handed me a clipboard.

"I'm Lina. Just give me a little info about yourself there."

"Nice to meet you. I'm Jack."

She smiled. I sat down and filled out the paperwork. Minutes later, the doctor entered through the double doors and called me in. Lina and I said goodbye, and I followed the doctor. She took me into the exam room and asked me all the regular doctor-kind-of-questions. I told her the whole story. She looked at me puzzled but calm.

"Listen, we could run tests and take ex-rays but it's going to cost money. Maybe you'd like to lie down in the waiting room for a while and give it some time before you spend your money. From what I gather, you might have had a reaction, maybe to one of the foods you ate, maybe a pollen in the air you haven't been exposed to. Sometimes people develop allergies out of nowhere. This could also be stress from all the anxiety of your trip. How about giving it a rest out there and waiting it out?"

"Thank you, doctor. I'll give that a try."

I went out to the waiting room again. Lina greeted me.

"How did it go in there?"

"Well, I'm feeling a bit better now, but I'm still a little shaky. The doctor said I should rest awhile."

"Oh, good. What did she think it was?"

"She thinks I had some kind of reaction. I still don't know what the hell happened to me out there."

"Good, then relax awhile. Keep me company."

Lina came out from behind the counter and sat with me on a waiting room couch. She held her hand out, and I shook it gently.

"So how did you find yourself here on the nightshift?"

"I'm a couple of years out of high school. I don't think I can do this forever, but the nightshift is quiet and pays more. I have to take care of my mother. She has Lupus. How about you?"

"I go to college in Portland, but I'm heading south to visit friends. I'm originally from New York. I'm sorry, what's Lupus?"

"Ah, that's where that accent is from. Lupus is a disorder where your immune system attacks your body. It can be painful."

"I'm sorry to hear that. Will she be all right?"

"Probably. It's just a lot of extra care."

We talked on until suddenly a woozy feeling overcame me. I tried to stand, but my knees started to tremble and dizziness took over. I lost my equilibrium. Lina helped me lie down. I sprawled out on the couch stomach first. She stroked the top of my head running her fingers through my hair.

"Do you need the doctor?" she asked.

"Just a wave of something. I'm probably just overtired, that's all. No need for the doctor, not right now anyway."

"Lie down here and take a nap. I'll go get you some water."

"Thank you so much. You're very sweet," I said.

"You're welcome. It's my pleasure. Get some rest, and I'll be right over there if you need anything," Lina said.

I drifted off for a while. When I came to, I looked over at the counter to see Lina doing her paperwork. I sat up and felt drastically better. There was a cup of water waiting for me on the table.

Lina looked over and then came over to me with a smile.

"How was your sleep?"

"I feel much better. I haven't slept like that in ages."

"That's great to hear! You were out for a couple of hours."

I stood up and shook off the sleep.

"Let's take a walk outside for some fresh air. See how you do on your feet," she said.

"Good idea."

Lina hit the switch, and we walked outside. Above us the stars shined brightly in the cold mountain night. I was entranced.

I had lost myself, found myself, and lost it all over again.

"Do you think you'll be able to travel on now?"

"I do. I feel much better."

We gazed into other's eyes.

"Do you believe in fate?" she asked.

"I do."

"Then let's see what happens. Give me a call when you pass through on your way back," she said handing me a slip of paper.

"I will, for sure. Thank you for everything."

Lina and I said goodbye. She walked inside and watched as I got into my car. Starting the engine, I looked back at the doors and caught one final glimpse of her as the twin doors closed between us. With that, I drove away. I slid in Heart's *Greatest Hits*. Meeting Lina reminded me of the roadside romance in the video for "All I Wanna Do Is Make Love to You" minus the baby and the melodrama. I hoped we'd have a nice second get together when I returned on my way back up to Portland. "Alone" came on as I drove toward the California border, and I couldn't help thinking about someone else, from the deep past.

Head On Out

The following day was spent on the road. I meandered down to LA and made it to Andy's doorstep by 9:00 p.m. Andy and his brother Jeff greeted me, and we took my bags in for a two-week stay. After settling in, I told the guys about my wild road story and the young lady named Lina. They probably thought I had gone berserk out there on the road, but they were entertained.

"So enough about me. How are you guy's doing?"

"It's a big change, but LA is feeling like home," said Andy.

"After community college, I finished my program at the tech college. Things were looking bad though. My girlfriend and I broke up. And then mom passed away," Jeff said.

"I'm sorry again for missing that. I really wanted to come."

"No worries. We knew you were in Portland," Jeff said.

"Things have been good here. I'm really liking the sunshine," Andy added. "I'd never go back."

"I feel the same about Oregon and New York, even without the sunshine," I said.

"I don't know how you do it with those clouds," said Andy.

"The summer is the pay off," I said.

Andy had some days off, and Jeff was in between jobs, so we all got to hang out a few days. They showed me around the city. We spent one day at Venice Beach. It was a whacky scene. Muscle-heads pumping iron on the beach. Some guy buzzing around on rollerblades with a wired electric guitar. Hippies. Surfers. Beach bums. It was a circus on the beach.

Jeff and I went out a couple of days while Andy was at work. We explored the city. I had been there a couple of times, so I showed him my usual spots. Santa Monica. Malibu. The rock star's house in the hills. Hollywood. We drove all over blasting The Ramones *Brain Drain* and the new green Weezer album. We walked up and down Sunset and Hollywood laughing our heads off. Then we stopped in a bookstore for a more cerebral moment.

"You like this guy's books?" Jeff asked pointing to a Chuck Palahniuk book titled *Choke*. "This is a crazy one."

"I haven't read him yet."

"He's a Portland writer! Hey, this is a signed copy. It's a must," he said and handed it to me.

"If you recommend it, I'm buying it. Besides, that title sure is familiar. It reminds me of my trip down here."

"I thought so."

On another day, I slipped out to go meet with Sarah. She met me where we had had lunch years earlier. We hugged and sat down for lunch. I thought of all that had happened since we had last seen each other.

"I was so surprised you called. It's so good to hear from you all these years later," she said.

"I know. I'm sorry. So much time has gone by."

"Hey, that's life."

"I know, but I could've…"

"What's new? You have some friends here now?" she asked.

"Things are good, I think. Sometimes I'm not sure. I ended up in Portland for college, as you know from our letters. My two childhood friends live here now. I needed to get out of Portland and take a trip."

"That's great. You look healthy," she said.

"You too."

Sarah looked older and more mature now.

"Thanks. I moved out of my cousin's, and I'm living with a guy now. It's been about a year."

"Wow, serious," I said with a smile trying to play off my surprise. She hadn't told me this in our letters.

"Right? I guess so. Life happens," she said.

"Hey, as long as you're happy. That's what matters."

"Will you be going to Ventura on this trip?" she asked.

"Oh, do you mean to see her? I don't think so. I think that ship has passed."

"Does it ever?" she asked.

I didn't know what to say to that, so I just shrugged.

Our meals arrived and we got into eating, and then we talked about the world.

"I get the sense the world is about to change," she revealed.

"You mean, like the new millennium and all?" I asked.

"Not even. Maybe it's part of it, but I just feel like things are about to get turned upside down for everyone. Maybe it's just me."

"This year has already been shaky. We had an earthquake up there."

"Yes, I heard about that."

"And things are getting a bit whacky at college," I said.

"Parties?"

"Yeah, too much sometimes."

"You can always say no and turn it all off for a break. It's okay to do that. What would Alex P. Keaton do?" she asked.

We laughed.

"Thanks, Sarah. I'll remember that."

"Like I said, I think the world is about to change, but let's hope for the best."

"Well, you know where I am if you need anything," I said.

After a while, it was time to say goodbye.

"It was so nice to see you," she said and hugged me goodbye. I wondered what might have been if I'd never left her.

"Yes, let's do this again sometime," I said, and instantly realized how unrealistic it sounded now that she was in a relationship in a new life. She politely smiled.

I left knowing life was stretching us, all of us, in different directions at all times, and I knew how difficult it was to stay on the same path with others. People would come and go. There were all these clichés about fate, but I wasn't so sure about anything. Who was who? I thought of all the times I was so sure about someone or something. Maybe it wasn't about anyone else. Maybe you had to be sure about yourself.

I was eager to find out more about Lina on the way back up to Portland. What would become of my visit?

☆

The two weeks slipped away, and it was time to depart north for home. Andy went to work early, so I said goodbye to him the night before. Jeff and I spent some time over breakfast.

"You know, this was a great couple of weeks with you guys."

"Thanks for coming down, Jack. It was perfect timing, and dude, that new Duff McKagan bootleg of the unreleased album is rad. Genuine punk."

"Yeah, great stuff! Best wishes here. It's a new beginning."

"I know you had a hard time this past semester. Just keep at it. You're almost there. When you're done, who knows where you'll end up. Maybe here!"

"Maybe so! It's been the summer of my life so far."

"Crazy, but no matter how long we go, it's like no time apart. But let's still get together sooner than later," he said.

I hugged my friend goodbye. Then I hopped into the Toyota and slipped in the new Izzy Stradlin album *River*, which I had picked up at Jeff's favorite record store. I departed LA at noon heading north on I-5.

The Izzy album was awesome but short, so it was over by the time I hit Ventura County. I slipped in the latest Iron Maiden album *Brave New World* from the previous year. The songs reflected what was on my mind— the thrill of the road with "Ghost of the

Navigator"— my childhood buddies and "Blood Brothers"— my old life in "Brave New World"— mysterious Lina in "Dream of Mirrors." As hard as it was, I drove past Ventura again. I started to feel something in my throat. So as Ventura faded in the rearview mirror, I sipped some fresh water and slipped in a lighter album by a cool California guy from a TV show. The Jamie Walters album had super melancholic songs like "The Distance" and "Perfect World" as well as a few cool road trip songs that helped me relax.

Just north of Sacramento, I stopped at a motel for a nap. I mostly wanted to wash off the road and change into fresh clothes. I fell asleep for about five hours, showered, dressed, and then headed back out. Lina was now just five hours away. I considered calling her but decided to surprise her as she got off work.

I arrived in Medford, Oregon around five a.m. I accidentally missed her exit and had to turn around to retrace my steps. Driving around and around, I couldn't seem to find the hospital. I stopped and ran into a convenience store to ask for directions.

With new directions, I found my way to the hospital. It was 5:30 a.m. and the sun was just coming up. I parked and walked up to the door to knock. A woman answered, but it wasn't Lina.

"Hello, may I help you?"

"I'm looking for Lina."

"I'm so sorry. She had to leave early. Can I take a message?"

"No, it's okay. I'll give her a call. Is everything all right?"

"Yes, just family matters."

"Okay, good to know. Thanks."

I drove over to a payphone at a pancake house to give her a call, but then I realized it was early in the morning. Would she be up? Would I be disturbing her? I sat with some coffee and French toast to think this one through. I didn't want to miss an opportunity to see her, but it wasn't about me. I couldn't be selfish. Maybe she was in the middle of something. I decided to head home to Portland and call her later. As I raced back onto the interstate, the sun was above me.

All My Friends

When I returned to the building, there was a stillness. Leslie was about to leave the next day. She made her rounds of private goodbyes. When she came by my room, she brought a slip of paper.

"I want you to have this poem by Shelley," she said.

On the paper was a sonnet titled "Ozymandias"—

"I met a traveller from an antique land,
Who said—"Two vast and trunkless legs of stone
Stand in the desert...Near them, on the sand,
Half sunk a shattered visage lies, whose frown,
And wrinkled lip, and sneer of cold command,
Tell that its sculptor well those passions read
Which yet survive, stamped on these lifeless things,
The hand that mocked them, and the heart that fed;
And on the pedestal, these words appear:
My name is Ozymandias, King of Kings;
Look on my Works, ye Mighty, and despair!
Nothing beside remains. Round the decay
Of that colossal Wreck, boundless and bare
The lone and level sands stretch far away."

I read the poem and thought of the past year. I wished we had all spent more quality time, instead of all the time we spent beating ourselves up. I told her this, but she comically told me not to beat myself up over it.

"Don't worry. We all have this foundation to build on. Remember Mariel's melting sundae," she said.

"The sundae of life!"

We laughed, and almost cried, and hugged goodbye. In the morning, Leslie was gone. A bus took her off into the distance.

☆

Jill didn't take it so well. She was broken up over her friend leaving. She went back to her room and cried. When I knocked an hour later, there was no answer.

I decided to take a walk downtown. I roamed around the streets, dodged the Max train, ignored some beggars, and went to the mall. After looking around for a while, I went to the food court to get some pizza.

Mally was on the other side of the court having lunch with some hipster guy. She couldn't see me where I was seated, but I watched her for some time. A feeling of regret overcame me. I wondered if I had messed up something good, and once again quit too easily. Eventually they got up to leave. The guy leaned over and kissed her and took her by the hand. They dumped their trays of garbage and walked off hand in hand.

☆

When I got back, I met the new young lady moving into Alana's old room.

"Hi, I'm Jack, welcome to the neighborhood."

"I'm Keyta. Nice to meet you."

"Getting ready for fall classes?" I asked.

"Yes, I'll actually be doing a summer class too. I just got in."

"Where from?"

"DC."

"Get out, really? I'm from New York. East coast!"

She laughed.

"Yes, this is quite different. I like it though. I spent a few weeks in Seattle last year and loved it."

"In the summer?" I asked.

"November actually. For an internship."

"So you know the rain season well," I said.

"It's definitely a big part of the culture here."

"It was a tough first year for me."

"Better now?" she asked.

"Getting there. Say, this is my old friend Alana's room. I guess that means we have to be friends."

"East coast. Of course."

We slapped each other five, and she went back to unpacking. I was going into my room when I heard Jill's door open.

"Jack, was that you before?" she asked.

"Yes. I guess you needed some time."

"Can I talk to you?"

She came into my room and sat on the bed and told me her plan to leave Portland, just like Leslie. I was losing my friends.

"Jill, are you sure? Maybe you're just upset. Give it a day or two, and you might feel better."

"Actually, I've been thinking about it for a while. I even told Leslie about it. I didn't want to tell everyone at the same time because I felt like it was Leslie's goodbye. I had already decided."

"Are you going back to Utah?"

"Yes, I want to be close to my family. Life is too short. You guys all gave me a great experience I'll never forget. I will cherish this past year."

"Thanks, Jill. You touched our lives too. We'll never forget you."

The Tyger

My four-week summer classes started. I was taking Professor Mariels' class on William Blake and one other class titled Tragedy. They were like night and day. Professor Mariels was as insightful as ever. He covered Blake's biography and then started to work through all the poetry from *Songs of Innocence* all the way up to *Jerusalem*. Blake had created his own universe. It was both mad and fascinating. When I was out at Djangos looking for bargain CDs, I came across a giant framed poster of a real tiger's face with the first verse of the poem at the bottom.

> *Tyger Tyger, burning bright,*
> *In the forests of the night;*
> *What immortal hand or eye,*
> *Could frame thy fearful symmetry?*

I brought it back to my room and hung it on the wall. The tiger was now looking over me with big piercing eyes.

I was sad that Leslie wasn't there to experience the Blake course with me, but I'd write her with the highlights.

This would be my last class with Professor Mariels, since I'd taken every course he taught. This would also be my last chance to earn an A. I started with a B with Contemporary Literature, a B+ with Romantic Lit I, and an A- with Romantic Lit II. I was working my way up.

> *On what wings dare he aspire?*
> *What the hand, dare seize the fire?*

The Tragedy class, on the other hand, was a tragedy. This was another professor who had gone to school on the east coast, like the Literary Criticism professor from the spring, which I barely passed. I thought I'd have better luck with this professor because she was from Queens. I introduced myself.

"....and my mother was born in Queens."

"Where did you live?"

"Long Island."

"Ah, one of the rich kids."

"Rich? I don't know about..." I tried to finish my sentence, but she had already walked away.

> *And what shoulder, & what art,*
> *Could twist the sinews of thy heart?*

The content was interesting and covered tragedy in dramatic writing from Greek literature to modern British works. The brash professor meandered around the room in snow boots and paced from time to time. Her lectures were fairly organized and detailed, but most of us had no idea what she was going to test us on. She only talked to one or two students. One of these two was an older more confident man, who had obviously returned to the university after a long time away. The other was a young witty philosophy major. Both were extreme extroverts with enormous background knowledge of the subject. Everyone else was shut out. When I mustered up a question about the tragedy of the Romantics like Blake, she just nodded and told me to take the Blake class with her colleague. Her class was a fight for survival. If you were the introverted reflective type, even of great intellect, you were going to lose this fight.

> *And when thy heart began to beat.*
> *What dread hand? & what dread feet?*

Dead Leaves and the Dirty Ground

Mid July's weather was stunningly pleasant. If you could survive the rain in the winter, Portland was paradise in the summer. Alana showed up at my door to pick me up for another concert. This time we were seeing The White Stripes at Berbati's Pan. We packed a bag of drinks for the walk.

The venue was small. It only fit five hundred, but there were about five hundred and fifty. We got right up into the middle in the front. Meg White pounded the drums producing an unforgettable live sound. Jack White plugged in his guitar and wailed on it like three guitarists. I had no idea how these two people sounded so full and rich. It was so complete. This was an extraordinary show.

I was going to take a cab home, but I decided to walk off my energy. Alana caught a bus home from the next block over.

Before we said goodbye, Alana leaned down and gave me a big hug.

"That was a historic show. One of the best I've ever seen. Thanks for coming. We've seen some great shows together."

"Thank you for introducing me to new music," I said.

"You're my concert buddy."

"Absolutely. I hope many more!"

"You've been such a good friend, Jack. We really connect. If only we were in different bodies."

"Yes, I guess so."

We laughed and went our separate ways.

☆

In late July, a friendly guy from Thailand named Derek moved into Leslie's old room. He was short with dark hair. He liked his music and video games.

The rooms were filling up. A new crew was taking over. Jill's room was yet to be filled, but soon someone new would become my third neighbor on that side. I was nervous because a new neighbor could be a blessing or a curse.

Derek met all of the gang in a hall party that final week of July. Anthony and Robin welcomed him to the floor. Michael and Marion came by. A few guys from the second floor came up as well.

A girl we didn't know came through the crowd at some point. She was already drunk and slurring her words. She pointed to me and asked me what I was going to college for.

"I'm an English major."

"What are you gonna do? Sell letters?" she slurred.

"Maybe. But I'd like to teach college classes."

"Oh yeah, you're going to be a teachaa... What are you gonna teach me? Huh?" she asked as she burped up some vodka.

"Probably how to take better care of yourself," I said.

"What? What did you say?"

"You're a bit drunk. Maybe you..."

"Maybe you're just lookin' to fuck me," she interrupted. "Are ya? You gonna bring me upstairs? Teach me, teacher."

Some of the other folks in the hallway heard the commotion and laughed. I looked to Marion for some help on this. Alana would've put the girl in her place by physical intimation if she were still on our floor. Marion had a persuasive way of talking to people. Nobody disliked Marion. She saw my warning alert and came over to us. She put her hand on the girl's back to calm her.

"Hey, let us take you upstairs to your room," said Marion.

"Yeah, he's gonna fuck me," the girl said.

"No, I don't think so. Let us help you up there," I said.

Marion and I managed to walk her upstairs. There was no way we were going to get into the tight elevator with her. We got to her room. I stayed in the doorway as Marion tried settling her down, but the girl stripped down until she was naked. She was bony thin, light skinned, and blonde. Only a month ago, I probably would've been having dirty, vodka-stinking sex with this drunken college girl. But now something repulsed me about her. Marion calmed her and told me to go. I fled down the hall.

Marion safely returned about thirty minutes later and assured me the girl was sleeping. I was safe. After a few more drinks, I retired to my room for the night.

I tried to call Lina again. This was the second time I got an answering machine. I had left a message, but she still hadn't called back. I left another message, just in case the first one had been accidentally deleted. I hoped she wasn't mad for me showing up there that night without calling first. I started to think I'd never hear from her ever again.

I sat in the dark. Nobody was home.

☆

Summer classes ended. Tragedy class ended with a B+. While I appreciated the tragic tales of Oedipus and Hamlet, the class was a bummer. In contrast, Blake was beautiful, and I got my A. I'd never forget Professor Mariels and how he brought William Blake to life. As he explained the Blakean experience of a necessary fall, he diverged into an explanation of Plato's *Allegory of the Cave*, which reminded me of Professor Kohl and my first English course back in New York so long ago.

There is no going backward.
If we try to go back down into the cave, we are shunned.
We are alienated, cast away without a home to go back to.
We can't be part of that family anymore.
We've left the tribe.
We must go forward to the light, the sun, the truth.

Schism

One night in August, Alana invited Anthony and I over to a party at the house. The place was a madhouse. Alana rented a room in the house with two guys and a woman. One scruffy guy named Tim was messed up on more than one drug for sure. The other guy was an eccentric screenplay writer, who drank little but smoked a lot of pot. The woman was from New Jersey, so I assumed we would hit it off with an east-coast tri-state connection, but that wasn't the case. She actually seemed like a lousy person. Alana didn't like her much and was convinced the woman was involved with both men.

The guys decided they would break out the butter knife and start knife-hits. This was a method of inhaling a massive amount of pot smoke, which some bored pothead invented one day while his parents were at work. Tim lit the stove and placed a bit of marijuana on the end of a butter knife. Holding the knife over the flame, he heated it until the weed began to smoke. He then took an empty soda bottle, which was cut off a short way down from the open cap. He placed his lips to the cap and positioned the knife under the bottle. Letting the smoke drift up through the open cap, he took it all in straight to the lungs. Tim coughed and gagged and then laughed. Then he asked me if I wanted to try one.

"Yeah, why not," I said.

Tim set it up for me and I placed my mouth on the open cap of the bottle. The smoke drifted up through the bottom. I inhaled, gagged, coughed, and pounded my chest. I had nothing to laugh about. It felt as if I had swallowed flames. I half smiled, thanked Tim, that fucking asshole, for his generous sharing of the lung-scorcher, and walked on into the living room where a bunch of people were getting rowdy over a video game. Ten minutes later, after watching graphic car chases, shooting battles, and brutal murder scenes, it all hit me, like a ton of steel and glass.

I went and locked myself in the bathroom and fell at the toilet. My lungs felt heavy. My body was shaking. My heart was pounding. My stomach began to purge its contents.

Half an hour later, I pulled myself up and opened the door for Alana and Anthony to show them how sick I was. Alana couldn't take it and walked out. Anthony followed, but he said he'd be back to check on me and to not lock the door.

Anthony returned a short while later with a boombox radio on his shoulder singing along to "Welcome to the Jungle."

My friend was lowering me into my grave.

I wiped my mouth with my wrist, wiped the tears from my face, and yelled back at him, "I'm already on my knees. Get the fuck out. Shut it up. Get the hell out of here."

Anthony said sorry and left. I went back to my suffering at the bowl. Good thing they had another bathroom in the house, because I would've been out in the backyard.

Anthony returned a while later, this time with a stinking bag of McDonalds. I violently heaved at the stench.

"You hungry, Jack? Figured you could use some grub."

Now my friend was packing the dirt on my grave.

"What do you think? Get out! Get out of here!" I yelled.

Anthony said sorry again and left.

After another half hour of heaving and examining the urine stains on the inside of the dirty toilet bowl, I began to feel my ass give way to an explosive excretion. For the next hour, I went back and forth from crapping to throwing up in the now stuffed-up toilet. My body was giving way.

Wet and messy, I eventually fell asleep on the cold tile floor with a devastated bathroom rug as a blanket. I thought I was long past this kind of debauchery.

Alana came in a while later and leaned over me.

"What's going on?" she asked.

I awoke and opened my blurry eyes.

"Your roommates. The knife-hits... I'm..."

"Clean yourself up. Come on, Jack."

Alana looked down on me. There was a fierceness in her eyes I had never seen. For a flashing moment, I recognized the eyes of an old friend I hadn't seen in years. Anger. Misery. Hostility.

She was annoyed that I had destroyed her bathroom. Pick better roommates is what I thought.

She stormed out and left me there reeling.

I quickly drifted back to sleep and was undisturbed for another couple of hours until Anthony came back for me. I was cold and trembling, but ready to make the ride home in his car.

"Sorry for yelling at you, man. I was really sick. Still am, I think. Can you take me home?"

"It's really okay. Sorry for being a dick. Let's go, bud."

A bottle of poison would've been more exciting. A blowtorch up my butt would've been a better time. The time my friends and I smoked an angel-dust-laced joint and forgot how to walk was more fun than this.

Anthony carried me over his shoulder for at least half the way up to my room. It was a long, hard climb to the third floor, even with an elevator. At some point on the way up, I told Anthony how I had decided to never do knife-hits or any other brilliant drug user's homemade invention ever again. And how even smoking pot seemed behind me now. And how I also decided to steer clear of Tim and his house, which meant I wouldn't be seeing Alana much anymore. And I told my friend I needed to change.

Throwin' It All Away

Everyone was getting together to party at another building on campus, but I decided to hang back and spend some time alone. I was still jolted from the knife-hits from two nights earlier, and I was feeling really low. I walked up to Safeway and grabbed a cheap bottle of white Zinfandel. I returned, popped open the bottle, and put on some music. I sat down and drank the whole bottle. I was laughing, smoking, singing along to "People are Strange" by The Doors. And then the dark thoughts invaded my head.

What was I doing here? Was I in the right place? Was I really living the best possible life? I had always thought college was the safe solution that could save me from a mundane or difficult existence, but then I saw what it did to Gil. I saw what it was doing to people around me now.

I got into wondering whether these people were even my friends. When you enroll in college, you end up on campus where you're assigned a room often based on what you can afford. Would any of us be talking to each other if we hadn't ended up here? Were alcohol and drugs the only glue that bonded us?

I was full of doubt. I looked down at the street below. This high up and yet I still felt like a prisoner in a cell. I was trapped by my fears, caged by insecurities, and terrorized by my own mind.

I thought of Alana. In her eyes, I saw an old friend from my old town. Anger. Misery. Hostility. I was haunted. Not by the people, but by the emotions that got the best of us.

I thought of Jane. I took out a slip of paper. I picked up the phone.

The phone rang and rang. I stared at the paper with Jane's number on it written in Sarah's handwriting so many years ago. I didn't even know if it was still the right number. The phone rang and rang. I didn't even know what I'd say. I didn't know what she'd say. The phone rang and rang. And just in the moment before I placed the phone back down on the receiver, I thought I heard a voice.

I thought of Anthony and Alana, and all the other recent friends who had come and gone.

All the Portland women. Moments of love.

Sarah in California.

Then my mind moved back again in time to New York. I had given up on old friends and walked away. Some of them were beyond my help. But I quit too easily.

Then I thought of my other love, Elizabeth.

I needed to face this.

All this running. All this driving. It had led me thousands of miles away to the point of zero. No magnitude. Total absence. The lowest point. The point of departure in reckoning.

What had I done?

Every day was the same cycle of destruction. My back hurt in the morning from the alcohol attacking my kidneys. My hands shook from the pot of coffee I drank every day. The heart palpitations would start up after eating the fried fast-food. The raging waves of delusion and panic returned every time I smoked pot. At night, my mind raced with anxiety exacerbated by the rush of nicotine from the two to three cigarettes I smoked every waking hour. My lungs started to wheeze from the smoking, and I thought of Mrs. Kennedy and her air tank. Alcohol and tobacco, marijuana and bad food — just because they weren't cocaine and heroin didn't mean they also weren't killing me. Mind, body, and soul— broken.

I went over to the mirror and looked myself in the bloodshot eyes and asked myself how I really felt. What if I took better care of myself? Really loved myself? Couldn't I be a better friend then too?

I decided I was finally going to live.

Until I Wake Up

I went to a motel for three days and stayed in bed. The first day I didn't eat anything and barely had any liquids. I just slept and slept like I hadn't slept in years. On the second day, I drank nothing but water. Gallons of water, it seemed. On the third day, I drank smoothies and vegetable juices from a juice shop a few buildings away. All at once, I had weened myself from caffeine, nicotine, and alcohol. My appetite had changed too.

When I returned to campus, I went through my mini fridge and threw out the milk, soda, and TV dinners. I went around the hall and knocked on Ryosuke's door. I remembered his rice cooker. I asked him what he could cook in that thing, and he explained that I could easily steam vegetables in addition to rice. I took a drive to Fred Meyers and bought a rice cooker, a big bag of brown rice, a big bag of white rice, and an assortment of vegetables. I also bought a portable burner, since I would have to stop using the microwave if I wanted to cook real food. When I returned to my room, I made myself a bowl of rice and cauliflower with lemon. I heated up some Great Northern beans and enjoyed a feast.

Then I went for a run. I was exhausted after a few minutes and my lungs hurt. I knew my body would be sore, but I needed to start somewhere. My run turned into a long walk across the city. Every once in a while, I'd start to run again. This was going to take some time.

Back at the building, I knocked on Chang Soo's door. Ryosuke was there. They invited me in. I told them about my metamorphosis.

"Are you an alcoholic?" Ryosuke asked.

"No, I don't think so, but at some points I went thirty-something days of drinking. My kidneys felt it. My whole body felt it. Even when I didn't drink every day, I'd still drink too much. I don't like it."

"Will you drink ever again?" asked Chang Soo.

"Maybe, maybe not, but if I do it'll be in moderation."

"I drink a little sake from time to time. All in moderation," said Chang Soo.

"Sake!" laughed Ryosuke.

"What about the caffeine?" asked Chang Soo.

"I was drinking a pot of coffee a day on top of soda. I couldn't sleep at night. I was starting to feel jittery. The coffee and cigarettes were giving me anxiety. I'm convinced now that that's what made my throat close up out on the road, like I told you about."

"I'd think so," said Ryosuke.

"Last week, I smoked pot at a party and burned my lungs out. I don't know if it was laced or I just smoked too much, but I got terribly sick at the party. I felt like a loser."

They both nodded.

"I understand the change," said Chang Soo.

"The cigarettes were the hardest to quit. They haunt me. Every new day is a step forward. But I know I can never go back. Just one and I'll be back to a pack and a half again, enslaved to Big Tobacco, making guys in suits wealthier."

I was drawn to these two guys whose cultures seemed so far away from mine. They had a calming way to them. I was curious about how they lived.

"Say, what do you guys do on weekends?"

Ryosuke looked at Chang Soo and they both smiled, turned to me, and said at the same time.

"Karaoke!"

A Clean Pair of Eyes

Chang Soo and Ryosuke took me to a building in Northeast Portland. We went around back and entered a dark hall and arrived at a motel-like check-in window. The man gave them a key with a number on it. We walked down the hall and found the room. Inside was a bench and a table with a book and microphone on it. I opened the massive binder with pages of song titles. On the wall was a computer where you'd enter the code number of the song you wanted to sing. Higher up on the wall was a screen monitor that read the song lyrics. Each song had a different color and background design.

They showed me how it was done, each doing a song before handing me the microphone. I made my selection "Movin' Out" by Billy Joel. The song kicked on. Something inside felt funny.

When I finished, I had a big long laugh. I couldn't stop. My friends joined in. We laughed, and I felt liberated.

"When you're ready, there are some bars around town where you can do this in front of a crowd," said Chang Soo.

"Do you guys go?"

"Sometimes. The nights get a little busier," said Ryosuke.

"I come here sometimes by myself to sing songs, but it's fun to get a big crowd sometimes," said Chang Soo.

"The bigger the group of friends, the better," said Ryosuke.

I realized the power karaoke had to bring people together.

"I'll put something together," I said.

☆

Keyta knocked on my door wondering how I was.

"I'm good. Thanks for asking. I made some big changes."

"Nice to hear that," she said.

"Things were getting a little out of control. A little foggy. I'm going to be clean for a while now."

"You mean no drinking?"

"No drinking, no drugs, no smoking. No caffeine. No junk food," I said.

"Straight edge. Wow."

"What's that?"

"It's like a punk culture. Some of it originated back in DC."

"Wait. I got this friend in LA who said those words a long time ago. I had no idea and he never really explained it, but he doesn't drink anymore."

"I guess he just didn't want to preach. Maybe it just happens to people."

"I guess I better call him later. I'm going to need to find new things to do. I'm trying to stay active."

"Hey, I saw this cool go-cart place outside the city and wanted to check it out. You want to go?"

"Let's go race!"

☆

We zipped around the track. The little cars were faster than I expected. The wind hit me right in the face, and the turns of the track were hair-raising.

Keyta and I hung around for a while after, talking about Portland, making comparisons to east coast cities.

"Are you feeling at home here?" I asked.

"Well, it's a lot whiter here, but I'm doing fine," she said and laughed.

"Not exactly a city of great diversity, eh?"

"No, but it's far better than other places I've been. There are people from other countries in my classes, which is cool."

"Believe it or not, I've never met more international people, more than I did in New York. Granted, I work in a computer lab and live on a college campus, but still," I said.

"Yes, even in the cities, we're still very separated, but it's getting better. Just look at us!" she said.

"How does it feel to be the only black person in a room?"

"Honestly, I try not to think of it like that. We're all human."

"Sorry, I don't mean to push..."

"No, it's really okay. It's better to talk about these things. Don't feel guilty about anything, especially if you're one of the ones making an effort."

We got into talking about my road trips and her travels around the United States, Europe, and Central America. I thought I was well traveled, but she was well ahead.

"Forty-four states is amazing!" she said.

"I'll hit the others soon, but you've got other countries!"

"My big dream is to go to the homeland. I have ancestry in Mali. I'll probably go when I graduate."

"That would be an awesome trip. I would love to see Africa. I've thought about a safari in Botswana or somewhere."

"You haven't seen Europe yet?"

"No, I guess I should. I think you've inspired me. Maybe I'll retrace my heritage in Scotland, Poland, Italy, and France."

"That's it! Backpack. Stay in hostels. Take trains. Do it while you're young," she said.

"I think I will."

We finished up at the track. On the way back to campus, I told her about my newfound passion for karaoke. I proposed she join Chang Soo, Ryosuke, and I on a group outing to hit the karaoke circuit. Keyta laughed and said yes.

Learning How to Smile

The Portland summer weather was perfect. I decided to go for a run through the city. I still wasn't in the condition for heavy running, so my run slowed to a walk after a few blocks, but there were still tough hills to climb and I felt good. I walked all the way up 10th Avenue until I got to the busy Burnside intersection. Then I circled back around on 12th Avenue. I got into whistling a tune or two. As I walked along a quieter spot, I saw a taller man approaching. I could clearly see his bleached blond hair and dark goatee.

I stopped whistling, and we were about to pass one another when I recognized him. Art was a local musician who had gone off to LA to become a rock star, but he still spent time in Portland. He had had several big hits with his band Everclear throughout the '90s. My eyes caught hold of him for a few moments. To my surprise, he smiled and waved when we met eyes.

"Keep whistling!" he said. "What is it?"

He stopped me in my tracks.

"You mean what song?"

"Yeah, let's do one together."

"Man, it was just something I was doing. Nothing famous."

"Alright. I don't want to walk away and steal your song, so help me out on this. I got this one stuck in my head."

He started whistling an unfamiliar tune. I only knew his big hits, and this wasn't one of them from what I could tell. It was catchy though. I started whistling along in harmony. I began to throw in some new notes. After another minute or so, we brought it to a close and had a big laugh together.

"Thanks! Maybe I can do something with this now. But if you beat me to it, the song is yours!"

"Thanks, Art. Love your work."

"Appreciate it. Enjoy your walk," he said.

Art smiled, patted me on the shoulder, and we walked off in opposite directions. I walked back to my building feeling like I was on a cloud. I remembered reading that Art had cleaned up his act early on and now lived sober. Another sign I was on the right path.

When I got back, I cooked up some vegetables and then called Jeff. I wanted to tell him about my encounter.

"Another one? First Izzy, now Everclear? Come on, what's the chances?" he said laughing.

"Right? I swear. It's luck, man," I said. "Hey, listen. I wanted to ask you about straight edge? Why didn't you say anything?"

"I did. You know I am, right?"

"Yes, but you never told me what it was. I just realized."

"You know I'm not a preacher."

"Man, I went through something when I got back from your place. I never got to see the girl. Everything went bad, but something woke me up though. I went and detoxed myself from everything. When I told my neighbor, she mentioned straight edge, and then I remembered I heard you say it a while back."

"It finds us when we're ready. I guess it was your time."

We talked on for a while. He gave me advice how to live the life, and updated me on his world. I told him to say hello to Andy.

My friends got together in the hall that night. I knew I couldn't hide away forever. Anthony offered me a beer, but I declined. He was surprised but cool about it. Robin, Michael, and Derek were there. A fun new smart girl from Canada named Ani joined Bonnie and Marion. I went around to say hi and then joined Keyta and Scott, who weren't drinking. Ani joined us near Keyta's door on one end. We all seemed divided into groups now, but I had a plan to bring us together. We were going to sing songs.

The Galaxy, Tuesday, 28 August 2001

Keyta, Chang Soo, Ryosuke, and I headed out to our first live crowd. The Galaxy was a club on the east side with a big star on the sign out front. This place had karaoke seven days a week. There was a stage up at the front facing rows of booths where people dined. The place had decent food and the sound quality was great. My friends ordered drinks from the waitress. I would be singing sober and serving as our designated driver.

Not everyone was there to sing. Some went for the food or to watch others. But for the ones who sang, most of them took it seriously. I was floored by their performances. Not the stereotypical disasters I'd heard about.

My name was called. This was it. The KJ handed me the microphone. I gripped the metal and brought it to my mouth.

"Are you ready, Galaxy? Ready for some 'Rebel Yell'?"

The music roared on and the room cheered on.

The beat of the bass drove me. I gave the Billy Idol song more of a Jim Morrison feel and sang with all my heart. It was over before I knew it, and I loved every moment. It was difficult to imagine life before or after this moment.

I cheered my friends on as they did renditions of their favorites. For my second song, I went with the more relaxed but still powerful "Interstate Love Song" by Stone Temple Pilots. Then I did "Love Her Madly" by The Doors as my third song.

"I don't want to go home," I said when I got back to the table.

"Ah, Jack, they're closing up," said Keyta.

"Don't worry, we'll be back," said Chang Soo.

Back at the building that night, I finally took the yellow radioactive warning sticker off my door. Alana had left hers behind, but when the building maintenance men came to clean up the room for the next tenant, they removed it. Anthony had his sticker up—he was on his own now. But I missed him and wondered what he was up to. Amazing to live right across the hall, a whole four feet across, and have no idea how the person is. Just as I was thinking of him, he appeared at the end of the hallway and wobbled over.

"Hey, champ, what's happening?" I asked.

"Just stopped at The Last Act for a few more on my way back from The Cheerful Tortoise."

"You know how I feel about that place. The name and all."

He laughed and yelled, "Jack Tortis owns the Tortoise!"

"Thanks. How have you been?" I asked.

"Good, I think. How about you, brother?"

"Better than ever. I liberated myself with karaoke tonight."

"Get out! Were you smashed?"

"No. I'm still not drinking."

"Stoned?"

"Nope."

"How the hell did you get up there and do that sober?"

"It was a high in itself. Ever do it?"

"Yes, but it's been a long time. Good times!"

"We should go. There are more places I want to try."

"Yeah. Yeah. Why not!" he said with his trademark laugh.

Anthony and I went into his room and got into talking. I started to explain myself and my recent changes, and how I didn't want anyone to think I thought I was better than them, how these changes were my own individual journey. I told him I was finding myself. I looked up and Anthony had fallen asleep on his couch. I leaned over and removed his shoes for him. I told him how out of control he was. I told him he was fired from the band. I told him I could help him. I told him he was still a friend, and would always be. But he didn't hear a word. And it didn't even matter.

Ramparts, Thursday, 30 August 2001

In late August, someone new had moved into Jill's empty room next door between Derek and me. Robin and I were heading out for something to eat when we met him. We invited him, but he said he already had plans. Abdullah was a tall, dark-skinned, twenty-three-year-old student from Saudi Arabia.

"Why here in the USA, in Oregon, in Portland?" I asked.

He explained how he had been in Indiana studying and that he'd chosen to leave there for Portland.

"I know more students here. I came here to learn more English and do more study," he said in a thick accent.

"From New York?" he then asked.

"Yes, how did you know?"

He pointed to the postcard of the Manhattan skyline taped to my door among the other various scenic pictures of monuments.

"Keyta told me too."

"Ah yeah, so you've met the others?" I asked.

"Yes, yes," he said nodding his head with a smile.

"Ever been there?" I asked.

"To New York? No, no, but I've been to Chicago."

"You'll have to see New York too. You seem well travelled."

"Yes, yes, I will. It's at the top of the list," said Abdullah.

"Welcome to the neighborhood. It was good to meet you. See you again soon, neighbor!"

"Yes, yes. See you soon again. See you."

Robin nodded and waved. He turned to me.

"And we thought we traveled far to come here?" he said.

The Boiler Room, Saturday, 1 September 2001

We busted into the next place called The Boiler Room. This was downtown right off Burnside, closer to campus. In contrast to the darker atmosphere of The Galaxy, this place was bright. The stage area was lower than The Galaxy's raised stage, but we still had a crowd of tables circling around the performance area. I heard Bon Jovi playing and looked over and it was my friend Candace from the library lab where I worked. I couldn't believe it! She was singing "You Give Love a Bad Name." I went over and slapped her five.

We put our numbers in and ordered some food. Chang Soo, Ryosuke, and Anthony were drinking tonight. Keyta decided to keep me company sober even though I insisted it was all right.

Keyta started us out with an awesome cover of "Smooth Operator." Ryosuke did a fun rendition of "Beat It" and even broke out some dance moves. Anthony jumped in with a hilariously fun version of "Body Language" and went around dancing with various women in the front row. Chang Soo had the whole place singing along with "Yellow Submarine." My song selection came on with a spiraling guitar and I slid right into the first verse, "Hey, little ..."

The crowd went wild. I couldn't go wrong with Billy Idol's "White Wedding." I ended the song with a giant "whooaaaa!"

As I waved and walked off, Anthony grabbed me by the shoulders, "That was unbelievable. Do another one!"

I agreed to and put another number in.

Candace brought the house down with "These Boots are Made for Walkin'" and then came over to sit with us. Then Anthony got called up, and we heard the acoustic opening of a great anthem.

"Come on up for a duet!" Anthony said and waved me up.

"Jon and Richie!" yelled Candace.

Anthony and I got into "Wanted Dead or Alive" and it was the time of our lives. We had practiced this song in our rooms, but this was a whole new level. It was a success and a great time. When we finished and returned to our table, I clinked bottles with him, ginger ale to ale.

For my second song, I had some fun with "Need You Tonight" by INXS. I added a little slide to my step.

Keyta got up for another song. This time she did the harder "Barracuda." She rocked it, and the whole place thundered.

My third number came up, and it was almost closing time, which made my last song even more special. I went up and took the microphone.

"It's not nine o'clock anymore, but there's a pretty good crowd, so I'll do this next one for all of you. Cheers!"

The piano started up and I dove into "Piano Man" by my hometown Long Island hero Billy Joel. I waited to get through the first chorus and then I broke out my surprise harmonica to play along with the song. The crowd loved it. At the end, the KJ named Brad declared it to be a historic occasion, and we all laughed.

We said goodbye to Candace and headed out on our walk back to campus. As we walked home, Chang Soo stopped us.

"After tonight, I think you're ready. Next Saturday is a big incredible event. Are you guys ready?" he asked.

"Like what?" I asked.

"Karaoke with a live band in front of a big crowd."

"Oh man!" said Anthony.

"Let's rock and roll," I said.

At This Point in My Life

I still loved walking through the Portland city streets. The odd people. The statues. The fountains. The smooth sidewalks being cleaned by men in orange suits. Music always nearby.

The sidewalks always led somewhere. They could lead to a bookstore so big you could lose yourself in it. They could lead to a music store you gladly set aside a portion of your monthly pay for. They could lead to a café to wait for your lover. It was a lively city, and to walk it was to live it.

The park blocks were only feet from my campus apartment. This was a series of blocks filled with tall trees where benches lined two paths that went right down the middle from north to south. Many spots were cool and shaded for summer sitting. A few open areas existed where you could sit in the sun too. I loved to sit in the sun in the nearby field to restore my vitamin D from the long grey winter. But on many days, I was content to remain under the shade of the trees in the park. I'd sit on a bench reading, sketching out ideas and poetry, dreaming, and people-watching.

A young lady appeared across from where I sat. She seemed gentle and calm. She sat with a book and got into her reading. Her petite leg crossed over the other. Occasionally, she paused to take a drink of her iced tea. Her dark hair was longer in the front, shorter in the back. Once in a while, she'd wipe the hanging portion of her hair from her face. She was angelic.

It was Sunday, and I wanted to hang around all day and watch her, but I had to go. I hoped to see her again.

☆

After the night out at The Boiler Room and a calm morning in the park, I dressed, and then met up with my neighbors for a Sunday lunch outing. We chose a local hotel restaurant and walked over there together.

I had gone around to each of my friends in our circle and asked them if they were willing to go out to lunch in a totally clean state without any drugs or alcohol. It was my way of finding out how we all behaved together without being high. It seemed whenever I saw Anthony, Robin, and Michael, they were already blasted on something. I had spent time with all the others sober, but the time together often led to getting intoxicated. Were our friendships dependent on drugs? Could we and would we be friends without the weed and the beer and the liquor? Could we still enjoy each other? I always heard about alcoholics and addicts who would be visibly disturbed if they weren't stoned or drunk. If no one had a problem, then they'd be fine. But more than that, we'd know for sure that we truly appreciated each other regardless of the external influences. The way I saw it, if this simple experiment failed, our relationships could not continue. They all easily accepted the challenge and welcomed the clean time.

Marion, Bonnie, and Scott were cool and calm, as were Keyta, Derek, and Ani. The biggest party animals Anthony and Michael were actually more pleasant and funnier with a clear head.

"You know, Jack, I think this was a good idea. I think we should do this more often," said Bonnie.

"I have no problem with this. I like it too. Feels good, like I'm going to church," said Anthony. We laughed.

Robin was quiet though, maybe irritated, but I could tell he was thinking. Maybe he would have to think about this some more.

"Thank you, all. It means a lot that you'd all agree to go out like this. I didn't mean to put you on the spot. There were no surprises here. I like you all just as much as I did when I was high and drunk. And I think and hope you all feel the same," I said.

"Cheers!" said Marion.

We all raised our glasses of water.

Optimistic, Sunday Night, 2 September 2001

Everyone always knew when their neighbors were home because the walls were thin. On one side, I would hear Keyta watching movies or listening to music. On the other side, I began to hear muffled Arabic voices. It was amazing how long we could go without seeing the person next door unless we bumped into them by chance in the hall, yet we always knew when they were home.

Abdullah's friends visited him frequently in his first three days. I bumped into him and his friends a few times in the hall in the final days of August. It seemed like he always had a new Saudi friend visiting him, and I never saw the same guy twice. Then Abdullah left for three days. We assumed he was out visiting friends to escape the claustrophobia of the room.

Abdullah asked us to come inside on Sunday night. Keyta and I accepted. Abdullah's room was much less lived in than ours. A pile of textbooks lay on the desk and that was the extent of personal belongings. It looked like he didn't even have sheets on his loft bed. Taking out a deck of cards, Abdullah showed us some magic tricks. Keyta and I laughed. Then Abdullah told us how we should visit his country someday.

"Is it safe?" I asked.

He laughed and replied, "Yes, I bring you."

"Hey, what about me? Can I go too?" Keyta asked.

"Yes, but you'll have to cover up your face on the street."

"Why?" she asked.

"Because they'll arrest you. It's against the law," he said.

"What would happen to her?" I asked.

"Prison or execution," he said.

"Execution?" I asked.

"Yes, some criminals get their heads chopped off."

"Damn, that's crazy," I said.

"Ah, what?" Keyta asked.

"Yes, they do it right in the street," he said.

"In the street?" I asked.

"You guys go, I'll stay here, thanks," she said.

"Jeez, you sure we'd be safe there?" I asked.

"You be safe with me. It's okay. It's okay. Really."

We talked for a little while more, and then I excused myself and decided to head to bed. Keyta also said goodbye and returned to her room. Then I heard Abdullah leave a little while later.

He wouldn't return for another few days.

As Far as We Can See, Thursday, 6 September 2001

I was just outside our building enjoying the pleasant September night by myself when Abdullah came walking up. We shook hands under the stars and had one of those moments you remember forever— that feeling of being part of something in the great wide world in which we live. I felt united with the universe. He and I sat on the brick bench and talked for about an hour.

"Tell me about New York," he said.

"It's a lively city. Much bigger than Portland or Seattle. Have you been up to Seattle by the way? Great place."

He nodded and smiled.

"My home is on Long Island, but I spent some time in Manhattan, which was about thirty minutes from where I grew up."

"How did you come here?" he asked.

"I wanted to see something new. Be closer to nature. Just experience something different from everything I'd ever known. I bet you feel that way."

"Yes, yes, certainly," he said.

Then he told me about his home, Saudi Arabia. We talked about foreign relations. He told me our governments were friendly with one another. I thought to myself how it was a strange distant world I'd probably never venture to. I wondered what could drive a person to go so far from home. I knew I had something in common with him— the desire to see new things— yet he had taken his interest to the other side of the world. I respected him for this.

"You know..." he stopped and reached out and placed his large hand over my forearm. "I have to..."

"Abdullah," called someone. "Abdullah."

His friend arrived to pick him up. The young man didn't acknowledge me and yelled from a distance. He shouted something of urgency to Abdullah in Arabic.

"Let me tell you some other time. I must go."

"Sure thing. Have a good night. I'll see you soon?"

"Yes, why not, right?"

My neighbor Abdullah walked off into the darkness and didn't return that night.

One More Cup of Coffee, Friday, 7 September 2001

I finally returned Alana's calls. She hadn't quit calling for a few weeks. She hadn't given up on me. She had moved out of the knife-hitting house and had a new rental home in southeast. I accepted her invite and went over to the house. We went out for a pleasant walk and ate some late afternoon breakfast at a café. A dwarf came walking in. Alana and I just looked at each other.

"Why does this always happen? What does it mean?" she asked.

"I know I'm not that tall, but I have no idea," I said.

"Listen, I know you got a little distant the past few weeks, not returning my calls as quick as usual. You're mad at me, aren't you?" she asked.

"Yes, I was. I was dying on your bathroom floor."

"I'm sorry. I know, I was a jerk. We're supposed to take care of each other. You always helped me with my moves and everything else. I let you down. I'm really sorry. I hope you'll forgive me."

"I do."

Then Alana told me about her bitter break with the knife-hitting house. The other woman had accused of her things she hadn't done. They were a malicious bunch. Alana moved on and found a nice home in a quiet southeast neighborhood with a few low-key artists as roommates.

We walked back to her house after breakfast. We crossed the street to the sound of a trumpet. A man standing on a corner played a jazz tune. We laughed and said we felt like we were in an old movie.

When we got back to her house, Alana offered me a beer or some wine, but I declined.

"Thanks, but I'll hold off. I'm staying clear for a while."

I told her about my new changes, and she seemed accepting of them. She seemed reasonable and in the best mood I'd seen her in since we met the previous year.

"We've been through a lot this past year. I'm glad you came over. I'm glad we can move past things," she said.

"Me too. I missed that opportunity with a lot of people in the past. I'm glad we can sit here and talk things out."

"Listen, Jack, a roommate is moving out next month. Do you want a room?"

Alana showed me the room, and it reminded me of the one I had the first year at my uncle Al's house when he took me in after I had returned to school. For a moment, I considered this room and knew how great it would be to get out of my building. I would actually have a real room in a real house. I missed having a room and a bathroom and a kitchen. I missed living closer to the ground.

But then I thought about signing a lease and being stuck there in a commitment. How dreadful it would be to get a sudden itch and have to move out and possibly ruin our friendship. What if we started to bicker over little things? Or what if I clashed with one of her already established roommates? With our friendship in mind, I declined the offer.

"I think I better hold on a little longer to see what happens next."

"I can respect that. Let me know if you change your mind."

"Let's get together again soon," I said.

We hugged goodbye, both relieved.

Dante's, Saturday, 8 September 2001

The night had arrived. The place was crazy and packed. There was a five-dollar cover charge to get in. At the back on a big stage, a band was playing. The singer was different on each song— karaoke participants from the audience.

Chang Soo and Ryosuke led the way into Dante's. There were painted flames on the walls. The audience area was dim, but the stage was lit with a spotlight. It looked like a real concert. Some of my friends hit the bar for drinks.

"Jack, you only get one song to start with, so go with 'Piano Man'," said Chang Soo.

"All right, thanks."

I walked up, entered my name and song, and then returned to my friends.

"Did you all put in a song?" I asked.

"No, we came here for you to win the trophy," said Bonnie.

"What? What trophy?"

"You just entered a contest. We're staying out," Scott said.

A guy with long dreads had just finished an impressive rap song when I heard my name called. I made my way through the aisle. They stopped me at the steps.

"No kicking the crowd or throwing anything at them. No stage dives. No spitting. No breaking instruments. Okay?"

"Okay."

"Everything else is game," he said and waved me up.

I jogged up the steps and the lights hit me on the stage. I stepped up to the microphone stand and looked out at the crowd.

"Here's a song for your Saturday night."

The piano player started and the crowd cheered. I started the song, and I was nervous. This was a packed crowd. I was high up on a stage. It was harder to hear on this big stage than it was in the smaller karaoke clubs. But I pushed on with confidence. It was all adrenaline. After the first chorus, I slipped it out of my pocket and burst into the harmonica solo. The crowd went wild and it was all a blurry freight train right to the end from there. The song ended. The crowd cheered. I could get used to this. I thanked the band and waved to my friends.

"Nice work. Unique!" Chang Soo said.

"The judges liked it. I could tell," Ryosuke said.

"Judges?" I had no idea what I had gotten myself into here. A few more songs finished, and a guy came up and announced three names and then mine. We would be the final four selected. We were instructed to select a new song, so I turned to my friends.

"Rebel Yell?" I got a dozen thumbs ups, and so I went up and submitted the selection.

The first singer did "Hungry Like the Wolf" by Duran Duran.

The second one did a vocally perfect rendition of "Dream On" by Aerosmith, and I was convinced I was eliminated.

The third singer did "Upside Down" by Diana Ross, a successful cover of an incredible voice that could end any of us.

Then I got up there and grabbed the microphone.

"Hey, Dante's, you gonna help me rip the roof off of this place tonight or what?"

The band kicked in and I started wailing to "Rebel Yell." I felt like I was burning up. It was incredible. At the final bridge, the band fell into a groove and I started bringing the crowd into a sing along. I reached out to my friends and strangers in the crowd for help. The room was on fire. When the song ended with a giant "whoaaa!" someone flickered the lights.

The four of us were asked to stand over to the side. Then the judges eliminated the Duran Duran and Diana Ross singers, to my shock. It was down to me and the guy who had done "Dream

On." His qualifying song was a magnificent version of "One" by U2. There was no way I was going to beat this guy.

The four judges announced they would be picking our final songs. The other guy got "Modern Love" by David Bowie and I got "I'm Still Standing" by Elton John. The winner would do "Holy Diver" by Dio. These final three songs were randomly selected, we were told. All three songs were from 1983.

My competitor did a flawless and fun version of "Modern Love" that had the whole place dancing. They loved it. I loved it.

I loved the Elton John song, but the most I had ever sung it was in the car. I remembered singing it somewhere in America.

I didn't know how this was going to go with the band, but they got right into it. They sped up the pace, but thankfully in a lower key than the original. The pianist did the back-up vocals. I put everything out of my mind and had fun with it. It's a lot easier when you've lived a song and relate to the lyrics. In the final chorus, after the word "standing," I changed the words.

I'm still breathing

I'm still seeing

I'm still hearing

I'm still tasting

I'm still feeling

I'm still walking

I'm still driving

I'm still loving

I'm still living

I brought the audience in for the last several lines of the regular chorus and they helped me to the end. For a moment, I was right back in the living room of the small apartment I lived in with my mother. I was seven years old, and she was twenty-four. She was playing this very song on her record player.

The music came to a close, and then the drummer started into a drum solo as the judges made their decision. The lights went down and the drums went into a light roll stopping with a big cymbal crash when they were ready to announce the winner.

"And our winner... Jackson Tortis."

I couldn't believe this. I'd never really won anything. I'd never expected myself to be up there singing on a stage in front of strangers. I went up and thanked all the judges. They handed me a trophy and a $200 check. One of them said it was the post chorus that did it. I still didn't know how the other guy didn't get it. They gave me the microphone to say something.

"Thank you everybody. Karaoke saves lives! Thank you to Chang Soo and Ryosuke for showing me this. A month ago, I never even knew this existed. It came to me at just the right time. Thanks to all my other friends out there. I see you out there. Keyta. Anthony. Marion. Bonnie. Robin. Scott. Derek. Michael. Ani. Candace. Candance is here. Now I'm thinking you all let me win. She would've won the whole thing! Well, thank you all. And let's give a hand to the young man who did awesome covers of Aerosmith, U2, and Bowie. Come on out. Future rock star!"

My competitor came out. He was a tall, dark haired, and good-looking kid. Up close I could tell he was younger. We raised each other's hands. He told me his name was Brandon.

"Are you from Oregon?" I asked him off microphone.

"No, I'm actually just passing through on a trip. I'm heading back to Nevada tomorrow."

"Nice. So I don't have to worry about you coming back to beat me next time?" I asked, and we laughed. "I'd have a drink with you, but I don't drink these days."

"Same here," he said.

"Get out! The winners of a karaoke contest are the only two guys in the whole place who aren't completely drunk?"

"Who would've thought!" he said.

"Well, let's go out for breakfast or something, on me" I said.

The judges sat down and the band called me up as management made some announcements about drink specials. The lead guitarist pulled me over to him and gave me a look.

"This last song is a serious one. It's tough. Are you ready?"

"Yes," I answered.

"I know your voice now. I know you can do it. Find your spots on the stage," said the guitarist.

. "This is your moment," yelled the bassist.

"If you kept up with the pace on that last one, you've earned this one. I'll keep it steady," said the drummer.

"Thanks, guys. I appreciate it. Let's do this."

The hot lights were shining down as I stepped out onto the front of the stage. The drummer counted down and we launched into our final song. They cranked up the sound for this one, so I moved around to try and find the right spot. The dramatics of each line of the Dio song were fun to sing on stage, and I didn't need the teleprompter for this one. We got into some kind of zone. Something happened up there, and I lost track of where I was. The lead guitarist ripped it up on the solo. This band was a beast.

When the song ended, I had no idea how I had sounded, but the band was happy and the crowd was cheering, so I knew I couldn't have ruined it. We said goodbye and I stepped off the stage, but something had been sprung in my heart and mind.

I met up with my waiting friends.

"That was operatic!" said Michael.

"Holy Holy Diver!" said Marion.

"That was like a punk version of Elton John!" said Anthony.

"I don't know about any of this, but I'll take it. Thanks, everyone" I said.

"Incredible! Let's go eat," said Chang Soo.

We went a few minutes down the road to The Roxy for breakfast. Brandon and his friend came along. He and I exchanged email addresses. He joked that we could send each song ideas and keep each other posted on karaoke wins. Keyta got into talking with the woman who did the Diana Ross song, so she came along too. Our voices were shot. None of us could talk or hear each other that well at this point, so we enjoyed a mostly quiet breakfast with some occasional jokes and laughs. Without a doubt, it was the greatest Saturday night of my life.

Hunting Bears, Sunday, 9 September 2001

The next morning, Keyta caught me in the hallway.

"That was incredible last night."

"Yes, thanks for coming out. It was a blast."

"Listen, he's gone again," she said.

"Who, Abdullah? Yeah, some guy picked him up the other night. He'll probably be away for a few days again."

"Think he might be involved in something?" she asked.

"Like what?"

"I don't know. Let's investigate."

"All right, Nancy Drew."

"You aren't curious?"

"I guess I am. It's odd for sure. Why don't we just go on in with my skeleton key," I said, kidding around.

Slipping my key into Abdullah's door, I turned it, and to my utter shock, the door opened.

Closing the door, we decided to think this over. We realized this was against the law. Worse though, we could be caught by Abdullah returning home, and anyone could become violent upon finding someone in their room. But we were desperate for answers, which we knew we'd never get just by asking.

I tried my key in every other door in our wing. The key only worked in my room and Abdullah's room. It was fate.

Keyta and I waited until late in the night before entering the room. There were clothes scattered around the floor. A couple of chemistry and calculus textbooks lay on the desk. Nothing but a couple of beers, a soda, and a box of Twinkies in the refrigerator. I looked behind the refrigerator and found a folder. Inside I found various notes written in Arabic, his college rental lease, a phone bill, a Kinko's receipt, a scuba diving instructor business card with phone numbers on the back, and a bank account statement written by hand confirming that funds belonged to Abdullah.

"What the hell are we looking for?" I asked.

"I have no idea," she laughed. "I hope we don't get arrested."

"Let me check up there."

I climbed the steps of his loft, and there on the bed was a yellow legal pad with the writing—

"If anyone finds this, please call the police. The factories are in danger in the big cities."

I showed it to Keyta, and she let out a gasp. I covered her mouth and told her to hush. Flipping through the other pages of the pad, I saw they were all written in Arabic. Climbing back down from the loft, I found a notebook in the desk and opened it. Pages were filled with mathematical equations, just as foreign to me as his language. In the back of the notebook was a folded paper. I unfolded it to discover a map of the United States with highlighted flight patterns. My head began to feel wavy, like the day of the earthquake, like the day I collapsed in the clinic with Ginny. Closing the notebook, I shook off the anxiety and moved to the closet, where I found a suitcase.

In one suitcase pocket, I found a passport and used plane tickets from London, Paris, New York, Chicago, and Portland.

"New York? He said he had never been there."

Keyta looked me in the eyes. "He's a liar!"

We opened an envelope of pictures and scanned through them. The photos were of all men but no one we'd seen. One picture was of Abdullah standing in front of a cornfield. Then we stopped at one picture. A young Arab man was holding a military-style assault weapon. The man wasn't at a military base though. He was standing with one foot up on a sofa in someone's living room. Flipping through more pictures, we stopped at another photo of a man hanging off the wing of a small, parked airplane. I stuffed a few in my shirt pocket. Keyta packed the envelope of pictures back into the suitcase. We left and locked his room. We stood in the hall bewildered.

"What the hell was that?" she asked.

"I don't know."

"Jack, we can't even tell anyone because then we'd be in trouble."

"What if we say we saw strange papers while we were visiting him in his room?" I asked.

"Are we overreacting? Would we be so worried if he wasn't foreign?"

"Maybe we should ask him some questions when he gets back?" I suggested.

But Abdullah wouldn't be coming back.

Side, Monday, 10 September 2001

We went out to sing at The Galaxy. I couldn't get enough. It was quieter on a Monday night, but some of the regulars still came out. I did ambitious covers of "Can't Stop Rock 'n' Roll" by AC/DC, "Beds are Burning" by Midnight Oil, and "Big Time" by Peter Gabriel. Somewhere in the middle, Anthony and I did our "Wanted Dead or Alive" duet one more time. Robin did "Personal Jesus" but more Johnny Cash style than Depeche Mode. Keyta brought the house down with "The Best" by Tina Turner. Marion, Bonnie, Scott, and Derek came along for laughs and something to eat. A few of us drank, a few of us didn't. It worked fine. We enjoyed each other.

On the way home, Derek suggested we stop at a building. He said he wanted to show us something. We climbed the tough stairs of a very high parking garage in downtown Portland.

"Could you imagine climbing the steps of the World Trade Center? I've never done it, but I took the elevator, and there's nothing like it. It takes forever and your ears pop like crazy," I said.

"Someone told me about this and showed it to me the other day," Derek said.

"Nice find," said Robin as we arrived at the top.

"There's nothing like being on the observation deck of the Twin Towers overlooking Manhattan. This so reminds me of it. But this is beautiful in its own special way, so beautiful," I said.

There was a spectacular view of the small yet bright city of Portland. We sat for a while at the top of our world before climbing down and returning home. At about three a.m., I fell off to sleep.

I'll Take the Rain

Keyta was screaming and banging on the door hard.

"Jack, get up! There's something going on in New York."
I rolled over and hollered back.

"What? It's early. I'm sleeping."

"A bad accident. Maybe an attack," she yelled.

"Yeah right, no way."

"Jack, get up, New York's being attacked. I'm not kidding. They're being bombed or something. One of the towers is on fire."

I sprang up, rushed to the door, and let her in. Then I lunged for my little TV set.

A gaping hole of fire was burning in one of the Towers. Suddenly a plane. Real horror. I ran my hands through my hair in disbelief and then sat in front of the screen. Others woke to the commotion and came in and out of my room for the next thirty minutes. Keyta sat with me and held my hand for a while.

A half-hour later, my head dropped through my chest. My throat closed. I couldn't breathe. I couldn't share that kind of horror, and my door soon closed and locked.

The Twin Towers had collapsed. A cigarette entered my mind, but that too was a different kind of evil I would resist. Last night, the world seemed so ahead of us. Now a void of uncertainty filled us like a valley after a broken dam. After a while, the phone rang, I picked up, and at once fell into a so familiar voice.

My Skin, January 2002

The world had changed. The winter had called. And even though I am leaving, I vow to someday return to the place where I found myself.

The mountain snowstorm was far more vicious than the city storm I had faced on my first voyage out of New York, or the southern rainstorm that had forced me to the side of the road. This storm had directly attacked me, but I held on tight and fought it back, pushing into the dark, with the deep belief that the further we get into the darkness of the night, the closer we are to the dawning of the day.

THE AUTHOR

Billy Lawrence has lived in many states, worked many jobs, and written under many variations of William. He was born and grew up on Long Island in New York. This is his second novel and a sequel to *The Punk and the Professor*.

Read more at www.wklawrence.com